THE MATTER WITH MORRIS

DAVID BERGEN

The Matter with Morris

A NOVEL

The International

2012

IMPAC
Dublin
Literary Award

HARPERPERENNIAL

A PHYLLIS BRUCE BOOK

The Matter with Morris
Copyright © 2010 by David Bergen.
All rights reserved.

A Phyllis Bruce Book, published by Harper Perennial, an imprint of
HarperCollins Publishers Ltd.

Originally published in a hardcover edition by
HarperCollins Publishers Ltd: 2010
This Harper Perennial trade paperback edition: 2011

Grateful acknowledgement is made for permission to reprint the
epigraph and excerpt from *Herzog* by Saul Bellow. Copyright 1964 by Saul Bellow.
Reprinted by permission of Penguin Group (USA) Inc.

The author acknowledges the assistance of the Manitoba Arts Council
and the Canada Council for the Arts.

HarperCollins books may be purchased for educational, business, or sales promotional
use through our Special Markets Department.

HarperCollins Publishers Ltd
2 Bloor Street East, 20th Floor
Toronto, Ontario, Canada
M4W 1A8

www.harpercollins.ca

Library and Archives Canada Cataloguing in Publication
Bergen, David, 1957–
The matter with Morris / David Bergen.

ISBN 978-1-55468-775-6

I. Title.
PS8553.E665M37 2011   C813'.54   C2011-903733-5
Printed and bound in the United States

RRD 9 8 7 6 5 4 3 2 1

To Larry

Parce que c'est toi, parce que c'est moi.

*"Oh, for a change of heart,
a change of heart—a true change of heart!"*
SAUL BELLOW, HERZOG

THE MATTER WITH MORRIS

1

Morris Schutt, aged fifty-one, was a syndicated journalist, well liked and read by many, who wrote a weekly column in which he described the life of a fifty-one-year-old man who drove a Jaguar, was married to a psychiatrist, played pickup basketball, showed a fondness for Jewish novelists, suffered mildly from tinnitus, had sex once or twice a week depending on how much wine he and his wife drank, and who cared for his mother, a hypochondriac and a borderline narcoleptic. There was a son as well, who had just turned twenty and who coloured his mother's hair every six weeks. He was a gentle, slothful boy. He had tried university, disliked it, and dropped out. He played online poker. He smoked too much weed. There was some concern that he might be dealing, though there were worse things than selling dope—like accosting old women and stealing their purses, or having sex with animals. Morris longed for the true and the beautiful and the good in his column, and though he could not be certain, he anticipated that we are saved by hope. Readers responded with hopeful thoughts. They appreciated

Morris's wry take on the world, his sardonic skepticism, his "straight shooting," his seeming annulment of the private, and his family's apparent openness. As is the case with most columnists, readers believed that because Morris wrote in the first person, the life he described was his own. They identified with the domestic dramas, the small failures, the financial burdens, and the difficulties of family relationships. Men especially recognized themselves and wrote to Morris as if he were a friend. As is also the case with columnists, Morris did little to dissuade anyone. As a journalist, he knew the fine line that existed between truth and fiction and he felt he was adept at walking that tightrope. Sometimes, however, he was brought up short by his apparent honesty, by his capacity to appear to be revealing the truth when all he was doing was offering the shell of himself. But he understood that he worked in a temporal, modern world, and if he had doubts or took the time to reflect on the thinness of his thoughts, it did not take long for him to push these doubts aside and then to sit down and write another column.

And then Morris's son joined the army as an infantryman, passed through training in Wainwright, Alberta, and within a year and a half he was deployed to Afghanistan. And he died. And everything changed in Morris's life. His wife let her hair go grey and she stopped having sex with Morris. She confessed that at night, when she knew that her two daughters and her grandson were safely sleeping, she imagined a dark place she might run to, but there was no place far enough, there was no corner dark enough. And

Morris, who had always cunningly told the world about his private life, began to lose his grasp of himself. The madness trickled into his columns, and in one of the last pieces he wrote in the late summer of 2007, he borrowed overtly from the seventeenth-century mystic Jacob Boehme, and he descended into the second-person voice, alienating many of his readers.

You are like a fugitive. *The hardness is fixed* and you are on a turning wheel, one part of you striving upwards, the other striving downwards, and you are full of both desire and will. So the wheel spins and has no destination and *there then results the greatest disquietude, comparable to a furious madness, from which results a terrible anguish.* You wish to bend time, to pass through it. Of course. You desperately wish to regain your son. Absolutely. You desire him, you want to experience your own reflection, and so you grasp, you lay out crafty plans, you manoeuvre and beg. Yet, to no avail, because your son is dead. The wheel turns and you have *no destination where to arrive.*

His agent, Robert, a rational man with a sharp chin and a distrust of anything contemplative, phoned Morris and said that his columns had become too wistful and he told him to retool them. "Everyone's threatening dismissal. Everyone. You're killing your cash cow here, Morris."

"I write what I write," Morris said. He said that he was not a word processor, that he could not just mass-produce essays on demand. "You have no sense of art."

"Your own life has seeped too much into these columns," Robert said. He liked to string together words like "seeped" and "too much." He smelled a loss of income and he was panicking.

"This is a first for you," Morris said. "All this time I've stolen from my own life, and not happily, I should say. I've sold myself to the highest bidder, to readers who are fond of human interest and self-reference and biography. Given them the aging mother who is based on my father, the remote spouse, the son who dyes his mother's hair, the pot smoking, the fumbled sexuality, the American brother who is a duplicate of my own brother, Samuel, and my grandchild whom I'm not allowed to see. And finally I offered up my dead son, hoping it would bring some peace. All of this, and now you complain about seepage? You are a philistine and you are, contrary to your highfalutin sense of yourself, astonishingly middle class."

"Before." Robert paused and then sighed, and Morris imagined him leaning forward as if to convey a secret. "Listen. Before, when you first began writing this column, you were generous. Of course you excavated your own life, but you did it circumspectly, with a kind of mockery. You nailed the truth in a lighthearted manner. Lately, you've become too serious. Bleak. Nobody wants to read about unhappiness. What the fuck is all this mysticism?"

"The reader doesn't mind."

"But he does. He's complaining. The letters! Numbers are way down. You're frightening people. Christ, you're frightening *me*. Take a leave. Sort things out. Better than losing the column completely. You need this column. You need the money. It'll carry you through to old age. Find a good person to talk to, and when you're ready to come back, your column will still be here. But take some time."

Morris closed his eyes, then opened them. "I've been thinking that I could just drop out of sight and there could be a note from the editor saying that I have cancer, or that I died quickly, without warning. Perhaps an aneurism."

"Jesus, Morris. You don't want to kill yourself. I'll handle it. It will be done tastefully. Keep writing the columns for yourself and at some point you will pass through this." His tone was wry. He had read Morris's piece written in the second-person voice and hadn't liked it and now he was mimicking him. But gently. He said, "How's Lucille? You talk to her?"

"We talk. Though not lately. She's seeing someone else."

"*You* should find someone else."

"I have. Ursula."

"She's married, Mo. To a dairy farmer. You had her once in a hotel room in Minneapolis. That's not a relationship. She's Dutch, for God's sake. What is it, you like guttural noises?"

"We didn't have sex. We talked." Morris was sorry that he had ever told Robert about Ursula. He had confessed it in a moment of weakness, or perhaps he had wanted to appear potent.

"You feed each other poison. This isn't good. Stop throwing bottles into the sea and think about your column. Your gravy train."

"I'm tired of talking about myself. I get nothing back. Anyway, Robert, the column's *your* gravy train."

"That's true, that's true. I don't mind admitting it. But I worry about you. I talked to Lucille myself yesterday."

"Don't. She's not part of this."

"She worries about you. She feels guilty."

"I can't be responsible for her guilt. Anyway, you're my agent, Robert, not my therapist. My private life is none of your concern—not Lucille, not my children, and certainly not Martin."

"Well, you did offer him up to the public. You wrote about him and you talked about him and you laid him out on a platter. I'm not saying this is a bad thing, but you use people in your column."

"You think so? This is sobering. Listen, I'm going to hang up and go smoke something illicit. Okay, Robert? I'm hanging up now." And he did, though there was a squawk from the other end, Robert trying to convince him of something, but he throttled the noise and laid down the phone. He leaned forward and removed his glasses. He was feeling old. His knees were sore. He'd played a game of noon-hour basketball yesterday at the Jewish centre, a collection of young men who were terrifically quick and a few older men like himself who had to measure their output, and who then later in the steam room complained about sex: too much, not enough, too quick, sometimes aborted. The men were Jewish, they made fun of themselves, they took the world and held it and studied it. They were both generous and hard. Morris wanted to be Jewish. He imagined that this might have made him a more interesting person; more spontaneous, passionate and complicated, though Lucille had already called him complicated in the extreme. (She said that his desire to be Jewish was a secret wish for tenderness and affection. "You're isolated, Morris. You think that love is over there somewhere, close to the menorah. But maybe it's right in front of your Russian Mennonite nose.") She might be right, Morris thought, but she didn't have to be so smug.

After a dinner of poached pickerel and wild rice, he made himself an espresso and drank it in one shot. Then he rolled a joint and smoked it on his third-floor balcony overlooking the street below. It was warm for September and in the sky to the west dark clouds were piling up. There were girls in tight jeans and sleeveless tops strolling along the sidewalk. Some had boys on their arms, some had big purses, and many had both. The boys were immature; they seemed coltish and awkward and were always half a step behind the girls. On the corner there was a patio bar that was filling up with mostly young people, though there was an older couple, perhaps in their late forties, who had found a distant table. They were drinking red wine and the woman was smoking and leaning towards the man, touching his arm and then stroking his face. Morris experienced an ache in his chest and stepped inside his condo. He sat down at his computer and began a column that was truncated and elliptical and was lifted from Petrarch.

You will stand safely on the shore, watching others being shipwrecked and hearing their cries in silence. The spectacle will indeed arouse your pity; but your own safety, compared with others' danger, will arouse just as much pleasure. That is why I am sure you will eventually get rid of all your sadness. Just so. But then you will think, What if I am not safe on shore? What if I am in the midst of the wreck? And you will have to reckon with yourself.

He did not write, as he always did, "This is the truth," which had been the four words with which he had ended every column. This particular piece was unfinished, and in any case, the claim to truth was fraudulent. He'd known this from the beginning, when he had first typed those closing words, but some greater force had guided him. Everyone—his readers, his editors, those who wrote letters back to him—all of them liked that he announced the truth. Only his family rebuked him. Lucille had said that he was exploiting those who loved him. She no longer wanted to be fodder for his writing. He'd argued that if he did not use what was in front of him, the clay of his own life, then he would have nothing to say. "Use your imagination," Lucille said. She had an office on the fifteenth floor of a downtown corporate building and she would come home and tell Morris about her patients. Though these people remained nameless, they were very real. There was the man who couldn't have sex unless he was wearing a red dress. The woman who kept changing her identity, using the phone book to discover new names. The adolescent boy who tried to kill his father as he slept. And there were those, ordinary people like him, who were overwhelmed by staying alive. They were addicted to the material, to commerce, to the comfort of stuff. The world was mad. He had used Lucille's stories, the people she worked with, as a taking-off point for much of his earlier writing. Very much disguised, these people had entered his column. And then there came the day—he can still remember the tiny quiver of recognition—when he began to use his own life, and though he suspected he was betraying his family, he saw himself harnessed to some great fated and unguided wagon. The astounding fact was that his readership grew. People were hungry for the personal and the private. He offered himself up as if he were both Abraham and Isaac, and he laid himself out on the altar and took up the knife as if to slay himself. And how he had succeeded.

Morris stepped back out onto his balcony and surveyed the street and the patio of the restaurant. The couple he had seen earlier must have just left, because their table was cluttered with dishes and napkins and the edge of the bill fluttered in the breeze. He examined the sidewalk, looking for them. He imagined that they would be heading home, that dinner and wine would be a prelude to a shot of liqueur or a glass of Scotch, which would lead to slow kissing and a removal of clothing and the sex that had been on their minds all evening. A couple of years ago he used to live like that. Now, he augmented his life with novels, occasional truncated sexual escapades, butter tarts, Petrarch, and long evening walks that led him into the depths of a city where two muddy rivers met, where the homeless slept under bridges, and where cars slipped silently by, their occupants vague shadows. There were times, as he came upon another pedestrian, that he willed eye contact, and when this happened the connection was brief, a quick glance and then a turning away. Perhaps he was too forceful, his head too large; perhaps he appeared as just another derelict in a silent city. He found that as he walked his anxiety was released. Past the wide grounds surrounding the legislative building, the late-night coffee shops, stopping at the corner store where an elderly Korean woman in a pale yellow shift read from her Bible, and on down into the guts of the city where young people swam in and out of nightclubs and drunks gathered outside the Occidental Hotel, parrying, sharing cigarettes and ribald stories.

Not long after Martin died, Morris, in a painful and irrational attempt to justify his son's death, had begun to stop people on the street and ask them, "Are you free?" It was not a casual question; in fact, it was a hard-found query, full of irony. Using the convoluted logic of politicians and generals, Morris reasoned thus: (1) Freedom is everything. (2) We are in danger of losing our freedom. (3) Our freedom must be defended. (4) We must seek young men to defend that freedom. (5) The young men will die doing so. (6) But they will preserve our liberty. (7) Therefore, we are free. And so Morris began to ask the question "Are you free?" which did not go well, because people misunderstood, thinking that they were being asked if they had a moment to talk, or as one young man said, backing up, "Get lost, fag."

And then Morris began to ask, "Do you have freedom?" and this too was difficult, but it was both general and personal enough to make people think. Or so he thought. "Sir, sir, do you have a minute?" he asked a man in a suit carrying a briefcase near the Trizec Building at the corner of Portage and Main, certainly a banker or a lawyer, and when the man paused and Morris asked the question, the man shook his flat head and he moved on. Morris looked down at himself as if to understand whether he looked like a panhandler, or appeared to be mad. He was wearing jeans and a dark jacket. He had shaved, though he might have looked a little grey around the jaw. He attempted to talk to several more people, two women and an older man, but they too snubbed him, although the man, bald and with rheumy eyes, did say that he would be free when he won the lottery. Morris discovered that an answer, any answer, was more possible if he approached those working as the slaves of modern society: waitresses, bank tellers, the barista at Second Cup, taxi drivers. He also learned to couch the question in less obvious ways, as an offhand curiosity, or as part of a random survey. A few people patronized him but most thought him foolish. He was astounded by the indignation, the lack of thought. Of the two people who talked to him at length, one was a drunk standing outside the Sherbrook Inn, the other was a young man on a bicycle to whom Morris offered one hundred dollars to answer one question. The young man refused the money with a smile. He was a Christian, he said. And then he proceeded, over the next half-hour, to try to convert Morris.

Lucille, when she discovered what he was doing, said that of course no one, absolutely no one, would answer that kind of question, especially when it was asked by some stranger on a city bus. "People are just trying to make it through the day. They don't want to be accosted," she said.

"But it was Martin, and boys like Martin, who made it easier for those people to make it through the day. Martin died so that Ian, our neighbour, could buy a new Lexus every spring. So that your cousin Annalena could send her daughter to Juilliard. So that Libby can be free to choose what colour of iPod she wants."

"Or so that," Lucille said, "as a girl, Libby can choose whether or not to suffer circumcision. Or to be educated."

"Oh, Jesus Christ, come on. It was the Muslims who saved Plato's writing from the Christian fanatics."

"You're sad and angry, Morris, and you're taking it out on complete strangers." She said she worried about him.

And still she worries, Morris thought. He sighed, went inside, picked up the phone, and dialled home. Libby picked up.

"It's me," Morris said.

"Hi, Dad."

"What are you doing?"

"Studying bio."

"What's that background noise?"

"TV. My iPod."

"Okay."

The girl was wildly talented. She was eighteen, in grade twelve, and she had none of her father's greed and calumny, or her mother's severity. She was interested in fish and marine life. Morris liked to call her Cousteau, a nickname she accepted with equanimity. The truth was that he had never used Libby in any of his columns, and he never would, though she would be the least likely to complain. She was innocent; a stark contrast to her brother, Martin, and her older sister, Meredith, who was twenty-five and angry and full of entitlement. Meredith lived with a younger man named Glen who disliked Morris. Or perhaps Glen was afraid of him. One couldn't be certain, though he thought that Glen was doltish and immature and had every reason to fear his girlfriend's father. Glen and Meredith had a child, a son of four, whom Morris adored, but he could only adore him from a distance. In a column, written almost a year ago, he had talked with affection about his grandson, Jake, and then he had described Glen as rabbit-like, soft and pale with a curious nose that twitched. When he wrote the column he had believed that it was more humorous than withering, but Meredith was furious and cut him off from seeing Jake. If he saw his grandson at all now, it was when Lucille had him and Morris happened to drop by. Mystified by his daughter's anger, he had refused to understand the strife he had caused. He missed the boy and now, on the phone, he thought he heard Jake in the background.

"Is Meredith there?" he asked.

"She is," Libby said.

"With Jake?"

Libby said yes. She said that Glen was there as well. Morris heard the warning in her voice and he suffered a moment of empathy for her. She shouldn't have to be privy to all this nonsense.

"Give Jake a hug, okay. Tell him it's from Grandpa."

"I will." Libby's voice was soft and low. "What's up?" she asked.

"Just checking in. Doing a father's job. How are you?" He wanted to keep her on the phone, hear her voice. She was the only one in his life who did not judge him, who did not see something dire in him, who did not want to wring repentance from him.

"I'm good."

"School?"

"Good."

"You still seeing that Mr. McKibben?"

"His name's Shane. He's actually a doctor of English, Dad. And we aren't *seeing* each other. He's just a friend."

"Of course. That's what I meant. It's just, now that you're over there and I'm here, I don't know what's going on. Not as much." He stopped talking, aware that he was asking for more than she wanted to give. Mr. McKibben was an older man, almost twice her age, who was a professor of English at the university, and Morris knew that they spent time together and were perhaps having sex. This worried him. Several times he had dropped by the university and gone to the English department in order to talk to the man, but all he'd discovered was a closed door and on the door the man's name: Shane McKibben. One time, late on a Thursday after his men's group, a sliver of light showed from under the door and he'd knocked and called out, but no one answered. He'd scribbled a note on a scrap of paper. He wrote:

Mr. McKibben, my name is Morris Schutt and I believe you are spending time with my daughter Libby, who is eighteen and in grade twelve. How old are you, Mr. McKibben? What do you imagine can come of this relationship other than some superior damage to my daughter? I am not threatening you, Mr. McKibben, I am simply advising and my advice is that you gently and kindly tell my daughter that you have made a mistake and that you will not see her again. Thank you. Morris Schutt.

Such restraint and decorum. He was pleased with himself. He folded the paper and slipped it under the door and then went down on his hands and knees to see if there was indeed someone in the room, if he might be able to glimpse a passing shadow. He saw nothing. He had expected that Shane would tell Libby about the note, but she said nothing. And they still kept seeing each other. Now, hearing his daughter say that she was only a friend with Dr. McKibben, Morris held back any speech he might have prepared and he said, "The debating team? That going well?"

She made a sound that was soft and very Libby-like, and he imagined that she was busy with something electronic, perhaps looking for a song, or texting someone, maybe sending Shane a message. He felt himself sink as he recognized that she might be pitying him.

"Is your mother there?"

"Hang on."

He heard her holler and then there was silence and finally the static of the phone being handed over and Lucille said,

"Don't you have your men's club tonight?" She sounded breathless, disappointed, as if she'd run a long distance, anticipating perhaps someone else.

"Tomorrow night. Thursday. And it's a men's group, not a club. Robert called. He said that my columns have become wistful and disjointed."

"Yes?"

"He said he talked to you."

"He did. Yesterday."

"So you knew this already. You knew I was being laid off and you didn't let me know."

"Morris, you aren't laid off. A hiatus—that's what they're calling it."

"And you agree? That I'm wistful?"

"Did I say that? I never did. You know I don't read your column anymore. I don't need to read fiction that is passed off as truth. I don't need to read about myself. Meredith was right to challenge you."

"How long do you think she'll stay angry? I miss Jake."

"You might try apologizing. Talking to her. And then talking to Glen and showing some kindness to him. Don't you get lonely, Morris? I feel for you."

"Don't," he said. "I don't need your amazing capacity to pretend to understand. And as far as the column goes, I told Robert that I was finished. I won't be writing anymore."

"I wonder sometimes." Lucille's tone crept upwards, ever so slightly, and Morris knew that she was standing, back arched, chin raised, with her left hand, the one free of the phone, held out from her body, bent a little, as if to ward off a blow. "I wonder if that woman hadn't lost her son, if you hadn't corresponded with her, if I had been more vigilant, if I hadn't settled into my own sadness, and if I had forgiven you, whether we would still be living in the same house."

"That's such an interesting word," Morris said. "*If.*"

"Why can't you answer the question, Mo? Why can't you dip a little into your thinking? Are you thinking?"

"Too much. Though my thinking is shallow. I have to think about my thinking."

"And you don't cry." Lucille's voice was softer now, as if she had sat down. He imagined her in the kitchen, or perhaps the soft red-leather chair in the den. "What will you do?" she asked. "It isn't good for you to have all this time. You're only fifty-one, Morris."

"Oh, I'll keep writing my columns for myself. Bob said that at some point I would move past the nonsense and rediscover the path of righteousness. The money path, as he calls it. He's a parasite."

Lucille ignored this. "You're taking Libby out for lunch Saturday. Don't forget."

"Hnnh. I remember." He studied his hand and said, "My right palm is all flaky. There're cracks on my fingertips, sometimes they bleed."

"Go to a clinic. It might be eczema."

"It was way easier when we lived together, don't you think? We'd play doctor. Give Jake a hug from me, okay?"

"I do. I always do. Lunch on Saturday. Pick Libby up at noon. Bye, Morris." And she hung up.

✧

Ursula was an American woman who wanted to be but was not yet his lover. She was six years younger than he was and he had come to know her in December of 2006, when she sent him a letter in response to one of his syndicated columns that he had written ten months after his son died. The column, one of the hardest he had ever written, and something he had put off for a long time, had been about a young soldier who was killed in Afghanistan. He had described the soldier's fear and his bravery, and he had referred to the boy's e-mails and phone calls to his parents in which he had talked about the good that the army was doing. He had also mentioned his own fear and the boy's doubt, the sense that people at home didn't truly believe or support what the soldiers were doing. "There are times, Dad, when *I'm* not even sure. I get scared, Dad. Scared that I'm going to be killed over here." The whole column was written in the third person, and only at the end did Morris write, "This boy? This beautiful twenty-year-old with his life ahead of him? This boy who was killed? This was my son."

He received Ursula's letter via his agent. She wrote:

Dear Mr. Schutt,

My name is Ursula Frank and I live on a dairy farm two hours from Minneapolis. This is not far from where you live, and though an international border

separates us, I feel very close to you today. I just finished reading your column about your son who was
killed in Afghanistan. My heart broke as you described
your son's death. I also had a son who was killed during the war, only he was in Iraq. His name was Harley.
He was nineteen and he was killed last year by a bomb
that exploded underneath the Humvee he was driving. He died immediately. When I heard about my
son's death and felt that first wave of shock, and then
waited and waited and finally watched his casket being lowered from the transport plane, all of that was
easy compared to what came after, and that's why I'm
writing you. It's amazing to hear from someone who
has lost a son to war like me and who is able to write
about it in such a public way. I've read your column
before but I've never thought, Oh, I should write him.
And then, when I read your last column, I felt that you
were sitting right beside me, telling me the story of
your son. I'm not sure how to talk about your son or
how to talk to you. Oh, I know that you are famous
and that I'm just small fry and that you probably won't
even read this letter, but I wanted to send it, I wanted
to write it on actual paper, using a pen, and I wanted to
fold it and push it into an envelope and put a stamp on
the envelope and drop it into a mailbox. These small
things are what save me these days from my constant
fear. Even though the worst thing that can happen has
happened, the death of my child, I'm still very angry.

And I'm afraid. In your article you mentioned the word "fear" and I thought to myself, Oh, he might be afraid as well. Is that true? Thank you for listening.

Sincerely,
Ursula Frank

Her writing was so formal and yet so clear and so moving that he wrote her back immediately. He too wrote on paper, with a pen, and mailed it to her through regular post, making sure his own return address was written on the top left-hand corner. He first talked about her son, and how sorry he was, and he said that he might be able to gauge her grief, though grief was personal and he didn't want to be presumptuous. He said that he did not see her as "small fry," not at all. And he certainly wasn't famous. And then he addressed what was most poignant in her letter, the question of fear.

Oh, yes, Ms. Frank, I am afraid of many things. Of sleeping and dreaming of my son and then waking to find that I was only dreaming. Of the darkness, of death, of life itself, of plodding through the day, always aware that I am alive when my son is dead. That makes me unbearably sad and it makes me fearful. And I am afraid of the possibility that I will lose my daughters as well, or my grandson, Jake, who grasps after life, though I do not see him often and have been told that I cannot see him. What kind of world is it that we live in where a grandfather cannot spend time with his grandson? And truth? I am afraid of truth, because if I truly look at myself, I will despair. Of happiness as well, because if I am happy, then I have let go of my sorrow.

I was walking by the river the other day and I saw the ducks and they were diving for food, their tiny rumps pointing to the sky, and I stood and watched them, little things, no need of lodging or clothing or money, just the feathers on their backs and their webbed feet, such intricate elaborate instruments, and for a brief moment I forgot who I was, and when I returned to myself, I realized that I had been experiencing happiness, allowing my emotions to whip my reason, and I was filled with panic. I am full of betrayal and selfishness. And you. I am afraid of you, Ursula, because you allow me to speak in this manner, freely, with no editing, no red pencil striking out the emotion. Are you Jewish?

Morris

And so began a correspondence that was intelligent and flirtatious and raw. And hidden. Morris did not tell Lucille about Ursula, and because he was the one to retrieve the mail, Lucille remained unaware. The privacy and the secrecy allowed his imagination to soar in the letters; so different from the mundane scribblings of a columnist. He was starting to see that by confessing to the public he had damaged himself and his family. At the time, he believed it had been healthy, that he was honest and worthy, that he was truer than the average man. Now he saw that he had been deceiving himself. This secret correspondence with Ursula left him giddy and alive. He talked about Martin and she talked about Harley. She told him about her life as the wife of a dairy farmer. She'd met her husband when he spent a year working in Holland. They fell in love; she quit school and moved to America, a country that was very different from the one she was raised in. "I never planned to be a farmer's wife," she wrote, "but here I am, in the middle of a life that I chose when I was too young to know better. I always imagined I would have a career of my own, use my education." She apologized; she hated whiners. She said that her husband Cal had closed himself off after Harley's death, and if she didn't have Morris to talk to, she would be alone in the world. He echoed these words and, in a moment of brilliant betrayal, said that he felt closer to her than he did to his own wife. This did not surprise or frighten Ursula. She agreed. They spoke of longing and loss and they spoke of sex. He said that ever since Martin died he had become more interested in sex, as if death had dredged up some hidden desire inside of him, as if this was his way of overthrowing his own demise. He said that his wife found his feelings contrary and frightening. She claimed that he was in denial and that sex was masking his grief. It wasn't normal to want to have sex when you were broken-hearted. "It is what it is," he wrote. "I refuse to be conquered by despair."

Ursula wrote back and asked him what he looked like, and then she described herself, but she did it in a circumspect manner, so that if Morris had been asked to make a sketch of Ursula Frank, he would have been hard pressed to do so. She said that she was not Jewish. "Funny question." Then she had given her height, five foot eight, and she said that her arms were muscular and that her bum was too big, but the other facts she offered were odd: the size of her feet, the difficulty in maintaining her nails, the mole below her right eye, a trait she had passed on to Harley. She liked to shop for fine clothes. Cal thought she spent too much money on shoes; she had no place to wear them. Morris was excited. He wrote that he loved women's shoes. He shopped for his wife, bought her boots and outfits of all sorts. He liked the feel of women's clothing. He liked to pass through a shop and press the cloth between his fingers. "Do you think this fey?" he asked. She responded and said that she had looked up the word "fey" in the dictionary and it meant "fated to die." What did he mean? He wrote back that he had meant "affected," as in, some gay men are affected. "Do you think that this behaviour is too effeminate?" She said that she did not like to think of him as gay or effeminate. That worried her. She had imagined that he was quite masculine, that he seemed strong, both physically and morally. She said that she felt guilty because she had not told Cal about her letters to him. She asked if he had told Lucille. She knew Lucille's name, she knew what Lucille did for a living, and she was intimidated by her education and status. He wrote back and said that Lucille did not know about the letters, that this was a private affair and none of Lucille's business. "It's not like you and I are having sex," he wrote. "We haven't even faced each other, nor do we truly know what the other person looks like, so why should we feel guilty for something that is non-existent?" She said that she disagreed. Their relationship was very real. She wrote: "I think of you often. I imagine changing this correspondence to e-mail so that you could send me a photograph of yourself. And then I think, No, this is better. I like the mystery, the sense of the unknown. So often the physical gets in the way, don't you think?" She said that her favourite cow, Meera, had taken sick and so had to be slaughtered. He asked if all the cows had names, and she said, "Yes, this is why it's so hard when they die." She got up with Cal at four thirty every morning to milk. They milked again at five p.m. "The cows don't go away," she said.

For several months they continued this correspondence and often the letters crossed paths in the mail. Lucille discovered one of Ursula's letters a few days after she and Morris had decided to separate. On the spring day that Lucille told him that she could no longer live with him, that their relationship as husband and wife was drawing to a close—she was so typically formal and uptight, thought Morris—they were sitting eating breakfast in the nook that had been built when Martin was three. The memory of torn-down plaster and lath, the empty hole for the large window that now looked out onto the garden. The dust and chaos and Martin wandering about, holding his toy hammer, banging ineffectually at the old lumber, imitating the workmen. Look at me. Such hope back then, no sense of needing to rehearse for what was to come. Morris had come to believe that he had failed to rehearse Martin's death. Certainly this must have been

Lucille's method. She was prepared, like Telamon, who said, *I knew, when I fathered them, that they must die.* She would never be surprised. She looked up from her newspaper and, without any preamble, wondered at what point he was going to admit that he had some involvement in Martin's death. She had raised this subject before and so the question was not unexpected. He laid down his knife, folded his own section of the newspaper, and looked at Lucille carefully. She was quite beautiful, wearing a sleeveless top that showed off the strong shoulders that he used to stoop towards and kiss. What a strange mind you have, Morris, he thought, admiring your wife, picturing yourself bending to kiss her shoulders even as she berates you. And then, suddenly, he was imagining the letterhead of some lawyer, and written beneath would be the words: "Morris and Lucille Schutt are separating due to incompatibility brought on by the anguish that arrived with the death of their son."

"Why are you doing this?" he said. "I know you're desperate to explain Martin's death, and that the simplest way to do this is to have me take the blame, but I wasn't there, I didn't pull the trigger. I did not kill him."

"I'm not saying that. You're putting words in my mouth, Morris, just as you put words in other people's mouths. Why haven't you ever written a column where you told the reader that your son didn't die during a battle, or from an improvised explosive device, but that he was shot by one of his own men? You claim to speak the truth and yet no one knows that you, the pacifist, pushed him to sign up, and that, horror of horrors, he was killed by one of his friends. But no, you'd rather talk about roadside bombs and snipers and the heat and the sand and pretend that he died a hero, or was at least shot by the enemy and can be made into a hero. You've never admitted that he was killed by friendly fire. Others had to announce this. Why are you so afraid of telling people?"

There were sparrows sitting on the feeder that hung from the lilac bush. Morris had been out earlier that morning, refilling the feeder, and he had felt, at that moment, a small sense of victory, both in himself and in the world at large, but now Lucille was ruining things. He said, his voice strained, "And what would that help? What could I possibly gain by this? I would only be hurting Tyler, a boy I've spoken to, as you know, and a boy you refuse to talk to. You sound so certain, as if you're the only one who knows the truth. I'm tired of laying out my life, and yours, and Martin's, before a bestial crowd that gorges on the personal. It's vulgar and it's wrong."

Lucille said, "I've thought about this a long time, and we've already discussed it, so it won't come as a surprise, but I want to live apart from you for a while. I'm quite willing to move out, to find an apartment, or I can stay here. You choose. I think that Libby would like to live with me, I've discussed it with her, but of course you would see her as much as you like. She loves you. She's devastated by this, but she's strong and she'll survive."

Morris was astonished. "You talked to Libby about this before talking to me?"

"We've discussed this, Morris. For half a year we've talked about it. This should not be a surprise."

"It *is* a surprise. I'm flabbergasted. You're so rigid. You are a miser, a collector. You give just enough to make sure that you get something more in return. Libby said that she wants to live with you?"

Lucille nodded. "She's not rejecting you, Morris." She reached out to hold his hand but he pulled away. "It's a trial," she said. "There's nothing permanent in this."

"I've heard that before. Exactly what your best friend Margo said to her husband Timothy and now she's happily ensconced in a condo by the river, entertaining young men with big dicks."

"Morris, this isn't about sex."

"I'll go," he said. "You can take care of this place." He waved a hand at the house, aware of the falling-down soffits, the peeling paint, the many unfinished projects that he'd been meaning to get to. What had been a novelty so many years ago, a house that needed a new kitchen, had now become a burden. The year before, a squirrel had made a nest in the eaves; it could be heard scampering along the gutters, storing up nuts and leaves and acorns for the winter. Morris had set a live trap, gently placing peanuts on the tripwire, and when he caught the poor thing, he drove it over to Omand's Creek and released it into the wild. Only to have it return. Morris swore that the squirrel made it back to the house before he did. And so he reset the trap and caught the same squirrel, stupid animal. He phoned Poulin's Pest Control and was told that a squirrel had a homing instinct of up to three miles. "Take it across the river," the woman told him. And so he did, dumping the squirrel into the unsuspecting laps of the folks on the other side of the Red River. And it worked. A house was a haven for crows and mice and ants and chipmunks. Come one, come all, thought Morris. He'd often suggested to Lucille that they should move into a condominium, where there was no need to shovel snow, to repair plaster, to redo the roof, or to make immigrants of squirrels. "We can just sit back and drink and talk and make love," he'd announced. But she'd balked at the idea of small closets and no garden. Where would she put her perennials? And so they had stayed on, and the house had continued to collapse around them.

"You're angry," Lucille said. "You know that I'm afraid of your anger."

"You, of all people, should be willing to work at this."

"Me, of all people. I'm not perfect, Morris, I don't have the answers."

He was on the verge of begging, and he hated it. He looked up quickly. "Is there someone else?"

"No. God, no. No one."

"Who's going to buy your clothes?"

She reached for his hand again and this time he allowed her to hold it. "We're not dead, Morris. If you want to buy me a skirt or a sweater, I'd love it."

"Who's going to watch you put it on and take it off? That's my dominion."

She smiled sadly and squeezed his hand.

And then, too quickly, within several months, she found someone else. Maybe she'd been searching on the Internet, slyly beckoning lovers to join her. And she ended up with the heart surgeon who, Lucille said, held her safely in his arms.

If there was any comfort to be found, it came from Morris's perception that he himself was stronger, more resilient than Lucille, that he was capable of grieving alone.

Morris had left the letter from Ursula lying on the kitchen table, opened and face up, a few days later. He had never intended to leave it there, though Lucille would have found something premeditated in the act, as if he had wanted to hurt her. The letter was meandering, a detailed description of calving a cow and then a brief account of a shopping trip to Minneapolis, dinner out with Cal, the purchase of new flatware, a haircut, and a bikini wax. When Lucille flashed the letter and threw it at Morris, he feigned astonishment, as if it had dropped from the sky, and then he said, "Oh this," and then he used the word "innocuous."

"*Innocuous?* What are you saying, Morris? She's talking about a bikini wax. Who *is* she?"

"She's one of my readers."

"And you send each other billets-doux? What century are you living in, Morris? What does she look like?"

"I don't know. I've never met her."

"You've never met her."

"That's right."

Lucille paused, calculating. When she did this she bit her upper lip, and this annoyed Morris because it made her look childish and wanting. "You have no clue if she's fat or short or ugly or old?"

"She's five eight. That's what I know."

"How old?"

"Fifty. Forty-five."

"Which one?"

"Forty-five."

"Oh, Morris, have you gone stupid? I see this kind of behaviour too much not to recognize it. And I always thought that you and I were somehow above all that. Now who's the stupid one?"

"I haven't done anything."

"You write her letters. She writes you back. How many times?" Her hands were beginning to wave in the air, her face had become slightly pinched.

"A few."

"I want to see them. How long has this been going on?"

Morris looked away. He sighed and said, "Half a year."

Lucille dropped her hands into her lap and folded them, and as she did this, she closed her eyes. She looked quite old at that moment and Morris had to turn away so as not to be too pleased with how ugly she appeared, which would be another level of deception. Absurdly, he was happy that she had told him that she was leaving him before she found out about Ursula. And yet he was not happy to discover that she could in fact be surprised; it made her appear unguarded, and this saddened him. Her eyes came open. She was raging again. "You—you spend the last six months talking to a strange woman, and yet you can't say a word to me? We don't talk anymore, Morris. Haven't you noticed? I certainly noticed. I always thought it was all my fault, but now I find out you're telling secrets to a strange woman who's not so strange that she can't tell you she just had a bikini wax. You want me to get a wax? I'd be glad to." She began to cry.

Morris reached for her. "I never asked her to get a wax."

"You prick." She pushed him away. "Who is she?"

"She's from Minnesota. She lost her son in Iraq, and when she read my piece on Martin, she wrote me about her dead boy. That's all."

Lucille had wiped her face, her cheeks and her eyes, which suddenly brightened with rage. "You talked to her about Martin? You told her about me, about our life, our children, our sadness? It wasn't enough that you told the world, but then you had to go and tell this woman you say you barely know. What were you thinking?"

"It's not important, Lucille. *You're* important." Was this the truth? he wondered.

She pointed her finger at him. "I never lied to you, Morris. I gave everything back to you. I tried to talk, I wanted to find a way back to you, I wanted to cry with you, to hold you, to talk about Martin, but instead you were talking to her. All your energy was going down there." She waved her hand south. She looked up, astounded. "You've slept with her?"

"No, no. I told you, we've never met."

"But when we were having sex, you were thinking about her. You were. I could feel it. I remember now. You had gone away."

"That's not true, Lucille. Ask me if that's true. Don't tell me what you think is true."

She nodded slowly. "You love her, don't you. And I mean that in the biggest way. Even if you haven't met her, you love her for what she writes, for how she talks to you, for the secrets she tells you. You whisper secrets to each other, and how can I compete with that? Should *I* write you letters, Morris? Is there something secret about me that would still interest you? Or am I just like one of those animals she milks. A cow. Is that how you see me? *Do* you see me?"

Morris shook his head throughout this entire speech, until she was finished, and then he said, "I do see you, Lucille. I see you."

Her eyes were clear and hard. She said, "I'm so glad Libby's going to live with me. And I'm so glad that I already told you that I was leaving you. If I hadn't, if I had found out about this affair and then left you, I'd be even more ashamed."

"It's not an affair."

She laughed. "Yes. It is. And you called *me* a miser."

They had sex that night. They had talked throughout the evening and late into the night. At dinner, Libby had been aware of a tension, but then, she had become accustomed to this since Martin's death. She ate quickly and excused herself. Morris watched her carry her plate to the kitchen and he felt sorry for her. Lucille asked again if she could see the letters, and Morris said that they were private.

"No, they are secret," Lucille hissed. "That's different than private. Private is moral and honourable. A secret withheld from your wife is treachery."

How quick and good she was with her words. He

couldn't keep up, never had been able to argue adequately, except in hindsight.

"I can't betray Ursula," he said.

"You ass."

She left the room. He could hear her banging around in the kitchen as he sat cold and culpable in the living room.

That night, in bed, her voice whispered, "What does she give you that I don't? Is she stealing your heart?" It was a hot spring day, very humid, and the fan turned slowly above them. Lucille wore a thin T-shirt and no underwear and Morris was naked. Even though they were leaving each other, they still slept in the same bed. Neither of them disagreed with this. They lay under a sheet. Morris again told her that he had not met Ursula and so nothing about this was real. He thought, but didn't say, that it was like doing card tricks without the cards. "She talks. I talk. There is no heart involved," he said.

"Talk to *me*," she said. "I *need* you to talk."

He lay there, words falling abstractly through his brain, and he opened his mouth but now nothing came out. He thought some more. Opened his mouth again. Nothing. Finally, he said, "She's a voice, that's all. And an ear. I throw a ball at the wall and the ball bounces back. Something solid out there."

Lucille began to cry, deep sad sobs dredged up from her belly, and he held her head as she wept.

She sat up suddenly and began to pummel his chest. "You set Martin up. Did nothing to stop him. You let him run off to a filthy country to shoot a gun at men who have a different God. And you don't even believe in God."

She turned away from him and fell asleep quickly. She had always been adept at that. In the middle of the night she woke him and said, "Hold me." He did this, and she kissed him and he kissed her back. So familiar she was, so easy. He knew her shape, what pleased her. At some point she climbed on top of him and put him inside her. She called out and pushed her face against his shoulder. Then she slid away and lowered her head and wet the pillow with her tears.

When he had told his psychiatrist, Dr. G, that he was corresponding with a woman who was a dairy farmer, Dr. G asked, "Is she dangerous?"

Morris chuckled. "How could she be dangerous? She's sad. She's broken up over the death of her son. She needs someone to talk to."

"And Lucille? She knows about this?"

"There's nothing to say. I don't even know what Ursula looks like, smells like, how she walks, how big her breasts are."

"Why are you talking about her breasts?"

"She's a woman. She has breasts."

"Perhaps she's had a double mastectomy. You haven't seen her."

"Well, and perhaps she's a seventy-year-old male."

"Okay."

"She's forty-five. She has no reason to lie."

Dr. G was short and balding with grey tufts of hair over his ears. He wore corduroy pants. A docile Weimaraner lay

at his feet. He was Jewish. Morris was pleased that his psychiatrist was Jewish, though non-practising. It made him feel
somehow closer to Freud, a source of healing.

"It appears you would like to have your cake and eat it
too," Dr. G said. And he smiled.

Morris moved from the house that he'd lived in with Lucille
for over twenty years into a newly renovated condominium on Corydon. He bought two leather chairs and a small
kitchen table, a few utensils and a frying pan, some cutlery
and plates, drove his library over in the back of his Jaguar.
He kept only the books he valued greatly, and he arranged
them alphabetically. Adorno, Babel, Bellow, Buber, Coetzee,
DeLillo, et cetera, Kincaid, Kosinski, Lessing, McCarthy,
Nabokov, Niebuhr, O'Connor, et cetera, Roth, Updike, et
cetera. All necessary companions. For a bed, he purchased
a solid futon that left him stiff and irritable in the morning.
The antique bureau and the dining room set that he'd inher-
ited from his parents were delivered by a moving company
that he hired. His walls were bare and so he rented a number of paintings from the art gallery. Two watercolours he
placed in the living room, the third, titled *Bouquet,* he hung
above his bed. The quiet surprised him. He missed the sound
of someone else puttering at the edges of his life. He found
a few good choral CDs and played them throughout the day
because the voices made him feel less lonely. One day in
June, Lucille dropped off his mail, noting with disdain that

there was a letter from *the farmer's wife*. "But then, you're free to do as you please now."

In his last letter, Morris talked about the failure of his marriage, Lucille's reaction to the correspondence and his relationship with Ursula. He said: "She calls it a relationship. In fact, she says we're having an affair. She likes to think she is right in most everything, but in this she might be wrong. How can you have an affair with someone you've never met? Please, tell me."

Her response was brief, hastily written. She asked him if he would meet her in Minneapolis the following weekend. "This must seem very cheeky and it probably won't work," she wrote, "but I believe you have to ask for what you want and then deal with the answer." She was going to be in Minneapolis by herself for two days and she knew that it took only seven or eight hours to drive from where he lived, and she wanted to meet him. She wrote: "I can feel a real bond between us. You've been so honest, and I sense that you need someone to talk to, just as I need someone to talk to. We have our sons in common and I believe that we have much more in common. I'm being aggressive, I know that, and I'll understand if you never write me again, but I think that it's important that we see each other, look at each other. Writing letters says only so much, and in the end we have to talk face to face. Don't you agree?"

He read the letter twice and then put it aside. He picked it up again almost immediately and read it once more, looking for a trick in the writing, a possible deception, but he found only a pure candour that impressed and excited him. She had said nothing about Lucille and though this was disconcerting, he imagined she might be shading in the spaces. She would be loath to describe the obvious. He had not felt like this since he was much younger and falling in love with Lucille. The world was suddenly full and vibrant. He felt foolish and alive. He wrote back and said yes.

Morris and Lucille met when she was twenty-four and in the midst of medical school. Morris already had an undergraduate degree and had just received a diploma in journalism from a small college in Vancouver. The world of instruction and training had replaced questions about formation of character, and though he still read hungrily, both for pleasure and learning, he was a practical man. He wanted to make money. After Morris graduated, he returned to the city he'd grown up in and found a job covering the law courts, a typically monotonous beat interrupted by moments of sensationalism and violence. The world he worked in was filled with commoners, losers, and madmen. He first saw Lucille when she was a witness at a murder trial. As a medical student that year, she had treated a man who had come into Emergency with knife wounds to the stomach. The man turned out to be the accused and she had, while suturing his wounds, engaged him in conversation. There was some suspicion on the part of the prosecution that a confession had leaked out and Lucille had been subpoenaed. In court, on the stand, she was collected and sharp. Her hair was swept up in an unfashionable chignon and she wore a dark blue dress and dark blue high heels, and Morris, from his seat in the courtroom, had first noticed the heels and then her hair. She was asked to describe the mood of the accused that day, the nature of his wounds, the nature of the man himself. She was asked if he had confessed to the murder. She said that there had been no admission of guilt. She did not suffer fools, and the prosecutor was a buffoon who pressed her, charged her, was aggressively suggestive. She never succumbed to his assault.

After, Morris had followed her from the courtroom and down the street towards Broadway. It was winter. A recent snowfall had left the sidewalks icy. She tottered along in her high heels, wearing yellow gloves and a too-large mohair coat that he learned later had been her father's. He loved that she seemed, with her lack of hardy boots, to scorn the cold. He was taken by her thin ankles. At one point on the witness stand, she had said to the bumbling prosecutor, "I cannot offer the ineffable." And she smiled. She had tremendous disdain for ignorance. She was also extremely confident and Morris was attracted to confident women. Though his car was parked nearby, Morris followed her onto the bus and took the seat immediately behind her. From her bag she retrieved a book and opened it. He moved to the side seat so that he could peruse the cover and perhaps have something intelligent to say. The book was slight, with a barely legible title. He thought it might be a religious tract. This would be disappointing. He dropped a quarter onto the bus floor and, bending to retrieve it, he saw her blue shoe, partly suede, and the shape of her long calf in black hose, and on her lap, the small book, which was now closed. He looked up. She was watching him.

"Why are you following me?" she asked.

"Am I?"

"It seems so. You were in the courtroom, taking notes, and then you were following me, and finally you climbed onto the bus, and now you're crawling around on the floor, inspecting my legs. Unless this is all happenstance."

He sat back and said that it was true that he had followed her. He said that he had been intrigued by her use of the word "ineffable," and now he was even more interested because she had said "happenstance." "Not a lot of people I know use those two words within such a short span of time. Most don't even know what they mean. I wasn't looking at your legs, I was trying to see what you were reading."

She held up her small book. It was by someone called Norman O. Brown.

"I don't know that," he said.

That didn't seem to surprise her.

He held out his hand. "Morris Schutt."

She offered her hand, still gloved in yellow, and he felt the softness of the leather and the firmness of her grasp. "Lucille Black."

"You're a doctor."

"Becoming."

"May I ask a question?" Morris said. "Off the record."

She gave a small shrug.

"During the course of the conversation with that man, the accused, when you were suturing him, did he in fact confess?"

"To what?"

"To the murder."

"Like I said, he confessed to no guilt."

"That doesn't make him not guilty."

"You're absolutely right." She smiled briefly and spoke no more of it. This strange affect, of presenting herself as a model of clarity and yet not being completely transparent, would perplex Morris throughout their marriage, though it would not displease him.

She was attractive but not beautiful; her mouth was too wide and she didn't have the uniformity in her face that would have made her regal. She was quite tall and her legs were long and she walked through the world as if she were alone, as if she might always be alone. This independence would remain a problem in their relationship, beginning with the classic courtship. It turned out that Morris had to woo her. She would open the door slightly, and then close it. For a year, he took her to plays and movies and out for dinner and bought her flowers. Whenever they wandered through a shop and she pointed out something that pleased her, he would return the next day and buy it for her and either have it delivered to her or present it as a gift when he next saw her. She didn't seem overly thrilled by his offerings, but neither did she rebuff him. He was besotted. He couldn't wait to sit across from her and take her in. He held her hand as they walked. He finally kissed her after a dinner where they had both had too much to drink. She sighed and put her arms around his neck and she lingered and breathed in his ear. When he said that he wanted no one else, that he was absolutely in love with her, she said, "Of course you are."

He waited for her to say that she loved him, but she didn't. They played tennis. In the summer they met at the courts near the river, and in winter they played indoors at the expensive club she belonged to. Her father, a lawyer who had more money than Morris had ever imagined possible, paid for her membership. She was a tough-minded player who hated to lose, and she rarely did. Morris was an average player, more athletic than skilled. He was happy to have her win, happy to hear her chirping on the other side of the net, calling out the score, advising him to follow through on his backhand.

Tennis ultimately was the path to her heart. When she played, she was loose, suddenly in a world that did not require moral strength, and this made her more affectionate. One time, when she hit a passing shot to his forehand and scored a point, she called out, "Oh, Morris, I love you."

They married in the fall of 1980. Her father was quite ill and she wanted to marry before he died, even though Mr. Black had never truly appreciated Morris. He'd been judged harshly, thrown up against an impossible template. All Morris had had as a mentor was his own father, a Mennonite pastor who, when he met Lucille, couldn't believe that she would stoop to spend time with his own son. And neither could Mr. Black. But Lucille was wilful and sure. She had just graduated from medical school, and would move on to psychiatry, and so Morris would continue working as a journalist while she finished her studies. Morris was ecstatic. He was also looking forward to sex with Lucille. Though they had done everything from oral sex to sleeping naked together through the night, there had been no penetration because Lucille insisted that that was for the marriage bed. All of her friends were having sex; in fact, Morris felt that everyone in the world was having sex except him. He accused Lucille of hypocrisy, of wanting to live in a world of knights and princesses, where honour was rampant. She said, "Exactly. What better choice is there?" And she kissed him hungrily.

"Freedom" and "commitment"—these were Lucille's words and she asked Morris to accept them as well. She said that there could not be one without the other. "I'm freely choosing you," she said. "And this will bind us. After we are married, I will not go to anyone else. I will not leave you for another. Until death divides us." Morris had loved these words, the deep and abiding agreement, the commitment.

But now death, indeed, had divided them. As he packed his books into boxes and his clothes into suitcases in the last days of his marriage, he thought about the emotions of that earlier time: of the wedding night during which he had been naive and hasty and Lucille had been very tender, and how, finally, as they made love once again in the early morning, a window had opened onto his heart and he had experienced pure gratitude to finally be lying beside his wife; and of coming home happily from his office to their tiny apartment, to find Lucille sitting on the bed in her tank top and pyjamas, notes spread around her as she researched medical cases. Adoration. Pride of possession and certainty.

It would be Dr. G, years later, who would challenge Morris on his belief in certainty, stating dryly, "There is none, Morris. There is no certainty."

At the men's group on Thursday night, Mervine was the first to speak. "I've had diarrhea. Been about five days now and the doctor says maybe a virus and asks if I've travelled lately, and then he recommends Imodium, which can really bung you up, I hear. But the point is, the point is this, and there is a point beyond me having the shits, the point is that all this might be due to anxiety. My daughter moved in with her mother. She warned me, said, 'Dad, I love you, you know that, I truly love you, but I need to be with Mom for a bit'—you know, the girl thing—and I said, 'No problem, sweetie, you do that, I'll be fine.' And so she left, and I wander around the house and end up sitting in my tent that I've set up in the backyard, listening to some country station, because, because it feels safer. In the fucking tent."

Mervine was one of seven men in the men's group, eight if you counted the leader, Doug. Morris was sitting beside Mervine, whom he liked best of all the men there. Mervine was a runt of a man with a pockmarked face and dark blue jeans and cowboy boots who was a shipper-receiver for a trucking company. He was an epileptic. In one of the earlier sessions, he'd told the group the story of his first seizure. He was seventeen and it was three a.m. and he was waiting in a parking lot with a group of boys who were about to be picked up to go catch turkeys. He'd been eating licorice and laughing and suddenly he felt himself go shit-faced and a light descended and when he woke up he was in the hospital. Fellows told him later that he'd landed on his back on the asphalt and his cowboy boots were clacking like jackhammers and he was foaming at the mouth. Only other time it happened was when he was *shtupping* a woman who wasn't his wife. Not a good scene, though he wasn't conscious for most of it. "Don't worry," he said, "I don't expect to go all shit-faced in this group."

Morris asked if he was Jewish.

"Not at all."

"He's about as Jewish as a sow's ear," said Don, a burly man who claimed to be a financial adviser. He smiled.

"Damn right," Mervine said.

"It's just that he said he was *shtupping*," Morris said, and they moved on, as the group was wont to do, jumping here and there, their discussions not particularly linear, not always profound, rarely incisive, but usually worthwhile.

Mac, who was the oldest and who always asked a lot of questions without revealing much about himself, wondered how it was that Mervine ended up in his tent. What did he find comforting there?

"Well, it's clean and small and I roll down the flap so's I can see the sky and the stars at night, and sometimes I pull up a chair and survey my lawn and there's the smell of grass clippings and I build a little fire and there's nothing there to remind me of my wife, who I hate, or my daughter, who I love. I don't sleep in the house anymore." He looked around sheepishly, as if this were something he'd had no intention of speaking about. "Aww, man." He looked down at his cowboy boots.

Morris talked about his hands. He knew that, initially, none of the other men had wanted him in the group because he was a columnist and the group was afraid that he would use the confessions and conversations for his own gossip. "Nothing leaves this room," Doug had said. "No one takes what is said here and moves it outside. That understood? It's about the energy. If you take what is said here and bring it home to your wife, or your lover, or your brother, or someone else, then the energy gets sucked out of this space. I can't know what you're doing, but it'll be felt. Believe me, you will affect the group." He was talking to everyone, but he was preaching to Morris, who waved and said that he had enough fodder already. "I've got my own life," he said, and he grimaced.

Morris said that the flaking of his hands must be coming from worry and stress. "They bleed in the morning," he said. "I wake up thinking about Martin." He had talked about this before, but he once again told them a version of his pain. This time it was about the day in February when the people from the Canadian Forces had arrived at the house to give him the news. "My wife was working and I think now that I should have waited till she came home. I wanted to know at that moment why these two men were standing in my foyer, though I did know actually. It was like I couldn't wait to hear the bad news. 'Tell me,' I said, and they told me, and as soon as they told me, I was sorry they had spoken and I was sorry that I had not waited for Lucille, though how does one do that when the messenger is chomping at the bit? She was absolutely furious. And irrational. Sometimes I think that what destroyed our marriage wasn't Martin's death but me not waiting for her to come home to hear the news with me. She called it typical and selfish. I know that I'm selfish, but I don't want to be typical."

"Typical of what?" Ezra asked. He was sitting across from Morris and he was leaning forward, elbows on his knees. He was married to a beautiful woman who was a former model and he had potency issues. His wife was too gorgeous. His father had told him to marry a less beautiful woman, but he hadn't listened and now he was in trouble. He didn't trust her. Ezra said, "When are you going to get over this?"

"And when are you going to be alive again from the neck down?" Morris asked. He felt the rage located in his lower gut and in his crotch. He smiled. Ezra leaned back and shook his head and closed his eyes.

"Not fair," Doug said. "Too personal. Listen, men, we know that we can't use someone else's vulnerability as ammunition. How are we going to trust each other?"

Bill spoke. He rarely spoke, and everyone listened more carefully now because this was such a rarity. He did not speak of potency or sex or a spurned lover, but he talked about his father, who was at the edge of death. He said the words "edge of death" and Morris tilted towards him, as if there were something curious and interesting that had landed in the centre of the group. Bill said that he had always disliked his father, for his anger, his demands, his velocity. He was like a bullet ricocheting around a room and now the bullet had fallen to the ground. "The doctors say he's going to die within the week."

Doug said that he was sorry. Peter, a Filipino man in his late thirties who lived with his extended family, all of them crammed into one house, placed his hand on top of Bill's and left it there for three long seconds. Then he took it away.

"Thank you," Bill said.

Ezra said that his father had died two years ago of a heart attack and left him with a business that was overloaded with debt. "He up and dies and leaves the bank banging at my door. He did it on purpose."

"What do you mean?" Doug asked.

"It was like he wanted to be nearly bankrupt just before he died. So that I could suffer."

Ezra was Jewish, but Morris wished that he wasn't, because then he could hate him. He was a spoiled man-child who lacked the authenticity of those Jewish men Morris knew from the health club. There was no joking sanguinity, no self-mockery, only a deep-seated seriousness and a head full of negative numbers. Ezra knew nothing about the Pentateuch, or God, or Moses, or the King of the Jews, even though every Saturday he went to synagogue. Morris knew that he could easily beat Ezra at a quiz on the history of the Israelites. What kind of a Jew was that? He deserved to go bankrupt.

Morris said, "My father, who lives in a home for the disabled and the very old, is beginning to lose his mind. The other day he thought I was my brother Samuel and asked me to pray with him. And so I did, though I didn't want to. Meanwhile, the man in the next bed is beating himself off. And there I am, praying with my father, who thinks I'm Samuel, and I'm more interested in how both my father and I are aware of Cornie masturbating in the next bed, but we don't say anything. It's distressing for everyone. And then I worry that my father will descend into anarchy, like Cornie, his neighbour. I wonder if my father ever lusted. I never saw it. He was always faithful, never cheated on my mother, never told dirty jokes. I never even heard him swear."

Mervine laughed. "Great story."

Ezra fluttered his hands mockingly and said, "'Descend into anarchy'—that's just stupid. What does that mean?"

Bill chuckled and Peter, with suspicious eyes, just nodded.

"Lawlessness," Morris said, looking at Ezra. "Chaos. Disorder. That better?"

"Great fucking story," Mervine said.

Doug said, "I find it interesting that you imagine your father becoming like Cornie. He's given you no reason to believe that. Perhaps you see yourself becoming Cornie. This isn't about your father at all."

Was this true? Later, driving home, Morris imagined himself thirty years older and lying in a hospital bed, mind gone, asking some nurse-in-training to play with him. There must be some way to circumvent the subconscious, he thought. Some valve that could be turned on and off, at will, in order to release his longing. He was too clamped, too much like his father that way, seeking the narrow road and then stumbling on the thorny roots at the side of the path.

Back in late June, just west of Paynesville on the I-94 a few hours out of Minneapolis, on his way to meet Ursula, he had seen a billboard with a picture of a marine and the words "Devoted to a life of courage" and a Web address, "marines.com," and he'd been suddenly aware of the unfamiliarity of the country he'd just entered and he felt lost. Several months earlier, riding the bus one day to his downtown office where he sometimes wrote his columns, he had been rereading *Anna Karenina,* deep into the lives of Anna and Levin and Vronsky, and he'd lifted his head to see if his stop was near, and when he couldn't situate his place in the world, nausea hit him, then vertigo, and his head swam. The sense of not knowing himself had been so strong that he thought he might throw up. Upon seeing the billboard on the I-94 he had experienced that powerful feeling once again, the dislocation and the foreignness. In this strange world called America, courage was held up under a certain convoluted light.

He did not see Ursula as a prize. She was a tragic figure, like him, and when, in the stillness of her hotel room, she took his head in her hands and said, "You're a beautiful man," he was astonished that anyone could say these words. They had first met in the restaurant, shaken hands, and Ursula looked him up and down and said, "You're taller than I imagined."

"And you," Morris said, "you're not blonde."

She said that her parents were dark haired, even though they were Dutch. "Were you hoping for someone blonde?"

This startled Morris. He found it forward and accusing, as if she were sensing something about him that he himself did not yet know. But as the evening progressed he discovered that she was also clear-headed and guileless. They both spoke of their sons, but Ursula was more vocal, more willing to reveal herself. In fact, at some point Morris felt that her son was sitting near them.

"My friends are tired of me," she said. "All I do is talk about Harley. Even my husband's tired of me."

"My wife and I had nothing left to say to each other," Morris said, and immediately he was sorry. He had not meant to say anything about Lucille and here he was, talking about her again. He wanted her to be gone. What a feast she would make of this. If he could be brave enough to enter her lair, the office on the fifteenth floor of that glass building, where her corner windows gave south onto the river and west to the Great West Life edifice, and beyond that the spire of the Westminster United Church whose bells pealed merrily out of key every lunch hour, announcing death and more death and then death again and finally life—if he could slip past her door and have her inspect his heart and soul, she would happily point out what was on his back. A big lie, a load for the beast. She wouldn't help him get rid of the burden. She would just point it out and say, "There you are, there it is." She wouldn't even say that it was a burden. She would cunningly let him discover it for himself. It wasn't her burden after all, it was his. He was the one who slept with it, who walked around the city with it, unaware, though all and sundry could see the malformed bundle; he was like the man who has suffered polio as a child and now must stoop his way through to death. The burden was many things: his tremendous pride, his fear, his love of sex and high-heeled shoes, his envy and rage, his shame.

He pushed away these thoughts and watched Ursula's mouth as she spoke and imagined kissing her.

She said, "My husband, Cal, he's always believed in the army. It's how he grew up. And it's how he raised our son. But now he's angry. The government's failed him and he's angry. He has guns." She shrugged, almost imperceptibly.

"What do you mean?"

"He's always had a gun, but now he has a whole sackful. One day he goes to Cabella's and he buys a hunting rifle and then the following week he buys another, an automatic. He has six in total, with ammunition and cases. He spends his evenings cleaning the guns and breaking them down. He shows Wilhelm the guns. They work together and Cal talks to Wilhelm about velocity and wind and distance. I don't think an eleven-year-old needs to know about this, and I tell Cal, but he won't listen to me anymore. He used to play music in the barn, milking the cows. But nowadays there's no music, just the sound of the milking machine and the bucket bunters knocking pails of feed around. Everything's changed since Harley died."

Morris said, "My father was a pacifist. He passed this idea on to me and I accepted it, and then I tried to pass it on to my son, Martin, who because he needed something to push against, I suppose, laughed at me and joined the army. I'm not against taking care of myself, of protecting my own, but I cannot accept, as you people seem to, that billions need to be spent on a war machine."

"Nobody's a pacifist." She smiled in the slightest way. He loved her voice.

She had one crooked eye tooth and Morris thought that this was very attractive. It made her seem more vulnerable. She excused herself and made her way to the bathroom at the far end of the lobby and he watched her cross the marble floor. She wore jeans and a light green short-sleeved sweater, and high black boots that made her legs appear longer than they were, and he saw her arms and her shoulder blades and her backside, and he wanted her. Imagination was the ultimate eroticism. It trumped reality.

Her room was on the nineteenth floor and, like his, it had a deep-orange rug and off-white curtains and two double beds and double mirrors so that everything, when you entered, was doubled once again. Her window faced onto Marquette Avenue and from that height one could see across to the structure of Westminster Presbyterian. She stood by the window and he was behind her. A foot of space separated them. He said, "There are churches everywhere." And then he asked if she went to church, and she said that she did. She and her husband attended the First Congregational Church in Alexandria, where they lived, but she had grown up Dutch Reformed. She felt safe in a church, she said. He asked if that was all. Did she just feel safe, or did she believe in something more?

In the restaurant, earlier, she had said, "Come to my room," and then she looked at him and held his gaze until he looked away, at the approaching waitress, and he'd been aware that she was more honest than he was. After the waitress had given them the bill and he'd paid, she said, "I'm not thinking that we have to have sex, but I'm not against it. Since Harley died, I've stopped waiting for the world to come and get me. I spent so many years putting my toe into the water to test it and then stepping back. I never really jumped. Now, I'm ready to jump. You don't have to jump. That's your decision. But I don't have time to get to know you, to play the flirting game. I like you, I like how your mind works. I know this because I've read your columns and your letters, and now, talking to you, I can see that you're a man I can trust." She paused.

"What about your husband?" he said.

She said that Cal didn't have to know. In fact, these days Cal might not even care, he was so taken with revenge.

"Is he dangerous? All those guns."

She laughed. "He doesn't even know who you are."

"You've never talked about me?"

"I have. I talk about your columns." She said that this wasn't like her. Usually she was up front and she'd tell Cal what she was feeling, but these days he wasn't willing to hear her talk about her feelings. She said that she had told Cal that she needed a weekend alone. She simpered slightly and moved her shoulders. "So, here I am." She asked if he had told his wife that he was coming down to Minneapolis.

He said that he was living alone. She didn't need to know.

"You're honest."

"Mostly."

"You wanna have sex with me?"

"It's not that simple."

"Sure it is. Do you want to have sex with me?"

"Yes, I do. But there's too much turmoil in my life, and sex with you would just make for more turmoil. We'll go up to your room and we'll take off our clothes and lie down together and press our bodies against each other and I'll enter inside you, which is the most intimate thing one can do with another person, and then tomorrow I'll drive home to Canada and you'll go back to your farm and your son and husband. And I will think of you, and I will think of you some more, and that is one kind of turmoil, and another is you thinking of me and wondering if I will return, wondering if I love you or if I have simply disappeared."

She laughed. "'Enter inside you'—who talks like that? Anyways, I don't mind. You think I'm being used by you, but I might be the one doing the using." She said the last *I* pointedly.

"There's that as well." Then he said that Lucille had always felt that marriage was for life, that when they had said "till death do us part," it actually meant something, but now he had begun to understand that the death in this case was not Lucille's or his own, but their son's. "This is not profound, but it is true." He placed the bill on the table and stood and held out his hand to her.

"Smell me," she said. She was at the window, looking down onto the street below. She had taken off her boots and thrown them in haste across the room and they lay stranded by the wall and the foot of the bed. She pressed her palms against the windowpane. The curtains were open and it was darker in the room than it was outside where the city lights were just beginning to glow. Over the last while, when he had found himself in a hotel room with a woman who was a stranger, a woman he paid for, there had always been a wall between him and the woman, and usually it took great effort for him to climb over that wall. With Ursula, there was no barrier.

He approached her and leaned forward, barely an inch from the back of her neck, and breathed in.

"All of me," she whispered, and she turned to face him, her arms in the air.

He smelled under one arm and then the other. He smelled the sweater that covered her bra and her breasts. He circled her and smelled the small of her back, and then her rump. Still, he did not touch her, not with his nose, or his tongue, or any part of himself. His hands hovered as he smelled her hips and then her thighs and finally her calves and feet. He was on his hands and knees now, aware of the texture of the rug, and he thought, Look at you, Morris Schutt. He took deep breaths. He had an image of the computer keyboard in his condo and of the "enter" key; one tap with the baby finger on his right hand. He had an erection.

He stood and faced her. He smelled her cheeks, her ears, behind her ears, her mouth, and her neck again. She held up her hands, palms facing him with her fingers slightly spread, and he smelled first the heels of her hands, and then her wrists and her fingers and between her fingers. He stepped back and she began to cry.

❖

Sadness had overwhelmed their desire. He stood before her and watched the tears fall, and he took her in his arms and held her as she wept. Then he led her to the bed and told her to lie down. She did this, and he took the blanket at the end of the bed and covered her and then lay down beside her until she slept. The light slipped from the room and he too fell asleep, and when he woke it was dark and his arms still held her. He rose and stood by the window that looked out towards the towers of the church in the distance. The movement of traffic below. A few human figures darkly walking. The history of the universe is the history of a man. To see everything in the light of the soul, to see those dark figures down there as souls, to understand that every human, every flower, every created thing, is divine. To understand that the Absolute is not the father, that the father begins to exist only when he produces the son. Take his own father, a man who used to write songs, and then, strumming his acoustic guitar, he would offer the songs to whoever would listen. And he wrote poetry with a clip-clop metre and a simple rhyme. He was a man who secretly yearned to be published. A man who observed his son become a journalist, a semi-famous columnist, and judged him for it. "Your sentences are fine but they are empty. Trite. There is more to the world than sex and irony and making fun. You have an audience. Talk to them about goodness." By "goodness" he meant the salvation of lost souls, the conveying of Truth. The poetry his father wrote was simple; it lacked polish and insight; it was deliberate, the opposite of what Morris wrote. His father's sermons were deliberate. His goal was salvation. It was criminal to dance around the edges of truth when at any minute death might come knocking; for you, for the parishioner in the pew, for the young person who is seeking answers. It took courage to be literal. Which, to Morris's mind, was nonsense. His father had been a purveyor of solace and selfishness; like all good preachers, he had promoted the fear of death and then promised freedom. Morris did not know courage, but he knew what it wasn't. It wasn't the erasure of death. It wasn't some middle-class idea of a pain-free life. It wasn't running down to Minneapolis to hold a strange woman in a hotel room on the nineteenth floor of the Hilton. That took very little courage. There was no courage in success either. He had editors clamouring for his columns, he had the ear of the reader, he was known, and he was rich; he carried in his wallet a sheaf of one-hundred-dollar bills that totalled in the thousands. His father had always been poor. Morris would not be poor. Nor did he wish to succumb to the danger of the fool who sees his own image in everything. Moderation in everything, except moderation. His father had been excessively religious, excessively devout, and excessive in introspection. Wanting to be a writer, he had instead chosen to be a minister of the soul, a minister of justice, a minister of spiritual health, Christ's own emissary finally crucified by his own sense of inadequacy. The world would not listen. It was Morris who became the writer, as if calling out to his father, "Look at me, Dad. I can do what you could not." The trick, the neat trick of it, was exactly this: His father was a father because Morris was the son. There was the other son, of course, Samuel the elder, who had received all of their father's attention. He had become the missionary, was pious, and unlike Morris with his verbal juggling, he didn't lay his family out on the public altar. Still, there must have been tenderness for the prodigal son in his father's heart. You love most that which you do not comprehend, or that which is taken from you, or denied you. He had an image of his father at a family gathering, standing in the corner, drinking dark coffee, a mixture of petulance and pride. A man too stringent, too intelligent for the clowns in his wife's family. Harshness has its merits. The sharpness, the incisive thought, all of Blake memorized, all of the Old Testament tucked away in his heart, and then much lost to senility, that horrid monster.

In the morning, Ursula's cellphone rang and rang, and then stopped. And rang again. She climbed from the bed and scrambled for her purse and found the phone. She flipped it open and said, "Hey, sweetie." Her voice was husky, full of sleep.

Morris, when he'd finally felt tired in the middle of the night, had chosen to climb into the other bed beside Ursula's, knowing that his own room would feel too blank. He was awake now, peering at Ursula who sat on the edge of her bed, her legs bare. She'd taken off her clothes at some point during the night and she was wearing black underwear and a black spaghetti-strap top. Her knees were round. Her shoulders as well. Her fingernails were long and painted apple red, and they glowed against the black of the phone. She saw Morris watching her, and she rose and wrapped herself in a sheet from her bed and went into the bathroom and closed the door, and all he heard was her muffled voice. He stood and went to her purse and opened it. Looking inside, he thought, Morris, Morris, and then he saw the gun and he put the purse down and sat quickly and stared at himself in the mirror. It was comical, he thought, snooping through her purse as if he could find there some secret key to Ursula Frank. The toilet flushed and she came back into the room. She had put on a bathrobe and knotted it double at the waist. She was no longer on the phone and she carried it in one hand and with the other she tossed the sheet back onto the bed. She stood, confused, it seemed, by the intimacy and the domesticity of the room.

She lifted her chin. "You slept in your clothes."

Morris regarded himself. He got up and went into the bathroom and sat down to pee. When he came out, she had dressed and started the coffee maker and she stood by the window.

"It's Sunday," she said. "People are going to church."

He did not approach her. Instead, he sat and put on his shoes and tied them and thought this thought: Everyone is scuttling into temples. Then he stood and said he would be going down to his room.

"There's coffee," she said, turning to face him.

"I'm fine. I need to shower, brush my teeth. I'll phone up later. Okay?"

"That was Wilhelm. He was throwing up. He wanted to know when I was coming home. Ever since Harley died, he does this when I go away. Makes himself sick so that I have to come home."

"So, you'll go?"

"Yes. Right away. I'm sorry."

"Why? There's no need. I should be the one apologizing."

"Really? What happened last night?"

"Nothing. You went to sleep."

"You were very sweet. Thank you."

He laughed. "Now that's something new. 'Sweet.'" He felt great desire for her. He moved towards the door.

She watched him and then lifted a hand and said, "I'll write you."

He did not hear from her for several months. And when she finally wrote, in late September, he had just lost his column and the weather was turning. Her letter picked up where they'd left off, as if the span of time had not been great, as if she had stepped out of the room for a moment and then returned to pick up the conversation. She said that she had talked too much about Harley.

Morris, you kept asking questions and so I talked and
talked like a real blabbermouth, and only later did I real-

ize that you hadn't really said anything about Martin. I feel that you were hiding something. Last Sunday, Cal and I finally spread Harley's ashes down by the stream that runs behind the barn. Before we did this, we sat on lawn chairs and watched two whooping cranes fly in from the south, one behind the other, and coast silently along the path of the stream. They were maybe three inches from the water's surface. The shadow of the first crane startled the fish in the stream and the second crane, following closely, caught those startled fish. The crane dipped his claws into the water, just like that, and scooped up the fish. The cranes did this three times in a row, and each time the second bird caught a fish. Cal said that the birds were like Cheney and Bush. Cheney's the one who disturbs the life beneath the clean surface, and then Bush goes in for the kill. When Cal talks like this, I get scared. That day, there was a tiny wind blowing, and when we spread Harley's ashes out over the water, after the birds had left, some of the ashes fell onto my boots and the ashes were still there in the morning and I didn't want them to go away, so I wrapped the boots in Saran Wrap and laid them in the closet, up beside the strongbox where Cal keeps his important papers. Is that crazy? I want to see you again, even though Wilhelm hates me leaving. I can plan to be in Minneapolis whenever you're free. Let me know.

✧

She was offering him a form of deliverance, this is what it felt like, and he wanted to crow call out to his neighbours, a young couple he met on the stairway every morning as they went off to work, very slickly, both of them in colourful coats, like Joseph before he was thrown into the well by his brothers, she in high heels, he in long-toed black polished shoes. A beautiful couple, without children, no worries, no one to lose, their future brightly beckoning them. He had talked to the woman, Beth Ann, at some length one afternoon, a conversation about food because Morris had just stepped over to the Happy Cooker to buy himself a new toaster, and now he was returning to his apartment to prepare a bagel. Beth Ann said that she and Tom preferred toaster ovens. And then they'd talked of grilled things and salmon and finally books. She was reading *Madame Bovary.* She felt sorry for Hippolyte, the one with the club foot. She felt not a spot of pity for Emma: "Emma deserved everything that fell down upon her head." Morris had been surprised and dismayed at Beth Ann's vehemence. Such moral indignation. He wondered if it should be "fell down *around* her head," but he didn't correct her. He said that interestingly he had just reread *Anna Karenina* and he'd always felt that there was a very natural bond between the two books; both about women who are trapped. Beth Ann smiled and said, "Well, they do both kill themselves, don't they? Anyways, Emma traps herself." And then she said that she and Tom were having a party on Saturday night, would he like to come? He had hummed and given an indefinite answer. Now he stepped out into the hallway, as if Beth Ann might miraculously appear and want to continue the conversation about nineteenth-century women, but he saw no one. He stepped back inside and phoned Mervine, from the men's group.

Mervine, in a moment of vulnerability, had recently asked Morris to help him write letters to his ex-wife. Mervine had said that he wasn't a very good writer, he didn't have a way with words, and he figured if Morris wrote something persuasive and forgiving and not too elegant, then his wife might be convinced to come back to him. And if not convinced of that, she might at least be persuaded that she shouldn't have left a man who could write such fine words. There was no answer and so Morris left Mervine a message and said that they should get together to play pool, or maybe have a bite to eat, lunch or dinner, it didn't matter to him. He had all the time in the world. He'd just been fired from his job. He sat in his leather chair, aware that his own flesh and blood, his family, existed out there in the city, living their lives, and he wondered if Libby was with Shane. He pondered this and as he pondered his anger grew. The man was an outright charlatan. Morris picked up the phone and called the university. The switchboard transferred him to Dr. McKibben's voice-mail, and when the message cut in, Morris waited and then said: "Mr. McKibben, this is Morris Schutt. A while back I left you a note about my daughter, Libby Schutt. I pushed the note under your door, and as I have not heard back from you, and as I know that you are still with my daughter, I can only imagine that the note was vacuumed up by a janitor and you did not see it, or I can assume that your silence is an admission of guilt on your part. What you are doing is wrong. You know that. Look at it this way. If you were seventeen years old, she would be a one-year-old. Would a teenager date a one-year-old? You see what I mean? Perhaps you are having trouble with attachment, or perhaps you suffered as a child, you didn't get enough love, or something was broken at a tender age. Figure that out, sir, but figure it out with the help of a shrink, or talk to a friend, or talk to your mother. Don't use my daughter to assuage your sickness. I will keep calling and I will leave notes, and if you don't act in a proper manner, I will have to take further action, the kind of action that cannot please you. Though I am a pacifist, in this case I would be willing to meet you in a back alley and use my fists. There are people I can talk to, sir. The ethics board. The president of the university. I know him. I could easily write a column about you, Mr. McKibben, and it would not be flattering. How would you like that? I didn't think so. In fact, you might try to sue me. Good luck with that. Anyway, that's all for today. I look forward to you making the right decision." Morris hung up. He was breathing heavily and his mouth was dry. He stood and poured himself some juice and drank it quickly, feeling the cold deep in his chest.

He still felt the need to talk and so he phoned Samuel in Idaho, which would surprise his brother because they rarely spoke. No answer there either. His brother was a teacher of Arabic who worked secretly for the CIA. He had done this for a number of years now, ever since the Americans had suffered that terrible loss on September 11 and then had decided that whoever was not for them was against them. And they proceeded to pillory all things Muslim. And Samuel, his brother, had benefitted. He had told Morris this when he'd last come to visit their father, leaning forward and whispering conspiratorially that he now worked for the CIA. This did not surprise Morris. As a young man, Samuel had studied to be a missionary and had learned Arabic as an aid worker in the Sudan and then he'd married an American woman, become an American citizen himself, divorced, and found a job in the States where he could apply his Arabic. Samuel had always loved America and things American. He considered Canadians to be weak and dependent. Morris left Samuel a message on his machine: "Samuel, Morris here. I'm thinking of converting to Islam. Give me a call."

Then he sat down and typed a letter to Ursula. He said that he would be delighted to join her in Minneapolis. Perhaps in late October, a month from now, though there was nothing in his life at the moment to keep him from seeing her sooner, should she prefer. "This letter," he wrote, "will arrive at your house in a few days, and then your response, should you decide to respond, will take another week, and so it seems practical to plan for a month from now." He said that her letter had pleased him greatly. He missed her. He said that he was less aware these days of Martin's absence, but that might be because he was filling his life with material things and material thoughts, and what a distraction this could be. He said that he had much to tell her, some things that might surprise her. "I am a difficult man," he wrote. Then he wrote "Love, Morris," as if that would compensate for admitting that he was difficult. Or perhaps he wanted to scare her. He did not understand himself. Ever since he had spent that night with her, first smelled her from head to toe, and then slept on the bed next to hers, he had had little desire for anyone else. She kept appearing in his mind. On the back of his eye. She surrounded him and this was frustrating his erotic life. There was a need to clear up the problem and his sense of relief made him feel capricious and volatile.

When he had told Dr. G that he paid women for sex, Dr. G had shifted in his chair and looked slightly bored.

"It's only been a while now," Morris said. "I started, almost by chance, after Lucille left me."

Dr. G lifted his head. "When you say things like 'by chance' and 'Lucille left me,' you make yourself out as a puppet."

Morris ignored this. "You're not shocked? You don't find me pathetic? Dirty?"

"Should I?"

"Well, most people would find it reprehensible. And yes, I do enjoy it. Most of the time."

"And you're not most people."

Morris shrugged. "No, I'm not."

"Why stop there? Why don't you drive downtown on a Saturday night and pick up a fourteen-year-old girl? Or hire three women at the same time?"

Morris sighed. "Lucille says I gorge myself. On grief and sex. She says that I was unprepared for Martin's death. That I should have seen that Martin was going to a death-dealing event, not a feast. She prepared herself, as if she knew that some rehearsal was required. I didn't, and so I was surprised by the unexpected." He paused, then said, "She's right."

"You've told her about hiring women?"

"Oh, no." He brightened. "Chekhov hired prostitutes."

"So you and Chekhov, you're equals. And your daughters? What about them? Wouldn't they be surprised?"

Morris leaned forward and touched the dog lying at his feet. A shudder. The wet mournful eyes pondered him. You poor fucker.

On Saturday, he picked up Libby at her mother's house and took her to a Vietnamese restaurant. They ate *pho* and spring rolls and drank green tea and they talked about Libby's debating team; she was the leader, and she told him about argument and riposte and speech. She said that often the content was inconsequential, like political debates, where flow and ebb and smoothness of the words could beat out intelligence. She didn't like that. She thought she might quit. It was taking time away from her reading, her pre-cal, her volunteer work. She was wearing a soft brown sweater, a turtleneck, and her hair was cut short, and she looked like her mother, same chin, though her nose was sharper and she was prettier than Lucille. Her eyes were brighter and she was more willing to smile and try to please people. Morris thought that that might be a problem, this need to please, which was why when she said she might quit the debating team, he didn't argue.

"Might be a good thing," he said.

"Mrs. Kualla, our supervising teacher, says I can't quit.

The team needs me. She's a Nazi but she's a good Nazi. You know what I mean?"

He didn't know, but he said he did.

She talked about her work at Deer Lodge Centre, where she read to a ninety-year-old woman called Minnie Pishker. "She has no idea what I'm reading, but she likes the sound of my voice. Her arms are like sticks, Dad, and she knows when I'm there as soon as I walk in. Lifts her skinny arms and says, 'Libby.' She makes a sucking sound with her mouth. She's blind yet she senses everything. No one visits her. I think her daughter comes at Christmas. It's so sad." She blinked and Morris imagined that she might cry. But she didn't. She continued, "She reminds me of Grandpa. Has a foul mouth like he does. She swears at me in Yiddish. Calls me *kurveh*. Mr. Fox, down the hall, told me what it means. But she doesn't know what she's saying."

For a year now, Libby had volunteered at Deer Lodge where Morris had put his father when he was too confused to take care of himself. Libby had chosen Deer Lodge so that she could see her grandfather more often. Every day she was there she went down to Grandpa Schutt's room for lunch and sat with him. At first she had been upset that he did not know her, that his mind soared in many different directions, and then one day she discovered that he liked to listen to her iPod Shuffle, that this quieted him and relieved his agitation. And as he became familiar with the music, he began to sing along in his baritone voice, quite beautiful really, chiming in to songs by the Pogues and Bob Dylan. "He likes ballads," Libby said. "Softer music. No techno, that upsets him." She was so matter-of-fact. She bought him his own iPod and downloaded some classical music and gospel tunes. Some country. His favourite was Leonard Cohen. One evening, Morris arrived for a visit and he heard his father grandly singing "Bird on a Wire."

Morris could learn something from his own daughter. He said now, "Your mother must be happy, you working in a hospital, a step closer to becoming a doctor."

"I'm not going to be a doctor. You know that."

"You're eighteen, Libby. You don't know that yet."

"Are you okay, Dad?"

"Oh, well, what a question. I'm pursuing happiness." He smiled and then shrugged. "I'm fine. Don't worry about your father." Then he said that he wanted to warn her. He was getting rid of his cellphone and his e-mail address. "Though I'll keep my land line. You can call me at home, but no message service."

"What are you talking about?"

"I'm cancelling everything. No more technology in my life. I'm throwing out the TV as well. And cutting off the Internet."

"Why are you doing this? Does Mom know?"

"She'll find out. It's not a big deal. I was standing in the meat line at De Luca's and the woman in front of me gets on the phone and asks her husband what kind of cheese they want, Reggiano or Padano. She can't even make a simple decision. The cellphone has become a soother, an umbilical cord, a clattering intrusion. If we're texting or talking, we think we're alive. So, kaput, mine's gone."

Libby said, "But I like being able to call you. I like knowing that you might pick up, or that I can text you and you'll get right back to me. This makes me sad. Why wouldn't you want to talk to me?"

"Libby, Libby. It's not that. We can talk as often as you like. You can write me letters. You can come over and walk in my door anytime. You can phone me at home, just like that. To tell the truth, if you were the only one in the world who had my number, I'd keep my cell. It's the others I don't want to talk to. My editor, my agent, your mother, Meredith."

Libby jumped on this. "Why don't you say sorry to Meredith? She's waiting. She told me that you're stubborn. Called you a mule and said that all you had to do was say sorry and she'd let you see Jake."

"She said that? 'Stubborn'?"

Libby nodded.

Morris spooned the last of the soup from the bowl. Little flecks of peppers, a remaining noodle, the last bit of shrimp. He said, "We did talk. She wouldn't really listen, but she did say I could see Jake. I'm taking care of him next Saturday. The thing about Meredith is she's inflexible."

"No, Dad, it's you. You say sorry and then you break into this long rationalization for why you said what you said or how it's the other person's fault for why you said what you said. Just say sorry and shut up." She wiped her mouth with a napkin. Said that she had to get home. She was meeting a friend. She wrapped a yellow scarf around her neck. Morris imagined that she would never find a boy good enough for her, which was why she was dating this Shane, who was probably a postmodernist to boot. She was too vulnerable, and though she would say she was unimpressed by credentials, there was something gullible about her. She loved her father, wasn't that a sign of gullibility? Though a daughter like her would forgive her father of much. Had already. She had never said a word about Martin, whom she loved, even after he and Lucille had sat her down and given her all the facts, even told her about Morris's anger and threats and the challenge to Martin to just go and join the fucking army already. She had said nothing. Just hugged her father and cried and said, "I'm so sorry. I'm so sorry." Who wouldn't want to be with a girl like that?

He dropped her off at home, watched her run up the stairs of the old house he used to live in, a three-storey Tudor style that was begging for a paint job. Perhaps Lucille's new man, a heart surgeon and handy at many other things, was also a scraper and a painter, and while repairing Lucille's heart, he could have a go at the house. Morris drove away, surprisingly full of good cheer. Libby had kissed him on the cheek and hugged him and told him to be good and to think twice about getting rid of his phone. He meandered happily through the city, torn between liberty and licence. He had in mind a tryst, someone who would offer him tricks, a prestidigitator, a juggler. He flipped open his cellphone as he drove and phoned the Fort Garry Hotel and made a reservation for that night, and then he dialled the 800 number by memory.

The woman who answered was efficient, as always, and Morris imagined her as the secretary slotting appointments into various daybooks. The time and the place was agreed upon. No credit card was required; Morris had an account with this company. When the woman asked what he preferred that night, Morris said, "Surprise me." When the woman called Morris back, she told him that Alicia would be joining him, and that she would arrive at midnight. Morris hung up and experienced the charm of humble awe. A brief meditation on the human soul. His soul. He saw that he knew nothing, and in acknowledging this he was suddenly at peace with not knowing. In the past, as a columnist, he had been expected to know something, had even presented himself as knowledgeable, and in pretending he had found prestige. No longer. Socrates had said something about ignorance: *All I know is that I know nothing.* Morris had been reading about Socrates lately, trying to make his way through *The Republic,* thinking that if he could understand the bigger questions, questions that soared above his own insignificant world, then he might not be so flummoxed by his own littleness. It was a bit of deception, this notion of knowing. Hah. And so, Morris thought, knowing that you know nothing makes you in fact a little wiser. He understood that the woman who would join him later that night, a woman with a false name and a sham of a smile, yet a willing heart, was not the path to love, but it would be a form of knowing, and it was a connection. He would reveal himself, offer his modest body to her, and she would not recoil. They would become acquainted. It was contact that he craved. He anticipated carnal love. He knew he was selfish and deluded and he wanted to remain so, at least for that evening and on into the night.

But first, in order to reclaim some balance on the teeter-totter that his life had become, he would pay his father a visit. With the gradual loss of his intelligence and memory, his father strangely was becoming more tender, as if the unforgiving walls had been broken down, and as a result, Morris himself could be more indulgent. He was learning to touch his father, to rub his feet and back. About a month ago now, on a Sunday morning, after an expensive Saturday night with a woman named Chelsea (it had become a pattern that he visited his father either before or after a night with his women), he had dropped in on his father and fed him a baguette that he'd picked up at the French bakery in St. Boniface. *As you did it to one of the least of these, you did it to me.* Together they had chewed the bread and then taken a drink of water from a plastic cup, and his father, sitting at the edge of his bed, his white legs bared, had mumbled something about Morris's kindness. "Ach," Morris said, "you're my father." And then he'd kneeled behind him and shampooed his father's hair and dried it, and then lifted his shirt and rubbed his back, and in doing so he was struck by his father's flesh, so loose in comparison to Chelsea's, and he remembered how, the night before, she had lifted her arms above her head as Morris bent to kiss her navel. On that Sunday morning, seeing the back of his father's small grey head, he suffered shame, for his own sexual vigour, and for the uselessness of his father's cock. Do not take me there, Morris thought. He read then, from a collection of poems by Frost that his father kept at his bedside, selecting pieces at random, because it didn't matter to his father, who simply liked the sound of what he believed was Samuel's voice. Morris accepted this, as he accepted the responsibility of taking care of his father. What affection and impatience he felt.

A few days later, when Lucille came by to check on him, he told her in an outpouring of magnanimity that he was becoming reconciled to his past, his upbringing. Everything that he had rejected in his father turned out to be true or correct: the parsimony, the frugality, the strictures, the chastity, the faithfulness. His father had been maniacal about living honestly and with integrity. He had recycled before it was in vogue. He had tithed more than ten percent. He had sheltered the homeless and fed the poor. He was not wasteful or degenerate. Many of these things Morris had rejected. He had thrown out the old and gathered up the new, the modern, the material, as if the past could be thrown out like a heap of garbage. It turned out that his father, in his stinginess and harshness, had been quite right about the world. It was damned.

Lucille smiled, briefly, something he had not seen in a long while. "You're scaring me, Morris," she said. He studied her studying herself in the bureau mirror. A memory of Martin admiring himself in this same mirror the first time he wore his dress uniform. What a clean-cut handsome boy, all done up for servility and for war.

"I'm scaring myself," he said. "Once, when Dad was sleeping, I thought how easily I could smother him. Just take a pillow and press it down onto his face."

Lucille turned. "Oh, Morris. That's awful."

"No one would know."

She looked at him carefully and then said, "Maybe it's me you want to kill."

He found his father sitting in a wheelchair by a window that looked out onto the street. There was a remnant of food on his blue shirt, near the left pocket. It was still damp, a green purée, and he took a Kleenex and wiped at it, cursing the incompetence of the workers. "Just a little something, Dad," he said.

His father studied him. "Morris?" he asked.

"Yes, it's me."

"Good. I was thinking about the house. I want you to dig down to the weeping tiles. The foundation is cracked. We'll have to tar and patch. Reinforce everything. Samuel can help."

"Samuel's in Idaho, Dad. He lives with Dorothy." This was not true, he no longer lived with Dorothy, but it was easier to maintain that memory.

His father considered this. Nodded. His eyes gleamed briefly, sadly. He said, "Do it yourself then. Get Martin to help." He brightened. "How is Martin?"

He took his father's hand and held it. Stroked the back of it, where the blue veins ran in bas-relief. His father was docile, the result of medication that had been suggested by the family doctor. After all, the old man couldn't just depend on music to calm him. His singing was bothering the other patients, and so the medication was an attempt at settling him down, and it was working. Too well. His father's eyelids dropped and he slept and then woke and said that he had to pee. He wheeled him to the washroom in his room. Helped him stand, loosened his belt, and pulled down his pants and underwear. Settled him onto the toilet and held his hand as he peed, while with his other hand he pushed his father's penis downwards so that he would not have an accident. He was aware of touching his father.

"I have to poop," his father said.

"That's fine."

"But I can't." He looked at Morris, so close that they could feel each other's breath. Clarity now, the knowledge of intimacy. His father said, "The Metamucil isn't working. I'm all bunged up. I'm so tired."

Fifteen minutes later, his father stood and looked down into a toilet bowl that held two small turds. Morris wiped his bum. Pulled up his pants and tucked in his shirt. Buckled him and straightened his tie. And then helped him back onto the wheelchair. Back in his room, next to the bookshelf that held the King James Bible and *Pilgrim's Progress,* he stood and drew the blanket up to his father's throat. Touched his brow and then bent to kiss him. Eternity. The rejection of modern man, but never his father's abjuration. His father had always fought the oblivion of infinity and even now, near death, he still fought it with utter ferocity. As his father's eyes closed, and then opened, and then closed again, he read to him from Ecclesiastes. A book of melancholy and despair, but full of gladness as well. A return to nature. *All the rivers run into the sea; yet the sea is not full.* And as he read, he thought about this young woman Alicia, who would come to him at midnight.

2

In the months that followed Martin's death, Morris had found himself walking the streets in the late evenings, looking into the lit windows of houses where people went about their domestic business, as if by peering into the private lives of others he could come to some better understanding of his own way of life. At some point, perhaps early on, though he could not be certain, he began to talk to himself and offer a version of what he saw in the houses. He only talked to himself in his head so that any passersby, though there were few, would not be alarmed. He told no one of this routine, certainly not Lucille, who would have declared him not only mad but criminal. He continued these walks through the fall and into winter. Later, living on his own, Morris had maintained these late-evening walks, and so it was one summer night that he stepped out of his condominium and walked up Corydon and then down towards the large houses near the local high school, and as he passed by the swollen lives of strangers, he paused at one point and saw a woman in a strapless dress, working in the kitchen. A man approached her from behind *and enveloped her*. The woman *poured coffee into china* and then she lifted the cups as the man whispered in her ear, and he released her and the two of them disappeared from view, into the other room *to lie side by side and nuzzle on a chaise longue.* On the next street, in a massive barn frame, Morris saw a man standing in a room, behind a couch, watching TV, *thinking about the cost of a new garage door.* The man was alone. *His wife was leaving him.* And then, much later, returning home, Morris came upon a family sitting around a table, eating very late, and the father, or what appeared to be the oldest man at the table and therefore the father, was wagging a finger at his beautiful teenage son, *asking him hypocritically to tell the truth.*

This city, so humble and resigned, nearly out of breath, made from Tyndall stone and fir and asphalt and brick and pine and white oak and cedar shingles and metal and glass, row upon row of houses both modest and hopeful, spreading out like a bloom, enveloping farmland where cows used to graze and shit, suburbs built on dung heaps, this city in the frozen soul of the country, a bitter and godforsaken place, not rich enough to defend itself, not important enough to require defence, a city neither soft nor prosperous, a city that held so poorly its countless poor, a city of thieves, a city of blight, a city of greed and garbage, of landfill sites where scavengers rose and fell, a stolen city run on voracity, a city whose heart was scooped out, and in that heart walked Morris Schutt, former columnist, imaginer of others' lives, clumsily recording his own life, the tread of his Ecco shoes on strewn streets, a group of boys clattering by on skateboards, the smell of weed, the ache in his heart: Who will protect me, thought Morris, who will be my neighbour, who will love me?

At ten o'clock Saturday night, Morris checked into his room at the Fort Garry Hotel. He carried a small leather bag into which he had put a change of underwear and socks, several condoms, a vial of pills for instant erections, a shaver and shaving cream, and a clean white T-shirt which he some-times liked to wear underneath his dress shirt. In his room he stripped, showered and shaved, took one Cialis, and then lay on the bed in a bathrobe and watched the beginning of an adult movie. At eleven thirty, he dressed again in his suit and put on his shoes and then studied himself in the full-length mirror. He wore the Hermès tie that he'd bought in New York the year before. It was striped pink and grey and was softly textured. He admired it and the cut of his suit jacket. At his age, fine clothes could only improve his look. He was almost handsome in a suit and tie, and he knew that this handsome-ness could not sustain itself as he removed his clothes, not that Alicia would complain. Her job was to prompt and carry on. What he looked like physically was of little consequence. This was a monetary arrangement, and though he would like to believe otherwise, he would be one more man on Alicia's path. Still, he was capable of fooling himself, otherwise he wouldn't be standing in this hotel room. He shook himself; this was a night to feel, not think.

She arrived at midnight. Her knock was light, and when he opened the door, she looked at him and said, "Mr. Schutt," and he looked at her and said, "Oh, Christ. Leah?"

She looked at the number on the door and then she said, "Maybe I have the wrong room." She glanced over his shoulder into the room to see if he was alone.

"Alicia?" he said.

She nodded slowly. She was thinking, he could see that, and then she smiled and said, "You wicked man."

"Yes," he agreed. "Unfortunately."

She laughed, very lightly, nervously, and said, "This is too weird. Icky." And she sucked in a small breath and asked, "Now what?"

"You can go. Don't worry, you'll still get paid. I'll pretend everything was fine, and we'll both try to forget this little meeting, though of course we won't forget it. I'm sorry about this. Really."

"Why are you sorry? Were you sorry before, like five minutes ago, just before you opened the door?"

"No, but five minutes ago I was a stranger, a man with no name. Now I'm Mr. Schutt."

"That's funny." She tilted her head. "Where's Mrs. Schutt?"

He made a motion with his hand, as if dismissing someone or something. "There is no more Mrs. Schutt. She kicked me out."

"Oh. So you're not being naughty."

"I am though."

She shook her head and smiled. "You want to think that. You want it to be true, because that makes it more exciting." She said this plainly, matter-of-factly, as if quoting a statistic. She asked if she could have one drink at least. "I'm all dressed up."

Morris studied her. "Do you want to? I mean, it would be only a drink, but I would understand if you want to just say goodbye."

"A drink. Yeah, that would be nice." And she shrugged and slipped her large purse from her shoulder and unbuttoned her sweater.

Morris stepped back and Leah entered the room. His brain was muddled, and though he believed that he should ask her to please leave at this moment, he took her sweater, with its Peter Pan collar, and saw that she wore a silky top with thin straps that revealed her smooth shoulders and fine clavicle bones, shoulders he would normally at some point during the night have kissed. He placed her sweater on the bed and asked if she would like some champagne. She said that that would be lovely. The word "lovely" seemed wrong for a girl who had once known his son Martin at school, and who had perhaps even kissed him, though Morris had always believed they were just friends. She had come to the house occasionally, even eaten a meal with the family, and Morris had been impressed by her composure and confidence. She was Vietnamese, the child of parents who had left their country in the early eighties, thinking they were heading to New York by boat but ending up in a Thai refugee camp for four years. She was born in the camp and spent her first year there. When she told the Schutt family her story, she had been nonchalant and almost dismissive, both of her parents' sacrifice and of her own history. Martin had been quite vocal that evening, surprising Morris with his political knowledge; it was as if Leah had loosed something in him. Now, in the hotel room, she stood by the window that looked out towards the small park eight floors below, a park that held large stones, the remnants of a fort from hundreds of years earlier when settlers had required protection. She parted the curtain and stood with her back to him and he recalled Ursula in that same position, looking down at the streets of Minneapolis and asking him to smell her, and as he thought of that now, he was aware of the space he took up in the world. She turned back towards him and giggled and said, "Wow. This is weird."

"Yes, it should be," he said. "And if it isn't, then there's something wrong with us, isn't there?" He removed the wire that held the cork and then popped it and poured champagne into each glass and walked towards her, holding out her glass. She took it and said, "Thank you." She dipped slightly, as if in deference. "Wow," she said again, and then she said, "Cheers," and held up her glass and he reached his glass out and said, "Cheers," and they drank. The champagne was expensive, and he wanted her to notice, but she didn't. She wouldn't appreciate the finer things in life. She drank greedily, as if she had run a marathon and was now drinking water. She held out her glass for more. Her hand was shaking.

"It's okay," he said. "I'm not treacherous."

"Oh, I know that, Mr. Schutt. You don't scare me."

"Are you disappointed?" he asked.

"Oh, no. No. Not disappointed. I don't think so, anyway. Why? Are you?"

"A little. Maybe. Or it might be embarrassment."

"For me?"

"No, no, not at all. Not you. It's me." And he raised his glass and drank as she sat on the edge of the bed and crossed her legs. She was wearing a black skirt. Her legs were bare and she wore high heels that he believed must be quite expensive and he thought then that this was not her first time, and this excited and dismayed him.

She said, "I guess we both have secrets."

"Secrets are necessary," he said, and immediately he cringed. He was standing outside of himself, observing, and he did not like what he saw. He did not like his words or how they came out of his mouth; he did not like his lack of hair or how his chin doubled when he lowered his head; he did not like the tie he wore anymore or his own luxurious shoes or how he was trying, yet failing, to impress her with pricey champagne. He did not like anything about himself and he felt a moment of panic.

Leah was nodding and she held her mouth in a certain manner, as if the situation she had found herself in was not at all surprising, as if she had experienced too many men who were trying to fend off boredom. How many? Morris wondered.

"Well," Leah said, holding out her glass for more champagne, "what's next?"

Morris held up the bottle. "We'll finish this and then you can go. How about that?"

As they drank, Leah wandered about the room. Morris sat on the chair by the desk and observed and listened to her as she wandered. She went straight to the point and asked Morris if he wasn't curious about her and why she was doing this, and then without waiting for an answer, she talked about her situation. She used the words "my situation" as if it were something that had fallen down upon her, as if she had had no choice, and Morris thought that this was wrong, but he let it pass, he wasn't interested in debate. She had removed her shoes and she moved about in bare feet. She had a bruise on her left calf, and later, when he asked her about it, she said that she played Ultimate Frisbee with friends. A sports injury, she said, and she smiled sleepily. That was later, but now she was talking about men and sex. She saw sex, this kind of sex, as less dangerous than sex with love. She said that she had been in love once with an older man who treated her very well, and the affair had lasted for a year, and he had flown her to New York for weekends and they had spent time together eating wonderful meals and going to plays and making love in grand hotels, but then the man had gone back to his wife of thirty years and had stopped calling her. This was the last time she had let herself go, the last time she had allowed herself to become crazy with desire and love. What she had learned from that experience was that she liked older men, that they were softer and more generous than younger men, who were often arrogant and egotistical. They knew nothing about understatement or coaxing. "I imagine that you, Mr. Schutt, know how to coax. Am I right?" And then she continued, not waiting for his response. "I plan on studying medicine in Australia. I need money for that and this is the best way to build up my bank account. I'm young, I have a beautiful body, I'm free, and I have no hang-ups about sex. Older men who have money, men like you, Mr. Schutt, they are men who can afford to pay me. They want to pay me, it makes them feel strong and helpful. I'm very close to my goal." She paused and then said, "So, that's me."

He knew that she was closing one door and opening another, and that it was now his turn to speak, but he did not have anything that he wanted to say. Her voice had lulled him into a sense of safety and ease and he did not want that feeling to disappear. He asked her if she smoked marijuana.

She grinned. "Weed? Of course I do." Then she said it would be terribly cool to smoke up with a famous columnist. "Cool," she said again. She looked up at the ceiling and around the room. "Isn't this a non-smoking room?"

"It is, but we just have to open the window in the bathroom. Whatever, the smell will be gone by the morning."

"Am I staying till morning?"

Morris lifted a hand. "Don't worry. We're not going to have sex."

"I'm not worried, Mr. Schutt. Everything's chill." She fluttered a hand, as if shooing him. "I don't have issues."

"But *I* do," Morris said. He took some papers and a pouch from his bag. Rolled a joint and lit it, inhaled twice, and then handed it to Leah, who took it willingly.

She smoked, luxuriating in the moment, and then she handed him the joint again. They smoked without talking, as if the ritual offered something beyond words, as if the sharing was a stepping inwards, a slide back into a shallow cave. At some point, she motioned with the joint, pointing at his chest, and said, "Love your tie."

"Hermès," he said. "God of commerce."

She lay back on the bed and patted the blanket beside her. "Come here. Nothing serious."

"Convivial," he said, and he rose and went to the bed and lay down so that they were side by side, both staring up at the ceiling.

"I don't know that word," she said. Then, "I don't know many things."

"You're too beautiful to be doing this. It means friendly."

"And if I'm ugly, then it's okay?"

"It doesn't bother you? A man like me? Not me, I know, but like me, desperate, lonely, old."

"Are you lonely?"

"Of course I am."

"And desperate?"

"I don't know."

She lifted her hand towards the ceiling and they studied it together until she let it fall back onto the bed beside them. She said, "I was at his funeral."

"I know. I saw you there."

"I cried and cried." She searched for his hand and held it. "I'm so sorry." She squeezed his hand and then pulled hers away.

"Yes," he said. "Yes, so am I."

"He was funny, you know. He made me laugh and laugh. He didn't like fake things and he wasn't interested in money or status. He wouldn't like what I'm doing. This. He'd give me shit for sleeping with strange men. The day he joined the army he called me and said he was going to go to Afghanistan to kill some fanatics. He was making fun of himself, of the world, of the army, of something. I didn't get it. I called him stupid. What was he thinking? That wasn't Martin."

"But he *was* stupid," Morris said. "And I was stupid. One time I got really mad at him and pushed him up against the refrigerator and told him that I could fuck him over, if that's what he wanted. He looked so hurt. So surprised. Even though just before that he had been saying fuck this and fuck that, but now that I was suddenly using the same language, the rules had changed. He said I didn't know how to swear. That the word 'fuck' sounded phony in my mouth. This made me even angrier, as if he was the only one who could be vulgar. What would he make of me now?"

"He loved you." Leah's words fell sideways and down the canal of Morris's ear. Her voice went up and down and it was lilting and soft and she did a little singsong thing at the end of some sentences, an inflection that implied a question but wasn't really a question, so that you weren't sure if she was posing some serious problem, or maybe just being playful. And even now, he wasn't sure if those three words were a question or a statement.

"He might have loved me, but he loved his mother more. They ganged up on me. Martin and my wife attacked my thoughts, my ideas, my words. They laughed at me. They were like lovers. And then Martin and I had a fight, a terrific argument, and I called him lazy, a coward coasting through life, and he called me middle class and boring and a liar. I told him he had to leave, go find his own apartment, or he could join the army. I was not serious, of course, but within a month he had signed up. He came home gloating. Showed me his uniform, wore his green beret around the house, throwing everything back at me. I'm a pacifist, you see. I was raised one, I'm still one, I will always be one. Martin understood my weaknesses. And he knew how to hurt me. The strange thing is, after he joined the army, he changed. He became clearer and kinder and he tried to respect me, but I didn't go along with it. I didn't believe he could alter his personality so quickly. But now, after, when it is too late, I see that he did change."

Morris stopped talking.

Leah said, "I never heard him say one word against you. It was only good things. If anything, he talked too much about you."

"What do you mean?"

"It could be tiring. My dad this, and my dad that. He thought you were brilliant."

"That's not the Martin I knew."

Leah reached for his hand and held it again, and let go. "Poor Mr. Schutt."

"You're mocking me."

"Yes. You feel so sorry for yourself. And you're scared. Like if you had sex with me right now, tonight, it would be the worst thing in the world."

"Well, that's true, it would be wrong. Because I know you, and because you knew Martin. I have a very narrow

view of myself. As a young man, I used to chant, 'Morris
must make money.' I saw money as a way of saving myself.
In fact, I have over a thousand dollars in my wallet. Right
here, back pocket. And this makes me happy. But even with
the fat wallet and everything it can buy, you for instance, I
am still the young boy who peeks through a keyhole watching the world at work. In another time, another era, I would
be the dirty old man at the peep show. The one eye of
yearning, the narrow glimpse. And so I plod along, aware
that others might wag their fingers at me. Outside opinion.
It weighs me down. Are you enjoying this?"

"You're funny, Mr. Schutt. I don't have a clue what
you're saying, but I love the way you talk."

"I was just thinking that about you. How your voice
slips down my ear canal."

She chuckled. "See? Like that. You say strange things."

He was silent. He wondered what kind of underwear she
was wearing, if any. Desire was a tricky thing. His words were
a form of seduction, of opening her up. "The grass was lovely,
wasn't it," he said, and she agreed, "Hmmm," and she placed
both her hands on her stomach and said, "You're what, forty-
five?"

He laughed. "Fifty-one. Why?"

"I add up the ages of the men I see."

"Where are you?"

"Nine seven three."

"Nine hundred and——?"

"Correct."

"Jesus." This was sobering. "Including me?"

"No, not you."

"So, I'm special."

"Yes."

"I saw a doctor after Martin died. I went to his office and I told him about myself. I was trying to understand my terrible sadness, and no matter how much I talked about Martin, I couldn't retrieve him. He was gone. And this wise man, a Dr. G, listened to me talk and talk about wanting to make myself disappear. If Martin no longer existed, then I also wanted to disappear, but I didn't have the wherewithal to walk away from my family and life, and so I thought I should perhaps kill myself. But I am useless, even at death. Pathetic. If I am both a romantic and a moralist, it is the romantic in me that is in love with love and with death. And he said that love is death. It has a beginning, a middle, and an end. He said that to want to disappear is better than just dying, isn't it? A mystery is more interesting than a suicide. He said that as a columnist I stuck my fingers in my own shit and held it up for the world to see. Not that the reader necessarily saw the shit, but that I perceived it as shit. Perhaps Dr. G was right. I don't know. I've stopped seeing Dr. G. He was an older man who was trying to make me see more clearly, but this scared me and so I walked away. He said, before I left, 'You seem to need someone to tell you that you have done the right thing, Morris. That you are a good boy. Why is that? And when we choose, there are various opinions of that choice. Yours, your wife's, your children's, Martin's. Martin chose to go to war because, you believe, in a moment of anger, you told him to go. And then you could not stop him. He died, and now you must come to terms with how you loved him. You cannot forgive yourself.'

"But I thought that he had misunderstood. I wasn't talking about forgiveness. I was only interested in making myself disappear. I had already disappeared, I think. I am still doing that. I don't have any friends. I live alone. I have poor relations with my daughters. I sleep with escorts. I have a woman I write to in Minnesota, not far from Minneapolis. Her name is Ursula. She is close to my age, and if I were sensible, when I next see her, I would fall down into her arms. What is there to lose? I ask you that, what is there to lose?"

He stopped talking. Leah had fallen asleep and she breathed peacefully. Her hands, still lying on her stomach, moved up and down with her breathing. Morris sat up and Leah stirred, but she did not wake. He stood and pulled the top blanket over her bare legs and her torso. She turned on her side and pulled her legs up towards her chest. Descended into a deeper sleep. Morris sat on the chair and watched her as he drank the last of the champagne.

Two days later, on a Monday, Morris cancelled his credit cards, threw out his BlackBerry, disconnected the Internet hookup, packed away his television, and terminated his newspaper and magazine subscriptions. He went to his bank and closed his corporate account and asked for everything in cash, American one-hundred-dollar bills. He called Jonathan, his financial adviser, and told him he would be cashing in all his mutual funds, RRSPs, and any GICs that weren't locked in. As well, he wanted to put a stop payment on all three of his life insurance plans. "Three," he said in astonished conclusion. "Who do I think I am?"

"This is pure foolishness," Jonathan said. "The fact is, Morris, your stocks have finally started to show some progress. This is no time to sell."

"For you people, there is never a good time to sell," Morris said. "There's only a good time to buy, and that appears to be whenever, however, whatever. Well, I'm selling everything now and my money's going under the mattress. I'll maybe purchase a few gold bricks as well."

"Have you found someone else?" Jonathan said. "Because if you have, we can just do a signed transfer. I won't be hurt. I'll be disappointed, but not hurt."

Morris laughed. "I'm not sleeping with another financial adviser. The fact is, I'm tired of slick operators. I'm paring down, going back to nature."

"If you go ahead with this, your taxes will be huge this year. And besides, anything attached to Lucille you can't touch. You know that, don't you? There is no safety in cash. It just disappears."

"Don't worry about me, Jonathan. If I'm mad, I'm mad, but at least I'm happily mad. Cash whatever's solely mine. Lucille can have the rest."

"You're jumping out of an airplane without a parachute, Morris. This isn't like you."

"Let me jump."

"What about Libby and Meredith and your grandson? I

would suggest putting some money into a trust fund for them. You could set it up in a reasonable way, so that funds could be withdrawn in increments."

Morris agreed. Like King Lear dividing up his kingdom. When everything was cashed and counted, Morris had three hundred and thirty-three thousand dollars, really a paltry amount for a man his age. He knew that Ezra from the men's group had close to two million in surety, and that even Mervine, a lowly worker, was more secure. Morris calculated that if he lived to the age of eighty, which seemed interminable, and made not a cent more in his life, which would not happen because he had royalty income from his columns, he could allow himself $11,404 dollars, thirty-one dollars a day to live on. Not at all shabby, and that didn't worry him. If the birds of the air didn't worry, why should he, Morris Schutt, be worried? He stored the money in the large safe that he had bought at Staples for two hundred and fifty dollars (shaving eight days off his life), and in order to move the safe up to his condominium, he rented a pickup (two days) and purchased a dolly (three days) at Home Depot. It took him an hour to roll the safe off the back of the pickup and up to his condominium. He squeezed it through the door and placed it in the living room next to his bookshelf, forming a tidy dialectic of learning and lucre. He kept one key for the safe in his freezer, another he hid in his sock drawer, and the third key he slipped into his wallet. The combination for the safe was the year of his birth, 1956. Finally, because it was both mythical and symbolic, he took fifteen thousand dollars and laid it under his futon.

He sat in one of his leather chairs and drank Scotch and felt the burden of the riches in the room. He imagined that he could hear the money moving, but it was the sound of his own breathing. He had dressed in his dark suit and slipped on a tie, and he had eaten lightly, a sandwich of pumpernickel with two slices of Swiss cheese, butter, mayonnaise, and lettuce. He ate standing up, looking out the front window towards the street below. It had been raining. The lights of passing cars. Wipers moved. A woman crossed the street, holding an umbrella, and then the wind took the umbrella and folded it upwards and the woman stopped, harried, and tried to bend the umbrella back into shape but failed. By the time she had reached the shelter of a nearby building, her hair was wet and her light blue jacket had turned dark from the rain. Morris wanted to help her. He wanted to climb down the stairs with a towel in his hand and offer it to the woman. He thought this thought and then let it go. The woman was wearing boots and her legs appeared to be bare in that space between skirt and boot, and he thought of Leah at that moment, who had removed her shoes and padded about the hotel room as if they had known each other a very long time. And so easily she had fallen asleep. When she woke she sat up and said that she was sorry, it was unprofessional to sleep. He said that he didn't like the word "professional," it was crass, and then he gave her three hundred dollars as a tip, money that she tried to refuse but eventually took and folded into her purse. He said that he had been thinking, and if it was okay, sometime soon he would like to take her for coffee, or they might go out for a meal, but only as friends.

"Can I use the word 'friend'?" he asked.

"Of course you can, Mr. Schutt. We're friends." And she had written her cell number on a piece of paper and handed it to him. The paper was still in his wallet. It held her small handwriting with her number, her name, and an *x* and *o*. A kiss and a hug. Something sweetly innocent there.

More innocent than Ursula, whose letter he had just received the day before. She had agreed that they should meet on the last Saturday of October, and then she had asked him if he was depressed. Something in the letter, in his words, had made her think that he might be feeling low. She said that she wanted to eat Chinese when they met. She said, "I'll try to be more fun. I want to face you." Then, as he had, she signed off with the word "love." Morris wondered if Cal would be protective and jealous if he knew of these letters. Not that there was anything to be jealous of. Morris was aware that he felt little emotion, that his thoughts were steely and cold and that they flitted helter-skelter. He wondered if he perhaps wasn't afraid of seeing Ursula again. She represented *amor* and death. When they wrote "love" at the end of their letters, what were they saying? Were they asking for more, moving beyond the formal into the erotic? Love was serious. Kisses and hugs were frivolous. And Leah, who was so young, should not be taking off her clothes in front of old men. He must save her.

In an effort to arrest this kind of thinking he read Adorno, almost immediately dozing off and then waking with a start, a trickle of saliva slipping from the side of his mouth. He continued reading and stumbled upon a paragraph that was striking. He reread the paragraph and at once phoned Lucille, who was not home, or perhaps she refused to answer. Undeterred, he left her a message. "Lucille. Were you aware that Freud was hostile to both mind and pleasure and that transference has now replaced erotic self-abandonment? This is important to speculate and reflect on. Also, incidentally, the only way you can now reach me is at this number. Or, by dropping by and knocking on the door. *Knock, and it shall be opened unto you.* Even to the destitute. See you."

He hung up and left his hand resting on the receiver, as if he were finding human contact there beyond his own physical warmth. He thought about Ursula and Cal spreading the ashes down by the stream. He wondered why he had allowed Lucille to keep Martin's ashes. They had been unable to decide on a suitable and worthy place to spread the ashes and so now the boy sat in a little wooden box on Lucille's mantel. He thought about a "mantle," which was a shroud and a responsibility, a function. Take up your mantle. And what was Morris Schutt's mantle? What responsibility did he have in this world? To care for his children. Absolutely. And he had failed. But he could still compensate. Take my own flesh and blood, he thought: *he died, he returneth to dust, the dust is earth,* of earth we make clay, and of that clay we create a sculpture. He knew a sculptor. He picked up the phone and called Lucille again. And again she refused to answer, so he left her a second message. He said that he had had a brilliant idea. Did she remember Ivan the sculptor, their old friend? "Wouldn't it make sense to have him create a sculpture, and in the clay used for the sculpture, he could mix Martin's ashes. This was better than throwing him to the wind. Or burying him. Or letting him sit shrouded on the mantel, which is the last place he would want to be. Think about this. Okay, Lucille?"

"Why are you whipping yourself so?" This is what Lucille would ask him when she finally returned his call. Her voice would sound perplexed, worried. She would pity him. He thought, suddenly and with horror, that it would be Libby who would pick up the messages, and he did not want that. She would not understand her father. Fathers were supposed to be strong and stalwart, and here he was, muttering about Freud and ashes and sculptures. This was not good.

He poured himself another Scotch, and using his phone like a lifeline, he called Mervine, who answered quickly, as if he had been waiting for someone, anyone, to call. He asked Mervine if he was in his tent. "I can hear rain. Aren't you wet?"

When Mervine said sheepishly that he was, Morris told him to get out of there immediately. "This worries me, Mervine. I see danger in this behaviour."

"I just got here. I ate my supper inside and then decided to come out here. I got a bit wet running across the lawn."

"Have you seen your daughter?"

"We went out for pizza last night. And then to a movie."

"That's good, isn't it?"

"She went against her will."

"Says who? Did she tell you that?"

"Her mother."

"And her mother knows her daughter's will?"

Mervine chuckled. "You should be my lawyer."

"I've been thinking about your request," Morris said. "The letter thing. I'd be willing to do that."

"Oh, I've given up on that idea."

"Why?" Morris's voice lifted like a cry in the wilderness. "It's perfectly reasonable. It could be very persuasive and romantic. Women like letters. Love letters move them."

"She might not read it, and even if she did, she wouldn't respond."

"That's not the point. Do you have a pen and paper handy?"

"Now? You want me to write the letter now?"

"Yes, I'll dictate it. We'll woo her. You'll see."

There was a pause, and then Mervine said, "Hang on," and Morris heard the receiver go down and then there was silence and finally Mervine was back and he said, "I have a pencil. It's all I could find."

"Pencil's great. It's softer, more intimate. You still in the tent?"

"No, in the kitchen."

"You lying?"

"I'm in the fucking kitchen. I can see the sink, the dirty dishes."

"All right. Ready?"

"I am."

"Christa."

"Not Dear Christa?"

"Absolutely not. Just Christa."

"Okay. Christa. Got it."

"Christa, I want to be good, I want to be the good man that you married so long ago, the man who took you in his arms and said, 'I promise to be faithful and true.'"

"Hang on. What do you mean? I never took her in my arms and promised that. I mean, I might have said words like that, but not exactly."

"Mervine, you're too literal. Here's the trick—you use metaphor to get at the truth. If you say in a romantic way that you took her in your arms and said those things, she'll believe you. She wants to believe you. Anyway, who's the writer here?"

"You are."

"Exactly. Where were we?"

"'Faithful and true.'"

"Okay, let's continue. After that there's a period. Then: I have not been faithful. Somewhere, in the last few years, I failed to pay attention."

Silence, except for the rustle of the phone against Mervine's shoulder. Finally, he asked, "Is that right? That I didn't pay attention?"

"Probably. Most men, if they were honest or being tortured, would confess to that. Isn't it a fact, Mervine, that you stopped noticing little things? You forgot to appreciate her, or you got possessive, or pouted when you couldn't have sex, or you didn't want sex, or you complained that she was getting fat. Isn't that true?"

"Yeah, yeah, I guess it might all be true. Except I never cared if she gained weight. I liked that."

"Fine, but the other things. You admit to that?"

"Yes, I agree."

"So then write it down."

"It's down. But *she* failed to pay attention as well."

"Of course she did. But this isn't a cross-examination. This is a plea, an announcement of adoration, an apology. You're trying to win her back, and accusing her of not paying attention is not going to woo her. You see?"

"Yes. Okay."

"What's your last sentence?"

"'Failed to pay attention.'"

"All right. Period after that. Then: I know that love is susceptible to the vagaries of time and place."

"What are you talking about? She wouldn't have a fucking clue what you're talking about."

"Okay, how about this: I know that love can change, that responsibilities and work and indifference have made our love ebb and flow, like the tides. But, Christa, I want you to know that my love for you is constant, just as the moon is constant. It will always be there. It might seem to disappear, to fade, but that just means it was hidden for a bit, like the moon is hidden behind the shadow of the earth."

"Christ almighty. Are you sure about this?"

"Absolutely. Write it down."

"I got lost there, right after 'just as the moon is constant.' That middle section. Go slower, Morris. I don't want to miss any of this."

"Okay. Something like, My love, like the moon, might seem to fade away and disappear . . ."

"That's fine, I have the rest," Mervine said, and he repeated the last line slowly, savouring it, finishing with "the shadow of the earth."

"Then," Morris said, "end it with a request to have a drink or coffee. She can choose the place, the time. No pressure. Just a friendly drink. Or you can offer to take her out for lunch."

"She loves my Corvette. Perhaps I should take her for a weekend drive."

"Yeah, great. Something like that."

Mervine was scribbling. Morris thought he heard panting as well, as if Mervine had been running quickly. Mervine finally said, "You think this'll work?"

"It might, or it might not. She could say no."

"You think so?"

"I think if she's got any brains about her, she'll read it and say yes. But I don't know her." Morris paused and then said, "One last thing, Mervine. Read it through and call me back and tell me if it's proper. Okay?"

Morris hung up and stood and walked to the window. It had stopped raining. He felt a fine sense of peace and well-being. Mervine had been so malleable, so keen and willing. The sentiments had been true. Morris could feel them as well. The letter had import and purpose and it was full of poetry. He had wanted to borrow from Solomon, to say, "Christa, I am panting like a hind for you," but this would have been lost on both Mervine and his wife. Pearls before swine.

When Mervine called back five minutes later, he said, "It doesn't sound like me."

"What do you mean?"

"These aren't my words."

"But do you believe them? Are they true?"

"Yeah, I guess."

"Well then, Christa will believe you. She'll see past the fancy prose, which really isn't that fancy, and she'll be unaware of the metaphor, the language. The sentiments will convince her that it is you."

"You're sure you're right."

"Right as rain."

The following week, rather than running to what Adorno called "chorus girls, *bohémiennes,* Viennese *süsse Mädel,* sweet wenches, and *cocottes,*" Morris had dinner with Leah. He met her on Saturday evening again. He had spent that afternoon with Jake, taking him back to his condominium and feeding him Kraft Dinner and ice cream, and then he had pulled the television and DVD player from the back of his closet and together they had watched *The Jungle Book.* Morris had watched the movie numerous times with his own children when they were young and so he knew all the songs and he sang them for Jake, who giggled and listened, trans-fixed, his tender mouth soft and open. "More, Grandpa," he cried and Morris kept singing. They fell asleep together on Morris's futon, and when Morris opened his eyes he was dis-oriented and then aware that he was late returning Jake to Meredith. He woke the boy, who remained grumpy during the trip home, and when they walked in the door, Meredith saw right away that Jake had napped.

"That's just great, Dad. Glen and I are going out tonight and the babysitter will have a hell of a time putting him down. Didn't I tell you not to let him sleep?"

"It just happened," Morris explained, refusing to be cowed by his own daughter. He wondered where Jake's sweetness came from, with a pinched mother like Meredith and dim-witted Glen. "We were watching TV and singing and then fatigue tackled us. If you like, I can watch him tonight. I'll have no problem putting him to bed, and if he doesn't want to sleep, we can stay up together."

"He has a regular babysitter." She took Jake's duffle bag from Morris. "Anyways, he goes to bed at eight. He can't be staying up all night."

They were standing in the doorway of the small house that Meredith rented. She seemed old to Morris. She was bossy and responsible and she had this house she'd found, and she was trying to make a life with Glen, who was a mechanic at one of the nearby car dealers. Good for her. Good for Jake. Good for everybody. Always, when he faced Meredith, Morris felt immature and irresponsible. In fact he understood in some perverse way why she would prefer that he not spend time with Jake. He was too careless these days.

He said, "I was thinking the zoo might be fun. Jake loves animals. Maybe next week?"

"Jake doesn't want to see Bengalese tigers in tiny cages, or crowded monkeys. It's abusive."

"It doesn't have to be the zoo. We can just go to the

botanical gardens and smell the humidity and the rot and listen to the tropical birds."

She shrugged, softening slightly, and surprised him by saying, "Maybe the zoo. Not next week, but the week after that, okay?"

He hugged Jake and leaned towards Meredith to kiss her on her cheek and she allowed this, though she seemed wary. He stepped backwards out the door, into the late-afternoon light.

In the evening, he took Leah to a bistro that was crowded and loud and in order to hear each other they had to lean in across the table on which were set small plates of appetizers and bread. They shared a bottle of red wine. Morris felt expansive and happy. He lived in a world where only a movie star or a certain politician could acceptably fall in love with a woman half his age, and though he thought that he wasn't falling in love with Leah, that his intentions were noble, he was aware of the other men in the restaurant, especially the older men, who eyed him with envy. At some point during the evening, Morris steered the conversation towards Leah's work. She said she wasn't interested in talking about that, this was her night off. He pressed on anyway and asked if she worked seven days a week, and she said, "No, three or four." He asked when her next night was, and she said, "Tuesday." When he asked her where, she hesitated and then said it was at the same hotel where she had met Morris. She asked if he was jealous. She said this matter-of-factly, as if it were a certainty, and he said that he didn't think so. He was curious, he said, and he asked her to tell him about her latest escapade.

She shrugged and said that she had been with a politician from Switzerland. She did not talk about the sex, she just offered details of the man himself, his age, his looks, the way he threw money around, his accent. "He was such a child," she said, and then she asked, "Why do you want to hear this?" He said that it offered him glimpses into her world. He was trying to understand her. She said that there was no intimacy involved, it was sex; in fact, she was more intimate with him than with any of those other men. "Talking like this," she said. "Eating. I have several rules, and one of them is, Do not eat with the men." This pleased him, made him feel special. He said that she was more than a flute girl, did she know that? She laughed and asked what he meant, and he said that long ago, when common men gathered to converse, they hired flute girls to play for them, to entertain them so that they didn't actually have to talk. "But you are more than that," he said. "You guide the conversation." They talked about love. Morris said that there was tragic love, which was deep and abiding, and then there was the love of comedy, which was a lesser kind. She tilted her head coyly and said that the story of her love life was a comedy. But she could live with that. She said that he thought too much about his ideas and his emotions, and if he would just let himself go, he would see that there was nothing bad or evil about fucking. She leaned back in her chair as she finished. She said "fucking" almost tenderly. There were mussel shells in the bowl beside her plate. Her wineglass was empty.

They walked back to his place, side by side, slightly drunk, while she told him about her father, who was extremely

possessive and who believed that she was working as a bartender in the evenings, and if he were ever to discover what
she actually did for work, he would probably murder her.
"He's old-fashioned," she said. "He taught me how to play
piano, made me practise three hours a day on an electric piano
that he bought at a second-hand store." She said that her parents worked in a furniture factory and she was an only child
and this had made her own life difficult because expectations
were very high, and at some point it was decided that she
would be a doctor. "My parents have sacrificed everything.
They don't talk about it but I can see it. And for my father
to know that I sleep with men older than him, this would kill
him. Still, he wants me to be a doctor, and this is the only way.
I've had three interviews for school here, and each time they
said no. So, I'm going to Australia."

They were walking through a light rain, and though
Morris offered Leah his jacket, she would not take it. She tee-
tered along in her red heels and skirt and a light sweater. Her
hair was wet. When they arrived at his condominium, he said,
"Come, I have something to show you." They took the stairs
and passed by Tom and Beth Ann's apartment, where the
door was open and a party was taking place. Morris recalled
being invited and for a second he considered asking Leah if
she would like that, go to a party, maybe dance, do something very healthy, meet people her age, but as they passed
by the open door, Morris glanced inside and saw the guests
and he immediately felt old, and he imagined being laughed
at, mocked, and so they went up to his condominium where
he poured Leah a glass of red wine, a Scotch for himself.

They sat in the living room and Morris said that he was worried for her.

"Oh," she said. "Morris."

He had asked her to call him Morris, not Mr. Schutt, and this was the first time she had tried it out, and it surprised him. Her voice was soft, yet underneath there was an edge of something else, perhaps impatience. The music from the party reached their ears.

"I would like to be your benefactor," he said. "Which means that I would pay for your education. At least part of it."

"Really, Morris?" She paused and considered. "What do I have to do for this?"

"Nothing. Well, actually, there are two things, but they are quite simple. You would write me a letter once in a while, from Australia, telling me how you are doing in school. Approximately every three months, simply for information. You would not have to flatter me. And the second thing is that you would stop working."

"My job?" One hand reached out and waved lightly, as if she were dismissing someone.

"Yes."

"But I don't want to."

"What do you mean, you don't want to?"

"You want to pay me to stop working. You *are* jealous."

"No, no, Leah."

"Maybe a little, Morris." She smiled and pointed a finger at him. "You silly man. You can't have me, so you want to stop other men from having me."

Morris shook his head. "It's not healthy what you're doing. In fact, it's dangerous."

"You do it. With other women."

"Yes. I did."

"And you will again."

"I doubt it."

"You will. I know how men work."

"No you don't, Leah. You just know a certain kind of man. There are other men, wonderful men, who do not pay for sex. They have children, grandchildren, wives that they love. You just know a certain kind of man."

"What were you going to show me?"

"It's okay."

"No, please, I want to see."

Morris pointed at the safe against the wall. "I had this plan that I would tell you my idea about being your benefactor, and then we'd open my safe over there, and we'd sift through the money and talk about your future."

"I'd love to see your money," Leah said. "Show me." She stood and walked to the safe and squatted. She asked over her shoulder for the number and he offered it easily, as a form of trust. As she twisted the dial, he reached for the key in his wallet and handed it to her. She opened the safe and began to remove the bundles of money, and as she did so, Morris stood above her and thought, This is my life.

"Wow," Leah said. "How much?"

He told her and she said "wow" again and began to make towers with the bundles. "Touching money like this makes me dizzy," Leah breathed.

"I used to feel light and happy, and my chest would swell," Morris said. "But not anymore."

She looked up at him. "You've given up?"

"Not at all. No. I'm taking stock."

"I don't understand."

"Of course you don't." Then he said, "You should go." She did not argue.

In the middle of the night Morris woke in a panic and he got up and went into his living room and opened his safe. Within the orange pool of light that fell onto the brownish bills, he haltingly counted his money. Perhaps she had stolen from him, pushed a bundle into her purse when he wasn't watching. But it was all there. He experienced relief and heartache. What was wrong with him? What did he want? Perhaps he really wanted Leah but was too afraid to admit it. She had all but offered herself to him. Or she might have offered herself because she couldn't have what she wanted. Human nature. For much of his life he had turned reason on its head and allowed passion to guide him. What was the rule? Reason first, then will, and lastly passion. If you live in that manner, you are a just man. But take Lucille, who lived that way, coldly, reasonably, and this sometimes made her extremely unattractive. She had no balance. She was *too* intelligent. He realized now that he had made a mistake in offering money to Leah, because his intentions had been misconstrued. She had not understood that he was a generous man and that the offer had been honest. She needed the money and he had extra. There had been no evil intended.

◆

The next day Lucille phoned. She said, "Oh, so you deign to pick up the one phone left in your life? What are you thinking, Morris? Jonathan called to say that you cashed in all your investments. Are you planning on killing yourself, because if you are, I want to be warned. I can't handle any more surprises."

"I'm not going to kill myself, Lucille. I'm freer now than I have been for years."

She laughed, and as she laughed he was hurt, because of course she was laughing at his folly. She said, "You sound very pleased with yourself."

"I'm paring down. Life is going to be simpler. Dr. Lange says I have high blood pressure, and that I should reduce the stress in my life. I'm beating back the world." Dr. Lange had, in fact, been concerned. He'd posed various questions, about his peeing, his sex life, his eating habits, whether or not he was getting exercise. Morris said that he walked to his office when the weather allowed it, and he still managed to get erections, no problem there, though he did take longer to ejaculate, especially when he wore a condom. Morris had admitted this softly, as if shame was hovering at the edge of the confession. "That's normal for your age," Dr. Lange said. "The plumbing gets weaker." He picked up Morris's chart and studied it, glasses tilted onto the bridge of his nose. Closed the chart and wondered why Morris used condoms. Hadn't he had a vasectomy? Or was he seeing other women? Yes, Morris answered, since Lucille had left him he'd been playing the field, and as soon as he said this he felt foolish. What an idiotic truism, *playing the field*. As if he was an athlete with tremendous prowess. Dr. Lange nodded and then he told Morris to buy a blood-pressure machine at the local drugstore, and to check his pressure three times a week. Morris had obeyed, except that he found himself trying to deceive the machine, sometimes taking his blood pressure four or five times until safer numbers came up. He found, as he wrapped his arm and pushed the button on the machine, that he was tense, anticipating the worst, and of course his pressure skyrocketed. "Breathe, Morris," he told himself. "Take it easy." He got the best results when he dozed off while testing himself. He was healthiest in a comatose state. What did that indicate?

Lucille didn't seem concerned that he might suffer a stroke. She could be so remote and dismissive. She said, "Libby's worried about you as well. She thinks that you're cutting yourself off, not just from the world, but specifically from her."

"No, no. Never. I'll talk to her. She can come live here. I've always said that my door is open."

"Except you have one bedroom, Morris. Why would you rent a one-bedroom condo, knowing that your daughter might want to live with you?"

"She can take the bedroom, I'll move the futon into the living room."

"Relax, she's staying in the house here. It's just that your thinking is all messed up. You say one thing and then behave another way." She paused and then said, "You sure you're okay? Do you want to meet for coffee or lunch?"

"We could," he said, though he didn't want to. He would end up telling her about Leah, it would just happen. It was like that with Lucille, she pulled things out of him, even the deepest darkest secrets. What scorn she would heap on him if she knew that he hired escorts. "What a dire confused life you lead, Morris," she would say. "You walk down the street, morally straight-backed, and all the while you keep whores in your closet." No doubt she would say "whore." *Let us be absolutely frank here.*

Lucille spoke again. "Are you still there, Morris?"

He shook himself out of this useless reverie and said, "Yes, I'm here." He said that the following week was busy, and then on the weekend he might go to the zoo with Jake, Meredith was more willing to let him spend time with Jake these days, and perhaps the week after that they could meet.

She agreed, and then she said that he should call her, anytime he wanted. Okay?

"Yes, I will. Thanks, Lucille."

And, in spite of all of this, he loved her still. It was good that she didn't take him too seriously. Just as his own mother had always tempered his father's melancholy, looking for the joke in life, remaining upbeat. It must have been exhausting, he thought now, maintaining constant happiness. Perhaps this is why she had died young. All that striving for joy had simply tired her heart out. Morris, in one of his sessions with Dr. G, had talked about his mother, had wondered in fact if he had married his mother when he'd chosen Lucille. "They're somewhat similar," he said. "Lucille bakes brown bread like my mother did, uses the same recipe, and, like my mother, she has weekly appointments with a chiropractor, and she cajoles me when I'm down, just as my mother humoured my father. Like my mother, Lucille runs from darkness. Or she used to." And then he'd talked about the habit his mother had, when she prayed, of offering God a litany of events and moments in her life, and then suddenly pausing and saying, "But then, *you* know all about this." Morris had laughed and Dr. G smiled, and Morris pointed his finger at the ceiling and repeated, "But then, *you* know all about this." He said that his mother had a wryness, as if she were winking at God, at the world, at her own husband. "Maybe she wasn't fond enough of me," he said.

"So this is the problem," Dr. G said. "Your mother didn't love you well enough. And now Lucille hasn't loved you hard enough. You want to apportion blame, rather than look seriously at yourself."

"I'm looking at myself," Morris said. "It's just not very pretty. I'd be way more content if I didn't always have to take myself with me wherever I go. I'm walking around in a fog, with my hands out, feeling blindly. I stand outside of the action, watching, all alone. I am alone."

A long silence that Morris refused to break. Finally, Dr. G asked, "You were eighteen when your mother died?"

"Yes."

"So, you were abandoned."

"Not intentionally."

"But you felt as if you were."

Morris shrugged. Looked out the window at the steeple of the church nearby. In this same building, just a few floors below, was the office of his endodontist, Jewish, and just down the street was his ENT surgeon, Jewish as well, who had performed two stapedectomies on Morris. And then there was Dr. Lange, who cared if he could still get it up. What an amazing and tender tribe of caregivers he had.

"Did you cry?" Dr. G asked.

"When?"

"When your mother died."

"I can't remember. I don't think so. I don't cry easily. Samuel wept like a baby."

"Your brother?"

"You know he's my brother. Why would you ask that? Did you have a memory lapse? Listen, there's not a lot to keep track of here, and if you're trying to point a finger at me, or poke me in some way, it won't work."

Dr. G had picked up his yellow notepad and was writing.

"Did I say something important?" Morris asked. "Or are you making a grocery list?"

Dr. G looked up. "Your father was what, in his early fifties?"

"I guess. About that."

Dr. G waited.

Morris nodded finally, and then chuckled.

Dr. G said, "Can you picture him hiring escorts?"

"It wasn't that easy back then. But no, of course not. Though he did go out with a woman from his church, briefly, after my mother died. Her name was Katya. Of Russian stock. Samuel and I thought it would have been good for him to marry her, but he kept holding up my mother as a template, and no other woman came close. Thirty-three years without sex. Poor man."

"You have a very narrow view of the world, Morris."

"I do? How old are you, Dr. G? Do you still have sex?"

Dr. G did not speak. He simply looked at Morris and Morris looked back at him, until Morris sighed and said that his father had been very good at denying himself pleasure. "He was terribly strong, to the point of foolishness. He made such a big deal of carnality that it became a mountain that he was constantly climbing. Eventually, he ran out of oxygen. Just petered out. Hah. Listen, I've told you pretty much everything about myself, and about Lucille, and about Martin and my daughters, to the point where I must be boring you. I might as well just say, 'But *you* know all about this.'" Morris smiled, suddenly pleased with himself. Though he was sad, and he wasn't sure why. He said that he'd cried when Martin died. "So I can cry. But what's the point? It doesn't make me feel any better. And it doesn't make me think any more clearly. I lead a slavish life, and so I try to elevate myself a little, through reading or reflection, but then I tumble again, and I slowly climb back up the same mountain my father created, and I too suck for oxygen. And if I find relief in the arms of a woman who will make my wallet slightly thinner by the morning, so be it. Cash has bought less important things. I'd rather bury myself in the arms of that woman than fork over two thousand for a leather couch. Don't lecture me about morality, Dr. G. Don't tell me I have a narrow view of the world. How the hell is that supposed to cure me?"

✧

Morris, troubled by his thoughts, showered, and once calmer, dressed and went down into the street and over to Second Cup. He picked up the newspaper, began to read a front-page article about a soldier who had been killed in Afghanistan, and he folded the paper and set it aside. Two young women with babies in strollers sat across from him. They were talking about breastfeeding and cracked nipples. He listened half-heartedly and then finished his coffee and stepped outside and walked up the street to a consignment boutique where he bought Leah a pair of pale blue high-heeled shoes, Dolce & Gabbana. He knew her size. The night in the hotel he had picked up one of her shoes as she slept, and he had smelled it, even touched his tongue to the smooth inner sole, and in doing so he had noted the number seven. The Dolce & Gabbana shoes had hardly been worn, probably previously owned by a wealthy woman, one of many who frequented this shop, and who had probably bought them on a whim during a trip to New York and then used them once or twice. And then, perhaps because he felt guilt, or perhaps out of pure generosity, he bought Lucille a pair of purple velvet pants whose cloth was wonderful to touch. They were size eight, exactly right, and the legs were long enough, and for a moment, as he was paying, he imagined delivering them himself and asking her to try them on as he watched. They had done this together many times before, in their earlier and happier life, before children and later, as the children grew up. Lucille, who could be harsh in public, softened immensely in the bedroom. The fact is that they'd both loved sex, and Morris knew that one of the best ways to get into Lucille's pants was to buy her pants. Morris would giddily shop, purchasing skirts that were too short ("Morris, do you think I am twenty?"), and coloured tights, and boots with narrow heels, and lacy underwear that whether Lucille liked them or not she had to keep, and thin camisoles through which her nipples were silhouetted, and earrings and bracelets, and one time a perfume that was subtly citrus smelling, like lemongrass, and she said, "Don't buy me perfume, Morris, I don't wear scents," but he explained it was for him, that she was to spray it between her legs when she was horny, their secret signal. And even today, whenever he cooked Thai, or he passed by the mound of lemons in Safeway, he was instantly aroused.

He had to admit that she was always generous, that she willingly tried on the array of outfits he bought, as if she knew and accepted that it was his own pleasure he was satisfying, as if he were dressing her up and making her into another, but not in fact another, because when he lustily and hastily removed the new clothes, she was still Lucille. And in her eagerness she became grateful, as if she had willed it, though nothing can be willed, and the clothing, the jewellery, the wishful look in Morris's eyes, made her appreciative, and they would tumble onto the bed, the brand new acquisitions crumpled beneath them. The thing about Lucille was that she had a ferocious imagination but it was stored away in a vault and it sometimes took Morris days or weeks to unlock that vault because the harder he worked, the more her stubbornness grew. Once, after a particularly long battle that finally ended with his head between her legs, he paused and sighed and looked up at her and said, "Is this worth it?"

Lucille had always gratified him, even as she bested him in an argument. She was intellectually fierce and intensely curious. "Morris," she liked to say, "we need to talk about our talking." She claimed, as she should, that he needed to have the words to say it. She would have made an excellent priest, though not being Catholic, he could not be sure whether the words uttered in a confessional were true words or if they were made up. Lucille did not pander to untruths, which was why she disliked Morris selling himself as a columnist. Poor Lucille, married for so long to a materialist.

And so, half aroused by these random thoughts and the smell and texture of the shoes and velvet pants, Morris walked home with a would-be lover in each hand, and he called FedEx and arranged a delivery of a package to Leah's address and then to Lucille's. It was like having two wives, though he was sleeping with neither. When a credit-card number was requested, he realized that he had cancelled all of his cards. He asked that if in this cashless contemporary world, he could pay the driver in hard currency. Would that work? The voice on the other end, a sweet child-man, said without a trace of disdain that the total would be seventeen dollars and thirty-three cents and it could be paid in cash, though exact change was required. The driver would pick up both parcels the next working day. Monday. Thank you.

❖

One of Morris's much-loved novels was *Herzog* by Saul Bellow. He had read it as a young man and then returned to it recently and been amazed at Moses Herzog's capacious soul. Here was a man going mad who suffered and joked and wallowed, and in the midst of his madness he wrote unsent letters full of playful and searing intellect to people both dead and alive.

Well, thought Morris, I am not Herzog. I am not a free-thinker, I am not out of my mind, and I am not particularly intelligent, but like Herzog, I am a survivor. I will persist. I will keep thinking and I will keep acting. And so he sat down and wrote a column in which he addressed the prime minister.

Dear Sir,

I noticed in a recent press release that Canada has agreed to donate twenty-five hundred surplus C7 rifles to the Afghan National Army, along with training and ammunition. Surplus? Are we so liberal that we have rifles lying around in drawers and sacks that we can donate them willy-nilly to our friends? Who are our friends, sir? And will those friends proceed carefully with these twenty-five hundred rifles? I am familiar with this type of rifle. Sir, all political action is aimed either at preservation or at change. The war we are fighting in Afghanistan is futile. It will not bring change, save change to the families whose dear boys are dying. Do you have knowledge, sir, or is it merely opinion? How do you elevate your poor self? I understand empire and I understand that your opinion echoes the empire south of us, and if I am sad, it is for my own loss, for the horrible change in my life. That change happened when my son, who was a warrior for our country, died in Afghanistan. He was shot by a C7A1 assault rifle, manufactured by Colt Canada.

You call yourself a Christian, Mr. Prime Minister, but what kind of a Christian are you? Do you see the mote in your own eye? I have no mote. Not anymore. It was removed the day my son died. I am no longer a Christian, yet I understand Christ's teachings. Do you? I envy you your son's health and vigour. And with envy comes wrath, as you must know. And so my rage provokes me. Can you imagine why? I think not. I think that you might read this as the mutterings of a madman. If indeed you read this.

No one would read it. His was a voice crying in the wilderness. A less than minor prophet, like Haggai, who in the Bible gets two chapters and the line, *he who earns, earns wages to put into a purse with holes.* Morris knew this purse. In a recent dream, one of those elusive I-am-dreaming dreams, Morris was caught on a busy freeway in a tiny Toyota and he needed to cross to the other side because he had discovered that he was going in the wrong direction. Finally seeing a break in the traffic, he reversed, and just as he crossed the meridian, he fell asleep, his foot slipping from the clutch, but before falling asleep, he saw a Greyhound bus bearing down on him, and though he saw the bus and knew it was going to hit him, only at the last moment did he pull himself up through the layers of sleep.

His life had become like that dream: he was descending through levels of consciousness into a blessed oblivion, without any thought of the future, only to suddenly become aware again of the tumbling of his present existence, and up he rose once more, ready to devote himself to a life of care and duty and misery, to a life of putting his wages *into a purse with holes*. The one and only time in his recent memory that he had descended and rested without action or thought was the moment when he had been lying naked on a hotel bed and Carla, the woman he was paying, a forty-year-old with red hair, had done as he requested and kissed him from head to toe. But that too had passed. It passed as soon as he thought to himself, This woman is loving me by touching her lips to my frail flesh. The unconscious becomes desire, desire moves one to act, action leads to thought, and in that moment, bliss evaporates.

Morris was never breastfed. He had learned this when his daughter Meredith was just born and his father, visiting the little family in the hospital and watching Lucille struggle with the child at her breast, had announced, completely out of character, that Morris's mother had not breastfed any of her children. Lucille, perhaps still swooning from drugs, had said that then she must have had the most gorgeous tits in the world. Grandpa Schutt's mouth had tightened and he cleared his throat and quickly changed the subject.

Only later in life, when Morris took the time to reflect, did he think that a baby at the mother's breast is experiencing bliss, that this was the one time in the voyage from cradle to grave that no thought was required. And he had missed out.

This might be the cause of much of his anguish and delirium. "What drivel," Lucille would say. But then she was trapped by her own shadow. "We're all alone in the ocean, Morris," she had whispered over the phone late one night. "Only you haven't figured that out yet." Then on another occasion, perversely proud that he had been tempted and remained a faithful husband, she had waved her hands furiously and cried, "Nonsense." They were still together and he had returned from a conference in Paris, a symposium of bacchanalian proportions during which he had *almost* slept with a columnist from England, until the columnist began to talk non-stop of the book she was writing on pet food and how she had four dogs, an Alsatian and three mongrels that she slept with, and at that point Morris, perhaps because he didn't want to be just another animal in her bed, or perhaps because he had an image of many distressing repercussions, excused himself and went up to his hotel room. When he told Lucille later about the lure of lust and then his moral rectitude, she had said, "Don't be foolish, Morris. You've always wanted a tit in every port."

Why of course—didn't every man? And yet, what were his motives? Especially now with Leah, who had become his unattainable ideal. This was not unique. Petrarch had Laura, Novalis had thirteen-year-old Sophie, and Kierkegaard at twenty-four fell for fourteen-year-old Regine. Phaedria used to wait in a barbershop for his zither player: *If only she, if she would only, would that she might only soon, soon come back.* The subjunctive was the grammatical form fullest of longing. Perhaps all of life hinged on those two words, *if only*. Take his father, who in the autumn of his life could not even name his own son, let alone his desire and lust. His father should have been more active, should have had more women and not settled for the perfect breasts of his wife, who was now dead; had fallen over in church one day, crumpled into the pew from a heart attack. Or maybe it wasn't about action at all. It might simply be the capacity to hold two contradictory thoughts at the same time, and understand that there were emotions connected to the thoughts.

If only I had been a better father, thought Morris.

Opportunity wasted. Though action could still be taken. There was Libby, and Meredith, and little sweet-breathed Jake. And there was knowledge to be gained.

Over a year and a half ago, at the end of winter, Morris's much-loved professor from his university days, a Dr. Karle, died of pancreatic cancer. Morris had not known that Dr. Karle was sick and so his death had come as a shock. He had seen Karle six months earlier, on the street, riding a bicycle that was too small for his six-and-a-half-foot frame. Morris had been in his Jaguar, idling at a stoplight, when Karle had ridden by, pedalling painfully, and Morris had felt in that moment a sense of embarrassment, though he could not know for sure if it was for himself or for the professor. Morris did not go to the funeral. He disliked funerals, not because he was afraid of death but because, as he preferred to say, he didn't want to waste his time on contemplating mortality and singing dirgelike hymns. And of course, Martin had died just a month before Dr. Karle. Still, in the weeks following, Morris had been sorry about his decision not to be present at the funeral. He heard through acquaintances that the service had been inimitable, that the message, given by a former student of Karle's, had asked the question, "What is the best life?" The speaker had then held up Karle's life and thoughts and teachings like a mirror to that question, the same question that Dr. Karle had posed at the beginning of Morris's first class. Morris had long ago forgotten the answer, and he had decided not to attend the funeral. At the time when he was drowning in his own sorrow, the answer had been thrown his way like a lifeline and he had missed it.

One evening, not long after Karle's death, Morris climbed up to his attic through the small hole in the ceiling, into the crowded space where mice played amongst the asbestos insulation, pure poison, as he had discovered long after he had allowed his own children to romp in the vermicular fibres, playing hide-and-seek. A poisonous sandbox. Perhaps Martin as a child had been affected by the asbestos and this is what had driven him to the brink. Perhaps all soldiers, like journalists and politicians, had some chemical imbalance, some toxin inside them. Morris had rummaged through dusty boxes and plastic garbage bags that evening, a flashlight clamped between his teeth, looking for his notes and books from that one class that he had taken so long ago, but all he found were children's clothes and old photos, one of his father as a baby in Russia. On the knee of his own father, who was dressed in the uniform of a medical officer in the Russian army. Morris pushed the photo into his pocket. He climbed down from the attic and discovered that Lucille, in one of her hell-bent cleaning sprees, had thrown out all the books and his course papers. He was devastated. Unmoored. He needed to know the answer to the biggest question. He was the age that Socrates claimed to be the pinnacle of openness and learning and wisdom.

And then, several months later, a sale of Dr. Karle's books was held in the small chapel at the university. Morris was one of the first to arrive and he scooped up academic journals, novels, books on philosophy, history, the social sciences, pamphlets, textbooks, and first editions. Surprising himself with his own hunger, he went home, stacked the collection against the wall in his study, and over the next while he methodically sorted through his acquisitions. He discovered that Dr. Karle had been a lover of marginalia. His handwriting was clear and clean and even his references were written, for himself, in the perfect style of the Modern Language Association. Semi-colons and commas all in place. For some reason, this greatly impressed Morris. It meant that the man was serious, that he cared. Morris had brought home Adorno, Buber, *The Republic*, Barth, and Tillich. Karle had, in Tillich's *The Courage to Be*, with its broken spine and its pages falling out and its minutest marginalia, noted a section on non-being, something that Morris sensed should be pertinent for him. After all, wasn't he struggling with exactly that? Parmenides sacrificed his own life trying to get rid of non-being; Augustine used the concept to point a finger at human sin—this was entirely familiar to Morris: Boehme, the mad mystic, said that everything is *rooted in a Yes and a No*. And Hegel's dialectic? Ha, of course, shouted Tillich. And so on, and so on, from Heidegger's *das Nichts nichtet* to Sartre's *le néant;* everyone was on the bandwagon now, except for Morris, the non-philosopher. If he were wiser and were to write a treatise, and if he knew what he was talking about, he would call the treatise "Non-being According to the Gospel of Martin." But Morris knew nothing now. He knew only anxiety. And fear, which he willed away. And craving, which smothered the fear and anxiety and choked briefly the inevitability of his approaching death. Read Berdyaev, he noted.

In one of those fall classes so long ago, Karle had addressed the students affectionately, had spoken of mimesis as a necessity in art, and then announced that if he succeeded in this class, the students would leave knowing how to die. "Fear of violent death," he said, "is a bourgeois idea put upon you from the day you are born." Morris recalled that there had been a very pretty girl named Natasha Khan in the front row who had full lips and wide wet eyes, and who, when Karle made this statement, had lifted her thin arm and asked if he was trying to scare them. Morris remembered Natasha because he had tried to ask her out and been refused. What a head of hair she'd had. If he recalled correctly, her parents came from Aleppo. She was Muslim in the days when that meant very little to the Western world, though it must have meant something to her because she knew that Morris was Christian in the broadest sense; had even alluded to it in her refusal. Professor Karle had not regarded her question as impertinent. He said, "I didn't say you were going to die today. Or tomorrow, for that matter. In fact, Miss Khan,

you'll most likely grow to be eighty-five, have seven grandchildren, perhaps marry several times, and travel the world.
Men might flock to you. You will be loved. But what you may
never figure out is the problem of death." He held a piece of
chalk in the air, arm poised. "And that's where I come in."

Morris wondered where Miss Khan was today. If she had
married. If she was in fact still alive, and if men had indeed
flocked to her. Or had she learned to die well and then done
so? He did not know what dying well looked like. Perhaps it
was simply on the back end of the continuum of living well,
though everyone, even the animal in its pen, was tumbling
down the river towards non-being. Was there a "best way"
to die, a more graceful manner than not to cut away from this
earth? Heraclitus, suffering from edema, treated himself with
a liniment of cow manure and then baked himself in the sun.
He died the next day and was buried in the marketplace. This
was not graceful. This was not "dying peacefully in his sleep."
All beings going and remaining not at all. What a perplexing
mystery was the world. Mysteries, Morris had discovered in
his reading over the last months, that could not be solved. But
books, particularly the old books, specifically Plato's *Republic*, allowed him to see with the *unarmed eye*. This had not
made him a better person, not yet. Questions flitted about his
brain, and sometimes, on the verge of grasping an answer, he
felt a moment of contentment. I am on the earth for no reason
other than to be Morris Schutt. He could not rid himself of
the goals he had set so long ago: to be rich, to be famous, to
live well. This had been, in his mind, the good life. He had
been mistaken. Goodness was a matter of habit. It required

practice, just as being an excellent basketball player required practice. You see, he thought, I am still envious and wrathful and I pay women to have sex with me, but at least I am beginning to think about what is reasonable and unreasonable. The fact that he liked his brand-new steel safe was unreasonable, but it gave him pleasure nonetheless. And as far as Leah was concerned, he was pleased that he hadn't slept with her. This was very reasonable, and so in these two cases he was batting fifty–fifty. Courage and moderation.

Because *The Republic* had formed the foundation of Karle's course, it was to this particular book that Morris keenly went now, seeking out the professor's marginalia, rereading each of the ten books carefully, as if the secret to living well might be found there, though he also understood that the secret was available only to the spirited and careful reader. The theme was justice, the form was dialogues. He had a sudden thought that Plato might be trying to teach him how to talk: to Lucille, to his daughters, to his friends. But this was undemanding thinking, too simple. Karle had written in small print on the title page: "'Socratic restoration: the feeding of the body and the senses is replaced by the feeding of the mind.' Leo Strauss, *The City and Man*." *The feeding of the mind:* this was Morris's intent, but oh, it was difficult. There were times, while reading late at night, when he closed the book and said aloud to himself, "Morris, you're a stupid fucked-up man." At times he felt as if he was looking for definitions, a blueprint, and he wasn't finding it and he would never find it. Insight was allusive, like trying to catch a fish with your bare hands.

◆

His thoughts unruly, he stepped outside again and began to walk, but this time away from Corydon and his neighbourhood. Up Wellington Crescent, past the houses of the wealthy, past the lot where a very rich man used to live. The man now dead, his house torn down to be replaced by some ugly behemoth of stone, his empire run by his sons. Morris had been fond of him. The man liked to play his clarinet in bars, he smoked in public, and he didn't care about appearances. Too many people cared these days. Morris cared. He had taken to wearing Crest Whitestrips in the evenings, until one day his teeth began to ache and he had to quit. He always checked himself in the full-length mirror that hung on his bedroom door before he went out; made sure that he was clean shaven, that his shirt was ironed, that his pant cuffs were dirt-free and straight. He did not want to appear soiled. Fine clothes could hide a turbulent soul. The first time he hired an escort, not long after he had left Lucille, he had dressed in his Hugo Boss suit and worn a dark shirt and a subtle pink tie. The tie was a signal that he could be soft, that he was not a typical creature. She called herself Rita and he'd found her, too easily he thought at the time, in the Yellow Pages. When she asked if he wanted to take off his clothes, he'd done so carefully, with his back to her, and then slipped under the goose-down quilt. He'd thought: Morris, you are a cliché and a failure. And then he'd thought: No one needs to know about this. He'd foolishly told Rita that he was a sociologist and that this was for research. He was writing a book. She asked if she was the subject or the object. The wordplay had surprised him and the surprise must have shown on his face, because Rita said, "You think I'm dumb, don't you?" That night and into the next day his tinnitus was elevated and prolonged. He wondered if there was some connection to Rita, to guilt, to exercise. He wrote this down in his Moleskine in the form of a question to be posed to his ENT doctor. "Does casual sex heighten tinnitus?"

The second time he met an escort it had been easier, less embarrassing, but only because he had smoked up beforehand. The tinnitus recurred with a fury, but he found that Advil helped, and so the squeal of bats faded and became the distant pounding of surf, the faint crackle of a radio signal breaking up. He was discovering that guilt could be chipped away; the blight on his conscience had lessened with the second woman. But now that secret life was gone, finished. There would be no more. Disappointment and Leah had cured him. She needed to quit too, to stop seeing strange men, men who were greedier than him, men less inclined towards kindness.

By now he was up towards the park, then around the park until his heels were sore. He sat on a bench and watched the leaves fall from the trees as two boys threw a football, swearing at each other and laughing. The light was pale, almost yellow, and there was the smell of burning leaves. A soft warm wind. The boys' voices had already slid into adulthood, so deep for such youthful faces, and he recalled Martin at that age, when they would play basketball together at the Jewish centre. Once a week they went there and had a game of one-on-one, a fierce tussle on the hardwood. He was heavier than Martin and used his weight inside, pushing his son around, depending upon garbage shots to keep the score close. But Martin was so quick and in such better shape that the final result was usually lop-sided. Still, he felt real pride in his son, revelling in the snap of the mesh as Martin dunked it and whooped with glee. One Saturday afternoon, as they were finishing a game, Morris slid sideways on defence and he heard the pop of his ankle as it turned, and he fell to the floor. He groaned and held his leg as Martin stood over him, asking, "You okay, Dad?" He remembered the moment not so much for the pain of the injury as for the look in Martin's eyes as he bent towards him, surprised that his own father could appear so helpless as he lay on the gym floor. Where had his power gone? And then Martin had picked him up and Morris, placing his right arm over his son's shoulders, had felt Martin's youth, the texture of his muscles through his thin shirt. What a beautiful strong boy, such solid material. And thinking of this now as he sat on the bench, he reflected that we are made of matter and that matter can be destroyed, will be destroyed, as his son was destroyed. All of us are marching towards non-matter, only some of us arrive there sooner than we should. What is crucial, he thought, is to understand how he could still grasp and hold on to the essence of his life, those around him, those who mattered, both dead and alive. And it was Martin, at that moment, who mattered most.

The boys who had been playing football were gone, had floated away like the coloured leaves that tumbled from the trees. The light had grown duller; grey clouds were moving in. These roiling thoughts were not happy, they were more than full of despair. Dr. G had encouraged him to draw happy thoughts, using the verb as if Morris were an artist who could conjure bucolic scenes. It made sense though, that word "draw," and Morris liked to apply it in a different manner, as if he were drawing from the well of experience. And yet, it so often happened that as he tried to draw happiness he felt himself "withdraw." Words were difficult. Like the argument they'd had one session about the language of sex. "To have sex, or to make love," Dr. G had asked. "Which do you do?" Morris had said that making love was a happier and healthier way of living, but perhaps he did not practise it. "I would like to though."

Dr. G said, "In order to make love you need to work outside of yourself, to lay your hands on the other person and let go, though not totally of course, because if you lose yourself completely, then you are only making half-love." And he smiled.

Then Morris told Dr. G that his first experience with sex, the first time he'd made love, was when he'd slept with his brother's girlfriend. And so he told Dr. G the story, but later, he'd been slightly sorry. How was it that the man pulled these confessions from him?

Sitting there on the bench, the odd leaf falling onto his head and shoulders, Morris thought again of his brother. Three months earlier, in late July when the crops were ripening in the fields, Morris had driven out to visit Samuel in Boise. A twenty-two-hour road trip down into North Dakota and then west through Montana and into Idaho. The landscape had shifted from moonlike rocks to rolling hills and wheat fields and then to the irrigated, bright green crop circles of Idaho. Too much time to think as he drove. Thoughts of the past, of childhood, of the teenage years with Samuel, of how he had, in his sixteenth year, stolen Samuel's girlfriend, Collette. Swooped down like those big birds, cranes, that Ursula had spoken of, and pulled Collette from the murky river. Without a bit of guilt at the time. Samuel had studied French that year and his tutor was Collette, an exchange student from Marseilles. She wore miniskirts and bright stockings and high boots, and Morris, after he had successfully wooed her, had affectionately taken to calling her Barbarella. Samuel had never been concerned with beauty other than, say, the beauty of the *Bescherelle* and its cold hard logic of verbs and their conjugations. Beauty, in the erotic sense, seemed to escape Samuel. And so when Collette showed an interest in Samuel, pronouncing his name in a drawn-out manner, the lilting effeminate ending surprised him, and then when she asked him if they couldn't maybe meet after school, he had been so bewildered that he had asked if his brother Morris could come along. Samuel loved Morris, confided in him, admired him, and so it made sense to include him. And this was how Morris met Collette.

On that day the three of them went to a small café near the school. Collette sat on a leather banquette across from the two brothers and talked to them in a mixture of French and English. She had short dark hair and she wore some sort of black tam or a beret and her head was too small for her body. Morris remembered her fingernails, which she bit furiously. Then they walked back to the Schutt house and sat in Samuel's room, which was always neat and precisely organized; books were stored alphabetically by author, magazines were stacked with the most recent on top, and underwear was folded into drawers next to freshly ironed shirts. Collette, touching the spines of Samuel's books, discovered various labelled cassette recordings. "*Qu'est-ce que c'est?*" she asked. Morris grinned and explained that his brother had always been hard of hearing, he wore hearing aids ("*Oui, oui,* I noticed," Collette said), and he had, ever since he was a child, kept a record of various conversations.

"He likes to eavesdrop," Morris said, but sweet Collette did not know that word. "To listen without being noticed," he added.

"In secret," Collette said, and she nodded. "What is this, '*Amour Nocturne*'?" she asked, plucking a cassette from the stack. Samuel took the cassette and placed it back on the shelf.

Morris grinned and said that that particular tape was a collection of recordings with the sounds of different animals having sex. "A bit strange, but that's you, isn't it, Sammy?"

Samuel said that it was science research. Someday he might write an article on it.

"Why French?" Collette asked.

"Our mother can't read French," Morris said. "Or perhaps it's because the French are very sensual."

Collette laughed and Samuel turned red.

Morris saw that she was fascinated by Samuel. She said

that he *was* like a scientist. Maybe a mad one. "*Fou. Complètement,*" she said. "It is like you are watching the world through a very strong lens. Do you know what I mean? Your heart?" She reached out and touched Samuel's chest. "Ahh, there it is. *Ton âme.*"

Morris came to know this word, and he came to know Collette. She lived on the top floor of a three-storey house that belonged to her sponsoring family. She occupied a single room with sloping ceilings. There was a single bed against the far wall, beneath the window, and opposite there was a small kitchen with a sink and stove and fridge and a table with two red chairs. She pursued Morris. She was new to the city, she had very few friends, and she wanted a Canadian lover. She told Morris this. She said that though Samuel might have been preferable, Morris was more available. She smiled in her dreamy disarming way. She said, past her small teeth, "I have a frisson of guilt. You are quicker than your brother, though not brighter, and you can provide me with easy company." He was hurt that she did not think he was bright, but this did not stop him. He went out of his way to find false ID in order to purchase cheap Italian wine and bring it over to her tiny apartment, where they sat on the floor, a candle burning between them, and talked. She said she knew that love and sex was a game for them. And she admitted that there was a corner of her heart that she reserved for Samuel alone, who did not play games.

Morris, far too young and hungry, did not understand that after this experience with Collette he would always be attracted to women who were independent, women who were strong and slightly off-kilter. He played guitar for Collette and sang unremarkable versions of Dylan and Neil Young, and he told her stories of his childhood in the Congo, where the Schutts had been missionaries. Once, he brought her food that his mother had made, scalloped potatoes and cabbage rolls, food she had never tasted before, and they ate this together, huddled by the candle, drinking wine from coffee mugs and smoking the Gitanes that she had brought with her from France.

She sometimes asked about Samuel, perhaps because she missed his strange presence, but also because Morris was a softer and kinder person when he spoke of Samuel. She said that he seemed to love his brother very much.

"My father adores him," Morris said. "And my mother. He doesn't ask for anything but just seems to exist in a place that he has created for himself. When I was seven, and he was eight, he was very sick with rheumatic fever. He was going to die, I remember, and my father took a picture of him lying in bed. They propped him up with pillows and told him to smile, and they took a picture of him and then one of us together. If you were to look at the picture now—my father pulls it out sometimes and shows it to company—you would see that we are smiling. Only Samuel is the happiest, even though he is sick and almost dead. By the following week he was better."

Collette was leaning close to him as he spoke and when he was done she put out her cigarette and stood and took his hand and pulled him up towards her bed. She lay down and said, "Come."

The memory of this time was like the photograph of his nearly dead brother; both had curled and grown indistinct. What was still clear was Collette's manner in bed, as if sex was like the trying on of another's skin, as if it were a piece of clothing that might transform her. She took him and she folded into him and beat her soft wings and she called out. He heard the sound of the November wind pushing against the small window just above her bed.

Samuel, when he learned that Collette was Morris's lover, never spoke of her again. She went away, back to Marseilles, and for a time she wrote Morris letters that arrived in thin airmail envelopes. Solid words written on fine blue paper. And then he learned that Collette was also writing Samuel and that these letters were much more intimate (he found and read them one winter afternoon; sinuous confidential letters that began "*Mon Chéri*" and ended with a declaration of affection, "*amitié*"), and whereas Collette talked to Morris about Samuel, she did not talk to Samuel about Morris. And he understood that the betrayal had been his alone, and that Collette believed this. She did not need to ask for forgiveness.

Just before Idaho Falls he took an exit, and after an hour of driving, he discovered that he was heading north to Butte rather than west to Boise. He pulled over to the shoulder and studied the map, then continued and followed a small highway west into a town called Arco, where, close to the railway tracks, he stopped at a souvenir shop and talked to a Vietnam veteran who was selling bowls shaped from sol-id rock. The man was in a wheelchair. He was voluble and lonely, and without any prompting he said that he had lost his legs in Vietnam. He talked about wars both past and pres-ent. He showed Morris his Purple Heart. "I love my coun-try. With all my heart. I'd give up my legs sixty times over for this place." He wheeled out from behind his table and pushed up close to Morris. Looked up at him. "It's a beauti-ful country. When you're finished with Boise, go south to Arizona, the Grand Canyon. Gives you faith in God."

Just what he needed, Morris thought, a return to a faith he had lost so long ago. "I'm not an atheist," he said.

"Of course you aren't." Too enthusiastic, this suffer-ing cripple. And in order to escape, Morris chose one of the bowls, the larger one with the blue lines. His brother might appreciate it. Outside, on the stoop of the shack, the sun beat off his head and made his eyes swim. Or perhaps he was tear-ing up. He had taken to crying lately, at the slightest hint of bathos, like his father used to do when he told stories to his children, gathering them around him, a sequester near the fire. Ancient stories, because those stories were the best. And the tears fell.

Farther along, winding amongst hills that were bare except for the occasional horse or a pickup moving slowly along a road high above, he realized that he would never be able to compete with the patriotism of the man he had just seen. The mythmaking was so engrained, so lacking in contemplation. But perhaps I am missing something, he thought.

His brother, on the other hand, had chosen this place, the United States of America, as his new home. And his brother was not given to irrational decisions. All his life, at college, in Egypt and then the Sudan and then Tanzania and back to North America, Samuel had, or so Morris thought, led a careful life. Perhaps he knew something that Morris did not.

His brother lived in a large house in a gated community with a three-car garage and in the garage were two cars, a BMW and an Infiniti. And inside the perfectly clean house, when his brother was at work during the day, Morris roamed and snooped, dipping into Samuel's dresser drawers, where he found a purple dildo and some lacy panties and a pair of handcuffs in a brown leather bag and a handgun, fully loaded. He took out the handgun and studied it and thought of Ursula and her gun, never spoken of. And why had he never spoken to Ursula about the gun? Had he been afraid? Lucille would have said yes, yes, he was afraid. She would have said that Morris preferred secrecy and deceit to full disclosure. Look at him now, snooping through Samuel's drawers, experiencing the fragile eroticism of a peeping Tom. He put the gun back into the drawer. There was a television that filled one wall, and a den with a set of Robert Ludlum's work, the Koran, the Bible, an Arabic-English dictionary, and a photo of his brother in the Sudan, standing beside a tall black man with a marvellous smile. Samuel had always wanted to work for the CIA. Dorothy's father had been a chief of station in the Congo many years earlier. This had benefitted Samuel. Perhaps he'd married Dorothy for this reason—to carry on the tradition of spying. As Morris stood in the middle of the house on an extremely hot day in late July, near noon, he realized that he was once again on the verge of tears. Where was the relevance? Imprudently, over the last month, he had been reading Cicero, one of the books he'd picked up from Dr. Karle's library. Cicero's daughter Tullia had died in childbirth and Cicero had fallen into a private mourning, against the wishes of his compatriots who wanted him to appear suitably sad but finally healed. But it was difficult to be healed. And from this sadness leapt great writing, and the line, *Unless the mind is healed . . . there will be no end to our unhappiness.* How so? wondered Morris. Would a clear and wise mind remove his grief and distress?

That night, sitting on the back patio in the dry heat, Morris drank gin and tonic as Samuel held a sweating glass of ice water. At some point the conversation turned to Martin, an inevitable and painful topic. Morris said that it had been a year and a half now and that there was no escaping the sadness because it just clung to one, you see, like a burr under a spaniel's collar. They had had a spaniel as boys, so the allusion was simple and effective. Samuel had shot the dog after it was hit by a car and lay whimpering in a ditch. He'd walked up to it, pulled back the bolt on the .22, put in a shell, reset the bolt, said, "Poor girl," and shot the dog. Morris mentioned this, but Samuel would have no truck with nostalgia.

"Lucille told me that she is worried," Samuel said. "That like this now, talking about a dead dog rather than Martin, you are distracting yourself and everyone else."

"Not facing it then, eh?" Morris drank and the ice cubes

slipped up the glass and banged his teeth. "I am though. In bigger ways than Lucille understands. She's the one who's distracted. She's fucking a heart surgeon."

Samuel had never sworn in public in his life, not that Morris knew, and so there was a great pleasure in pricking his ears.

"Things were rough long before you separated. You told me this."

"Significance?" Morris asked.

"She's been lonely."

"And I'm not?"

"She thought you might be. Were, in fact. She said that. Are you lonely?"

"No. Are you? We are more alike than one might hope, aren't we, Samuel? Both of our marriages finished. Both of us living alone. Good thing Dad is unaware. He'd be very disappointed." He leaned forward and asked, "How's the spying world?"

"I should never have told you that. Ever."

"Listen, Samuel. I have one friend, maybe two, and we don't talk about you. And I've never mentioned you in my columns. Would you like me to? Perhaps a little story about my brother who tortures infidels?"

"I teach Arabic," Samuel said.

"Do you agree with the methods?" Morris asked.

"Which?"

"Come on, Samuel. The torture. Your people are breaking all kinds of laws."

"Not at all."

"You're serious. So, if the regime asked you to interrogate a prisoner, you would?"

Samuel appeared to be thinking. The air conditioner hummed on the other side of the house. Samuel said, "If a man throws rocks through your windows night after night, wouldn't you try to stop him?"

"Well, I might ask why *my* windows? What have I done? I might even walk out into the street and try to talk to him."

"You're naive, Morris. He'd smash a rock over your head."

"He might, that's true. But I wouldn't know that until I stepped out onto the street and faced him. The most dangerous thing is to not know your enemy, especially as the enemy is usually yourself, or your own fear. I've always wondered when your thinking changed. We grew up with the same parents, we were taught the same things."

"Maybe it's you that's changed."

"Dad always taught us to be peaceful."

"But I am. He also taught us other things that you've rejected. So, who's changed?"

Morris said, "What happens is that ideas flip with each generation. Children need to push against the values of their parents. Look at Martin. Going to war after everything I taught him." He pointed at Samuel. "If you'd had a child, let's say a girl, she might be your opposite."

"Maybe, but I doubt that. I would have raised her in a clear way."

Morris chuckled sadly. "And I didn't raise Martin in a clear way?"

"Maybe not," Samuel said with a soft voice.

He took a sip and shuddered and said, "You don't know what it's like to be a parent. Suddenly you're a father and then you learn as you go. Maybe I failed, but it wasn't because I didn't try."

"I never said you failed," Samuel said. "Your daughters are beautiful."

"I wish sometimes I had your certainty. Not very often, because I'm not a big believer in certainty, but there are times when I wish for that. It must be nice to be right." And then, perhaps because he was on his third drink, or perhaps because Samuel had angered him, he talked about Collette. He asked Samuel if he had ever heard from Collette after she left Winnipeg to go back to Marseilles. "She taught you French," he said. "Clean words, dirty words. How to order food. The weather. *Il fait frais ce matin*. Where the hat was. *Le chapeau est sur la table*. All useful things, weren't they, Samuel?"

Samuel was watching Morris warily. "This is your grief talking."

"Yes, yes. And it is fresh every day." And then he said that he was sorry. He had brought up Collette because he had been thinking about her on the drive down, and he'd come to see that he'd been selfish. He must have hurt Samuel. "I did. I was greedy and young and foolish and I wanted to fill both of my hands, and so, impetuously, I stole from you." He faltered and waved a hand and said that he was trying to be clearer with himself.

"There were three of us, Morris. I have to take some responsibility. And Collette, well, she chose too, didn't she?"

"She did. And it appears that her heart chose you. Her letters to you were warm and caring."

"You read them?"

"Yes. I'm sorry for that as well."

"Stop beating yourself up, Morris. You live too much in the past."

"See? Look at you, your generosity, your forgiveness. I love you, Samuel."

Samuel seemed embarrassed. He was quiet for a moment, and then he talked about his first year in high school, how the boys had made fun of his hearing aids, called him "AM-FM," and how, at lunch, he was chased around the school grounds and often came home with bruises and black eyes. "And then the next year you arrived in high school, and the first time Butch Gaartner tried to beat me up, you stepped in and kicked the shit out of him. The boys left me alone after that."

"I remember."

"You weren't such a pacifist back then, were you."

"No, I wasn't." He felt a certain pride in that memory. He wished now that Samuel had told Martin this story. Before he ran off to war. Some meaning could have been made of it; Martin would have had reason to be proud of his father. Who needs guns when you have your fists, eh, Dad?

"You're too full, Morris. You stuff yourself with sadness. You have to learn to sit back and assess. I'm not dangerous. I'm just your brother, your own flesh and blood. The thing is, we don't get to choose our brothers, do we." And then he rose and said he was tired and he told him to lock the patio door when he came in. To make sure that the safety rod was in place as well.

Morris waved in response. He sat and listened to the night noises. There were crickets, and cars, and once, faintly, the sound of a woman crying, which reminded him of Lucille when she cried. A lonesome sound, the noise of a sad woman.

The light in the park had shifted from yellow to grey to the filtered shadows one might find in the corners of a poorly lit room. The afternoon had fled into the evening and all Morris had done was sit on a bench. He rose and walked quickly back towards his condo. As he entered the building he heard the sound of someone moaning and for a moment he imagined that he was still thinking of Lucille crying, and as he reached the third floor he knew it was Lucille—it was precisely her manner of weeping, a soft wail that descended into a hiccupping sniffle and then back up again—but then he saw the huddled figure at his door and he recognized his daughter Libby. She was sitting, leaning against his door, her legs pulled up and her face pressed against her knees, as if she were trying to compress herself, and when he said her name and she looked up, she burst out crying afresh. And then she stood and fell into his arms. "He left me, he left me," she wailed and then, hiccupping, she pushed herself against him and what he heard was a jumble of crying and finally, "Oh, Daddy, my heart, I'm going to die."

Morris held her and said, "There, there," while he thought, Of course it feels like you will die, that your heart will never survive. I have felt that too, but it's not true. Then he said, "Come, sweetie, come inside," and he opened the door and led her in and sat her down in the kitchen and ran her a glass of water and he said, "Breathe. Just breathe." He waited and stroked her hands and her hair as she finished crying, and then, just when he thought she might be ready to talk, she began to cry again, and he said again, "Just breathe," until finally she was ready to talk.

She looked up at him with her blotched face and her red eyes. "This morning Shane told me." She trembled, then continued. "He made me breakfast and after I ate he said that there was another woman and her name was Anne and that he loved her. Daddy, she's fifty. He made me breakfast and let me eat it and then he said that he had fallen in love with a woman who's almost Mom's age. He called me unripe."

"You were at his place for the night? Your mother said that was okay?"

She shook her head in disbelief. "What are you talking about? He's leaving me."

"Yes, I understand that. And I'm sorry. But you were there, at his place, and he waited until the morning to tell you? After breakfast?"

"Daddy, she's your age. Don't you see? She's probably got a daughter my age. I'm so ashamed."

"No, no, Libby. You have nothing to be ashamed about. *He* should be ashamed, the son of a bitch. What nonsense. 'Unripe.'"

"You know what else he said? He said she was amazing. I asked what he meant, stupid me, and he said she was amazing in every way. She was smart, she played the cello, she was great in bed, she made him feel complete. And then I threw my coffee at him."

"Good for you. You hit him with it, I hope."

"Oh, Daddy. Mommy said good too. When I told her she said, 'Good, he doesn't deserve you.'" And she began to cry again and he took her arm and led her to his bedroom and made her lie down, and he pulled the blanket up to her chin and he bent to kiss her and quickly, so quickly, she fell asleep, as if drugged, and in her sleep she must have dreamed because she shuddered and her left arm jumped and her eyelids, the softest and most delicate things, flickered. How young she was, what beautiful, beautiful skin, so perfect. Lucille had had skin like that once, so long ago, when Morris was first in love with her. They had taken so much for granted, as if she and he and their youthful blazing condition would last forever and ever. This is how one thinks at that age. Note, Morris thought, read Hobbes. The phone rang and rang and then fell silent. Morris did not have an answering machine; he had rid himself of that as well. The light was sucked from the room. He sat beside Libby and held her hand as she slept and he thought, Yes, this too shall pass, and he imagined writing a column in which he would describe a daughter's fall from innocence and the misogynist who had invoked it.

At some point, he released Libby's hand and he wandered about the condo with a heavy heart. He washed the few dishes in the kitchen sink, dried them, and stored them in the cabinet. He scrubbed three pairs of black socks by hand and hung them from the shower rod. Libby slept. The phone rang again but he ignored it. He sat down at his desk, turned on the lamp, and took out paper and pen and began to write.

Dear Ursula,

Today I went for a walk around the park and I sat on a bench in the afternoon sunlight and I reflected on my life and the life of my family, my brother, my father, my wife, and my children. I thought of you as well, though you came to me later, as an ideal almost, like a photograph one keeps in a special place and then, while rummaging about looking for something that was lost, the photograph is suddenly found by chance and there is surprise and pleasure in the discovery. That was you. I found I was pleased, I had soft thoughts, and I began to miss you. I recalled our conversation about duty and I realized that it was immoral of me to allow my son to go to war. Not because he died, but because he entered a world where he was a mere object, a commodity, an article of trade. My country said, "We need you, Martin Schutt, to put on a uniform and hold a gun and to aim that gun at the enemy, and for that we will pay you a certain amount of money and we will clothe and feed you and perhaps educate you." And then, when he was killed, they clapped the pitiful parents on

the back and said, "Well done, thou good and faithful fool." My country could not see that Martin Schutt
was more than an object to be manipulated. *I* did not
see that. When my case comes up in court, would I
want myself on the jury? I think not. I have stopped
living as if there is a relation between the way the
world is and how I ought to act in it. My father, who
could be wrong in so many ways, was right when he
preached that salvation was first and foremost about
clothing the poor and feeding the hungry. Are you
hungry, Ursula? I am. Hungry and thirsty, though I
am not sure for what. I ache, this I know. When you
said, "Smell me," it was the most erotic moment of my
life, as if your body might divulge some secret. Perhaps I was hunting for your soul. For we are more than
just skin and bones and cock and cunt and intestines
and grey matter and shit and blood, are we not? On
my knees that night, I smelled something more than
just your hair, your body, your beautiful skin, didn't
I? How ineffectual I am. How small. I do not mean to
frighten you, and you must be asking why I am telling
you all of this. I do so because I have come to a point
in my life where I must stop wanting. I must learn to
stand alone, to inhabit the space given to me and not
reach greedily for more. *I want. I want. I want.* This
has been my mantra for so many years, even when I
thought I was being altruistic. Even these words, my
mantra, "I want," these are not mine. They are the
words of a man named Henderson. And yet, I claim

them. You see, I am inauthentic, a charlatan. And so, I am telling you, with a sad heart, that I will not be travelling down to Minneapolis to see you again. I cannot. I have two daughters, a grandson, an estranged wife, a son I have not yet even buried, all of these people to take care of. But mostly, I have myself to care for and I am not doing a very good job. Placing myself in your arms is not the answer. You are good.

Morris

Morris put down his pen, folded the letter, slipped it into an envelope, and wrote down Ursula's address, which he now knew by heart. He stood and went to check on Libby, who was still sleeping. It appeared she might sleep through the night. He paced his small apartment, picking up a book and then setting it down, putting the water on to boil, making tea, and then placing it aside absent-mindedly. Finally, he phoned Lucille, who answered immediately and asked, "Is Libby with you?"

"Yes, she is."

"Morris, why didn't you answer? I've been going crazy. Is she all right?"

"She's sleeping."

"I did everything wrong," Lucille said. "I was unkind and mean. I was so happy that Shane was finally out of her life that I paid no attention to her sadness."

"She told me."

"What did she tell you?"

"That you were happy."

"Oh, I am, I was, but I didn't mean her. I wasn't happy that she was hurt."

"Of course you weren't."

"I'm so tired, Morris. I can't be the good mother all the time."

"She'll be fine, Lucille. She's a strong girl. I was watching her sleep just now and I thought of you when you were young. You have the same skin texture. Very lovely."

"Really? What else, Morris? I felt so bad, I thought she'd run away."

"She did. She ran over here. Your eyebrows are similar too, though Libby doesn't pluck hers."

"I'm glad you were there. I'm glad she has both of us."

"She was furious that Shane had found someone almost as old as her own mother. Such indignation."

Lucille laughed lightly, a sound Morris had not heard in a long time. He tilted his head and marvelled. "The woman's practically my age," he said.

"Maybe she's got implants. Maybe her skin's been stretched tight. Did you leave me because I was getting old, Morris?"

"*You* left me, Lucille. Remember?"

"Did I? I thought it was mutual."

"And then so quickly you were in bed with that heart surgeon." He realized as he said this that he was a cuckold. How did the heart surgeon leap so quickly into Lucille's bed when he, Morris Schutt, had had to wait over a year? Was it aging that had made Lucille reckless? But then, he too had been reckless. But that was before, before. These days he was attempting to achieve moderation. A change of heart.

"Shh, don't talk like that. Can I confess something, Morris, without you telling the world? Harvey bores me. He watches too much TV, football, men with tattoos hitting each other. He likes reality shows." Her voice dropped to a bare whisper. "And he doesn't like to go down on me." Morris imagined her annoyance, the haughty shift of her shoulders. Her voice rose again, assured now. "Don't get me wrong, he's a kind man, gentler than you. The other day he picked me up from work and gave me flowers and took me out for dinner. It was lovely, but something was wrong, like he was doing what he thought I might want." She sounded wistful. Made a slight noise, a throat-clearing, and said, "I got a Brazilian. Well, not quite, there's just a little landing strip. He doesn't like it."

"Really?" Morris's voice had gone husky. She missed him. "Can I land there?"

"You want to, Mo?"

"I do, I do." Then he said giddily, as if this were the confessional part of the day, "I left Dr. Shane McKibben a message a while ago. I'd been trying to find him to have a talk and he was avoiding me, so I left him a phone message. I said that if he didn't stop seeing our daughter I would take him to court, I would have his job rescinded, I'd report him to the board of ethics, call in the president of the university, and if that didn't work, I would personally meet him in a back alley. He never got back to me."

"Oh, that's awful." But she was laughing.

"Is it? I thought it would please you."

"What if Libby finds out?"

"She's said nothing, and she would have if Shane had told her."

Morris heard a noise, a little scrabble or scratch, and he looked up to see Libby standing in the doorway. She was puffy eyed, rubbing her face, looking about.

"Hey," Morris said. "You're awake." He held the phone in the air. "It's your mother." He searched her face to see if she had overheard him, foolish man. She looked stunned from sleep as she pushed her hand through the air, dismissing the phone. She shuffled to the bathroom and closed the door.

"Morris?" This was Lucille, calling out.

Morris came back to the phone and said, "She's still half asleep, she'll call you later."

"Why don't you have an answering machine, Morris? Why are you cutting yourself off? I told Harvey about the stocks, the RRSPs, the cellphone, and he said two words. 'Solipsistic' and 'selfish.' I agree."

"Nice alliteration. Harvey's suddenly a poet now? The man is gifted."

"Don't, Morris."

"*You* don't. Don't tell me what Harvey says. I don't need Harvey's psychiatric evaluation. I've got you and Dr. G for that."

"Have you been seeing him, Morris?"

"No. I stopped going. Last month."

"You must go back. He's good for you."

"Is he? Jacob Boehme is also good for me. I'm learning a lot from him. And Aristotle and Augustine. Have you read Cicero, Lucy? He writes very wisely about grief. He says that we must shed distress or it will bring *gauntness, pain, depression, and disfigurement.*"

She laughed. Not just briefly, but for a good number of seconds and with a hiccup in between. Then she said more soberly, "I have suffered all of those, Morris. The gauntness especially."

"Yes, I saw that the other day. You've lost too much weight."

"Size six now."

"Really?" And he thought of the pants he had bought that afternoon, suddenly the wrong size, and he wondered if he should still expedite them to her the next day, as a sign that he was thinking of her. The thought was of the utmost importance. She could return them.

She said, "You always wanted me skinnier. That was one of our problems. That you couldn't accept me for who I was."

"Is that true? I thought that you couldn't accept yourself."

She ignored this and then, just before she hung up, she said that she had thought of the perfect place to spread Martin's ashes. "Lake Atitlán," she said. "By my sister's rock garden where Martin liked to sit and look out at the water. The whole family could go at Christmas." She paused and concluded with "Think about it, okay, Morris?" and she hung up. He put the phone down and looked at his daughter, who had come back into the room.

"You were talking about me," she said.

"Were we?" He was anticipating the barrage, the accusation of meddling, the tears, but Libby was absolutely calm, as if she had no more tears to cry. She said that Shane had told her about the phone call, about Morris's threats. "He called you hysterical and hilarious. He said, 'Who does he think he is?' and I said, 'He's my father.' I didn't mind you doing that, Dad. I was secretly happy, but that's not why he left me."

What sudden wisdom from the mouth of this child. Or had she always been wise? Perhaps he had been blind, though he knew Libby was full of sympathy and grace, this was evident from her work in the hospital, from her treatment of her grandfather even as he babbled like a child. She was generous, she was naive; she believed that bad things should not happen in the world. Or was that naiveté? It might simply be hope and compassion, qualities that he strove for yet failed to achieve. He stood, suddenly alert, calling out, "I have something," and he went to the bedroom and rummaged through his bags and pulled out the Dolce & Gabbana shoes, pale blue with those lovely heels, and he brought them back and handed them to her and said, "For you."

"Daddy," she whispered, and she took them and laid down the left shoe very softly and she held the right and then leaned forward and slipped it on. Morris watched. She picked up the left shoe and put that on as well. She stood. She was wearing jeans and the jeans were tight at the calves, and as she walked away from him and then swivelled and walked back to him, he saw that they were perfect and that she was pleased.

"How did you know my size? Oh, Daddy, thank you, they're beautiful." She bent to kiss him on the cheek and he, like a charlatan almost on the verge of no longer pretending, ducked his head, considered, and then lifted it again and said, "You're welcome."

And why not? Why shouldn't his beautiful daughter benefit from his passions, his mistakes, his stubborn fantasies? To stumble and then correct oneself, this was a necessary and exquisite thing. She didn't need to know why he bought the shoes. She ought not to know anything about Leah. Ought-not, what a lovely little combination, so fresh it should have a flower named after it. I would like a bouquet of ought-nots for my sweet *bohémienne*.

And yet, the following day, when the FedEx man knocked at the door, Morris experienced a moment of regret as he explained that there was only one package, and as he spilled cash into the outstretched palm, he wondered if he should run down to the consignment shop and find Leah something equally desirable. Instead, he mailed his letters. One to Ursula, and the other to the prime minister, which was the column he had written in a fit of anger. It was important to send it, he had decided. The envelope was addressed: "Prime Minister of Canada, Ottawa, Ontario." There was a third letter, and it was addressed to the president and CEO of Colt Canada. Morris had written it in the early morning, when sleep would not come.

Dear Sir,

Last year, when my son was still alive and fighting in Afghanistan, he killed a member of the Taliban. He used one of your guns, a C7 assault rifle. I thought you should know that your weapons of war are working fabulously. So fabulously that several days later he himself was killed by one of your rifles. Accidents do happen, don't they? I noted that your company is located in Kitchener, Ontario. Wow. Right next to Waterloo, where a lot of my people live. The Mennonites. We like to think of ourselves as pacifists, but this is mostly lip service. We can be hypocrites. Are you a hypocrite, sir? Do you understand that evil is voluntary and this makes man intimately responsible? In any case, my two points were these: my son managed to kill someone else with one of your guns, and he himself was killed by one of your instruments. Congratulations. You're doing a fine job. One hundred percent.

Morris Schutt

This letter he sent as well. Why not? Though the devastation of the world was not the CEO's fault alone, he needed to take some responsibility. His *Weltanschauung* had to be challenged. Where would we be if we all abjured accountability, if we all laid the evils of the world on the foundation of contingency?

Excited and agitated, he dropped the letters into the

mailbox, and then walked over to the local cyber café and logged on and read the *New York Times,* the *Guardian,* the *Washington Post,* and the *Independent* on-line. Then, hesitantly, he perused a few of the newspapers that had syndicated his column, looking for his replacement, or some indication that he was missed, or that he would be back. There was a small note in a midwestern paper that stated Morris Schutt was on holiday and would return. A prick of pleasure, then a rueful dismissal. He wouldn't return. Not ever. In the national paper, where his column had appeared every Monday, was a guest columnist by the name of Otto Hyperion. What nonsense the man wrote, pop psychology, all about externals, poorly composed and self-serving; though the column was funny, and Morris had to convince himself that it wasn't. He felt rebuffed. He logged off. Then logged back on to check his stocks, forgetting that he no longer had stocks. He Googled himself and found the usual entries and several new ones, small articles declaring that Morris Schutt the columnist was on paid leave from his job. Garbage, thought Morris, I am not being paid. He went to Wikipedia and looked up "Morris Schutt." The usual facts—where he'd studied, his work as a journalist, a list of publications with links (who writes this stuff? he wondered)—nothing new, no mention of his most recent life. The entry was quite minor compared to rock singers, movie stars. Even certain other journalists had more said about them. Perhaps they regulated their own sites, made their own entries. These days, fame was all about shameless whoring. Morris clicked on "edit" and after his name, where it read "born 1956," he changed it to "1956–?," and farther down the page, aware that the good denizens of this space accepted only what was verifiable and not necessarily true, he wrote, "Morris Schutt has a wife, Lucille, two daughters, and a grandson. At times he can be an out-and-out cur. He was predeceased by his son, Martin, in 2006." He logged off again, paid, and stepped outside into a cold north wind. He thought, If man's purpose is to flourish, to stand stalwart against the buffeting storm and find a tiny local corner in which he can thrive, then he, Morris Schutt, was failing. There were moments in his days when he was brought up short by his failure to remember Martin properly, to keep him in the forefront, to hold him in his mind and heart, and when he did fail, when he realized that he had been, for a brief moment, happily absent-minded, he felt guilty and pushed the happiness aside.

And why not, Morris thought now as he bent against the cold wind, who else was to be held accountable for Martin's death? Why he, Morris, of course. But this was not a thought that he wanted to think. He just couldn't stop thinking. One night, full of anguish and unable to sleep, he had risen and sat at his kitchen table and written down what he believed, at that time in his life, to be fact. He wrote: "Justice is the most important thing. Justice means not harming others. Perfect justice is perfectly impossible, but that does not mean we should not know what perfect justice looks like. Evil is voluntary. War is voluntary. War is caused by humans. Martin's death was an accident. Accidents imply chance. I do not believe in chance."

He stood, retrieved a few of his books, and sat again. Man, he discovered, should be by nature *a rememberer, a good learner, magnificent, charming, and a friend and kinsman of truth, justice, courage, and moderation.* This from Socrates. But to find moderation was not easy. He knew that. Morris wrote, "The most just person is the one precisely aware of his failures." The danger, of course, was that this kind of thinking might lead to piety, which then led to fanaticism and the kind of behaviour that drove him, so long ago now, it felt, to ask people on the street the question "Are you free?"

One time, half a year after Martin died, in Toronto on a trip to visit his editor, Morris had taken a taxi from Chinatown to the harbour, and he began to talk to the driver who was quite dark and quite certainly Middle Eastern. He learned that his name was Hasim and that he came from Afghanistan and this produced a singular pang. What a strange symmetry. He had talked to the man's eyes which studied him in the rear-view mirror, and the man had talked back. They spoke of the weather, too humid, and of the price of gasoline, too high. And then he aimed the conversation in a certain direction. "I was at a party the other night and I fell to talking with a woman."

"Fell?" Hasim said.

"Began. I began to talk to her, and you know, I have this question that I ask. Are you free?"

"Ahh yes," Hasim said. "Free."

"Well," said Morris, "in this case the woman thought I was flirting with her, until I explained that it was a philosophical question. Do you understand what I am saying?"

"Yes, I understand. Say on."

Aha, he thought, a thinking man. And then, perhaps because of the coziness of the car, or perhaps because of the openness in Hasim's eyes reflected in the mirror and the sense he had that those eyes could be trusted, or perhaps because he could not truly see Hasim's face or the doubt and disbelief he might be expressing, he said that he had had a son named Martin who had been in the Canadian army, and that his son had been killed in Afghanistan. He told him the whole story, from beginning to end, which included his anger at his son for his defiant ways, how he had, in a moment of antagonism, told him to join the army, and his son had, and then how his son had written letters home detailing his fears, and how Morris had not really responded, at least not in good faith, and then his son had died, and there had been a knock at the door one day when he had been upstairs, writing. "I am a journalist," Morris explained. He said that when he saw two people in uniform at the door, he had not wanted to answer because he knew what the message would be. He talked on, even after they had reached their destination and the taxi sat idling in the heat, and beautiful people passed by on the sidewalk, and on several occasions some of those same beautiful people tried to open the door to the taxi, but Hasim shooed them off, saying, "I am on my break." And so Morris talked, and at some point he confessed that his son had been shot by one of his own men. And that was when Morris began to cry. He felt no embarrassment, no shame, and it was as if he knew that Hasim would not judge him, that it was almost as if Hasim had been dropped down into his life in order to be the recipient of this news. No disapproval, just a nodding of his head as he said, "This is a grave affair." When he had finally stopped talking, Hasim said, "I have a sister in Kandahar, and my sister has a daughter who goes to school. This could not happen if your son had not gone there to fight. Do you see? My sister's daughter is free. And my sister, she is free as well." He tsked and shook his head and Morris thought, Has this man heard me? Is he a spokesperson for the government? Is this what I want to hear? But Hasim continued, generously. "There is madness there. Morris, please, I would like you to be a guest in my house. Would you come to my house? To meet my wife and my two sons?" Then Morris saw that there was only goodwill, and he nodded and said he would like that very much, but perhaps the next time he was in Toronto. He would phone. Hasim gave him his phone number, written on a taxi chit, which he took and folded into his shirt pocket. Hasim got out of the taxi and came around to open the door for him, and when he tried to pay, Hasim said, "No, it is me who should pay you." They shook hands and Morris said, "You have a good soul, Hasim."

He misplaced the taxi chit. Or perhaps it got lost in the laundry. He hunted for it but could not find it. He called Beck Taxi in Toronto and asked for information regarding one of their drivers, Hasim, but it turned out there were seven men named Hasim working for the company. And besides, that kind of personal information was never divulged.

3

On the day he learned of Martin's death, Morris had been working at home, alone in the house. He was writing his weekly column, putting on the finishing touches, when the doorbell rang. He saved his file, backed it up to a memory stick, climbed reluctantly down the stairs—he disliked being interrupted while writing—and as he approached the front door, he saw, through the glass, two men in army uniform. He knew instantly and with absolute certainty the reason for their visit. He stood, several feet from the door that remained closed. He had the thought that if he turned away and walked back upstairs and returned an hour later, the men in uniform would have disappeared and that this moment would pass into eternity. His body began to shake and he heard a voice crying, "No, no, no." It was his own voice, he heard the timbre of it, the bass tone, and he stopped himself. There would be no scene, no indignity. He stepped forward and opened the door.

It had been an accident. Martin had died when another soldier's rifle unintentionally went off while they were on foot patrol. It had happened in the Panjwayi District the day before. The bullet had passed through Martin's jaw, into his brain, and exited the top of his skull. He had died while en route to the field hospital. The man who told Morris this was the padre. He appeared to be the spokesperson. He introduced himself at the door. He said, "Mr. Schutt, my name is John Fellows and I'm a captain and a padre with the seventeenth Wing here in Winnipeg." And then he had given Morris the news. Only later, standing in the living room, had he introduced the other man, a commanding officer who had been a part of Martin's training. But Morris, oddly, was focused on the padre, curious that he should first call himself a padre rather than a chaplain, as if he were some sort of "father," and curious also about the padre's demeanour: he seemed so calm and prepared. While he spoke, he leaned forward and studied Morris carefully, as if to ascertain some sort of possible damage. Morris had many questions, but he thought later that he had asked the wrong ones. He asked if Lucille knew. She didn't. They had come here first. Then he asked what that meant, "unintentionally." The colonel said that the soldier whose gun it was had fired accidentally while the unit was on foot patrol. He said that Martin had been well loved by the other men. He was a hero. Morris asked how this could be, how could his son be shot by one of his own men? Were they careless, stupid? His hands began to shake and he pressed them against his face, and then looked up.

"He's dead?"

The commanding officer nodded and said, "There will be an investigation, of course."

"And to what end? The culprit will be charged? Why? You say it was an accident. What's the soldier's name?"

He looked at the men standing before him. They were good people. They were doing their jobs, but they also had to deliver information that was more difficult than death due to an improvised explosive device, or death during a firefight with the Taliban. Without waiting for answers to his questions, he said, "I don't like the army, and I didn't want my son to sign up, but he did so to punish me. Look at me now. I'd say he's succeeded."

The padre made a clicking noise with his mouth. He reached out to take Morris's hand and he let him. He realized that these men had done this before; that whatever madness and grief and anger he threw their way, they had seen worse. And he also saw that his hatred of the army was nothing new. They had experienced this as well, were inured to this kind of reaction, almost dismissive, and this dismissal angered him. He turned to the commanding officer, a man about his own age, fifty perhaps, and asked him if he had a son. Then, not waiting for a response, he said that the people in power, the ministers, the prime minister, the generals, the colonels, all of them, they were the ones to blame for this. "Little war games," he said. "Plucking boys, innocent, gullible boys, who'll jump when you tell them, who'll leap into a den of lions if you order it, who'll bark and dance and beg and fetch, plucking them from the world of love and desire and goodness, and throwing them to the wolves." And he said no more. Only much later would he realize that his anger and his rage at his son's death had erupted at that moment in the living room, and that he had then dismissed and buried it; put it away.

The padre asked if he wanted to call his wife, or if he would prefer that they speak to her. He said that he would call. He went into the kitchen and dialled her direct line rather than going through her secretary, Joan. Her machine kicked in immediately and he knew that she was seeing a patient. He left a message. He said, "Lucille, it's me. Morris. Please call."

He didn't want to worry her, though he made his tone serious enough to warrant some suspicion on her part. He never called her at work and so she would be curious. But he certainly didn't want to give her any grim warning and have her thinking the worst. But what was worse than this? He thought of going through Joan, having her interrupt the session, or of leaving another message and saying that it was the worst thing possible, and she would know and come quickly, with utmost haste. He knew that Martin's death would destroy her.

They'd made love that morning, before she went to work. Now, facing these two men, he wanted to step back through the day to that moment when their eyes had met and she had clasped his buttocks with her heels. Back through time. Erase the day. Though Martin must have been dead already while they were having sex. For how long?

The padre was talking. He said that he would stay with Morris until Lucille came home. He thought it best that he be here when she heard the news. "In our experience, it's important to have someone else present."

What a terrible job, Morris thought, and he nodded.

The commanding officer spoke then. He said that the common practice was for someone to be with the family during the day. At least for the first while. To be a support, to talk to the press, to field questions. A family wasn't necessarily equipped for the hard questions at this time, for the snooping and prying. "Journalists are looking for a story, I'm sorry to say, and in our experience we are able to provide a buffer for the family. Is that okay? If we are here for you?"

Morris nodded again. He wanted to say that he was a journalist, that he knew the methods and the people, but he said nothing.

Lucille had been amazing. When she walked in and saw the three of them in the living room, she said, "It's Martin," and Morris had gone to her and held her for the longest time, and then she'd pulled away and sat down and said, "Tell me," and the padre told her. After, she cried. Morris sat beside her and held her hand as she cried, and then she looked up and said that she would make tea. Her hands were shaking.

The padre said that they didn't need tea, they were fine, but Lucille insisted. Morris watched her rise and walk towards the kitchen, and the commanding officer, softer in tone than his uniform and rank would imply, followed her. He heard them talking as the water boiled. Muffled voices, the occasional question. He felt proud of his wife. How solid she was, so fine in this moment.

Later that night, after the phone calls to family and friends and to his brother in Idaho, after Libby had come home and been given the news and cried and cried and then been put to bed with a hot-water bottle and two sleeping pills, only then did Lucille show her rage. "Why didn't you tell

Joan that it was an emergency? My God, Morris, you treat me like a child, like I'm breakable, and then you act surprised when I break. I should have been here. It was my right."

"That's ridiculous, Lucille. You're being unreasonable. I knew what they were about to tell me the minute I saw them."

"Did you? Truly? Oh, my. Oh, my." Then she asked why Sheila had to come back the next day. Sheila had arrived at the house after dinner, been introduced as the assisting officer, and stayed till midnight. She would return in the morning.

"It's how it works," he said. "They've done this before."

"He was shot by one of his own," Lucille said.

"Shh. Don't."

"How could it be an accident? Do you think they're lying? Do you think he wasn't liked by this unknown killer? What was the soldier's name? Maybe they're covering it up. Maybe an enemy soldier broke into the compound and killed him. I don't trust them, Morris. They want everything to be clear and certain and I'm not getting this story. Did you see the padre's eyes? He wasn't being straight with us."

"That man has a terrible job to do," he said, but he was thinking of other things. He believed that everything in the world, even the loss of his son, was necessary. Because, if it had been an accident, then it was unnecessary, and if it was unnecessary, then it became pointless, an event that did not fit into the larger design of the world. Which was nonsense. Because, for him, nothing could be accidental. Not the colour of Lucille's hair, nor the socks he had chosen to wear that morning, nor the shape of his son's ears, nor the coffee he had spilled at breakfast, the black stain spreading over the white tablecloth. An error perhaps, but not an accident.

Lucille's voice floated through the darkness of their bedroom. "Why did you tell him to go? Why, Morris? Why do you always have to be right? Did you ever think of the consequences? Oh, God. Why didn't you keep your mouth shut?" She began to weep. She sat up and wept and beat her hands against her thighs and he held her and shushed and said that Libby would hear. She didn't want to upset Libby, did she?

Then he said, "I loved him, Lucille. I loved him terribly. I just didn't know how to tell him. He wouldn't let me."

"He was twenty. That's all. He was twenty years old and he'll always be twenty. How does that work, Morris? Tell me. Please tell me."

"Come. Come here." And he pushed her back onto the bed and rubbed her back, felt the fine bones of her rib cage, the sharp shoulders, the elasticity of her skin. He talked to her, told her what a beautiful boy Martin was. He said, "Remember the day he walked into the house and announced he was going to Afghanistan. He was happy, Lucille. I've never seen him happier, as if he had found a calling, and no matter what we said we couldn't convince him otherwise. He was brave, Lucille. He had to be brave. Now it's us, our turn. Okay?" He kissed her forehead, her face, and tasted the salt from her tears. He held her head to his chest as she wept and then she stopped, and eventually she fell asleep, and he did not let her go because he feared she would wake.

In the morning, Sheila had reappeared. She kept a constant pot of coffee on the go, and whenever the phone rang, she made it clear that she was willing to take it, to screen the calls. Morris said that he could handle it. He had friends who were journalists, and if they wanted to call, he would speak to them, and if there were any unwanted calls, he would hang up.

"I understand that you're upset, Mr. Schutt," Sheila said. "And so is your wife. You're vulnerable to suggestion, and it might just slip out that you're angry with the Canadian Forces. You might end up saying something you'll regret later. We want to be united."

"Do we? And why? Because you are concerned about appearances? Well, I'm not, and I'll say whatever is necessary."

That evening Lucille told Sheila that she should leave and not return the following day. There was no point. "We're quite capable of talking to the press," Lucille said. "We know how to think. We stand side by side, and if our heads wobble a little, that's normal. But we know what we believe. We're not here to protect the army or to justify some war or even to claim our son was a hero. He might not have been."

Sheila said Lucille was wrong, that their son was a hero, and she found it sad that they couldn't accept that. Her cheeks were round and ruddy and her dress shirt was too small so that the button holes were stretched. She made a little popping sound with her mouth as she exhaled in exasperation. Lucille saw her to the door and swept her outside into the night. "Am I cruel?" Lucille asked when she returned to Morris, who sat like a puritan on a straight-backed wooden chair in the living room. But she did not sound sorry, and she did not want an answer to her question, this he knew.

The ramp ceremony took place on a cold and windy Tuesday at the airport. Morris was flanked by Libby and Lucille. Glen stood beside Meredith. She held Jake, who was restless and wanted to see the airplanes. The casket was closed; Morris and Lucille did not want a public viewing. They were given Martin's uniform and a flag. Morris had been surprised to see one of the pallbearers weeping. The drive from the airport to the funeral home was silent. He had read of the Highway of Heroes near Toronto, where the public gathered on overpasses and paid respects to the fallen war heroes, and as they drove down Sargent Avenue towards the downtown, he wondered how it was that he had come to live in a place where a fallen soldier was driven ignominiously past warehouses and big box stores and empty sidewalks.

Martin was cremated. Lucille demanded this. Bizarrely, she spoke of an article she'd read recently, about the discovery in ice of a prehistoric man, killed violently five thousand years earlier during a battle. An arrowhead had been found lodged in his shoulder. She said, "I want my son's ashes." And they had done exactly this. But first, after arriving at the funeral home from the ramp ceremony, they opened the casket and looked at Martin for the last time. His body had been prepared in Afghanistan and then been shipped to Winnipeg. He was in uniform. His face was flattened slightly, and at first Morris didn't recognize him. Then he leaned forward and kissed his son's forehead, his cheek, and laid his head against his chest. "Martin," he whispered. The rest of the family held hands after they'd all said goodbye. Lucille told Morris later that she had looked for the hole in Martin's jaw but couldn't find it. She said that she had wanted to crawl into the casket and lie with him. "But Meredith would have gone nuts. And Jake. He wouldn't have understood." And so they remained, resolute, said their goodbyes, and reluctantly turned away.

Martin had both a military funeral and a smaller memorial service. The military funeral was attended by close to one thousand people and Morris was astounded by the tributes and the respect Martin was paid. The padre who led the service spoke of honouring the fallen, and at some point during the service, as Morris held Lucille's hand, he became aware that the army had become Martin's family. What a good boy he had been. He was aware too of the sameness—the cohesion, the hardware, the perfection—of these men and women, which contrasted so greatly with his dead son, no longer able to wear the uniform of his country.

The memorial service, held two days later, was small, intended for family and close friends. Samuel flew up from Idaho. A few members of the Canadian Forces attended. They sat near the back and approached the family after the service, out on the parking lot. One of the men introduced himself as a soldier from Martin's company. He shook hands with Morris. Lucille, much to Morris's surprise, hugged him. Libby was the only family member to speak at the service. She was graceful, both in how she carried herself and in the manner she spoke, as if she were wearing Martin's death lightly. Her tone was even and calm and she told stories about Martin. She said that no sister could ask for a better big brother than Martin. "Once, when I was going out on my first date, at fifteen, he came into my room and told me that I should trust myself, that I was a beautiful strong girl, and that I should know what I wanted before I acted." Libby laughed and said, "I knew what he was trying to talk about." She blushed and paused, moved aside a strand of hair that had fallen over her eyes. "Then he said, 'Boys can be greedy, Libby. They want to have sex. I should know. I'm a boy.' And then he hugged me. He was wise. And carefree. He didn't know that certain conversations might be difficult, that there were rules." Here, Libby made little quotation marks with her fingers as she said "rules" and she smiled. "I would like to be as honest and forthright as Martin was. He was so spirited, so fervent, so curious. If only I could be half of what he was."

Libby's mouth, when she spoke, twisted slightly, as if she were suffering, but she did not cry. She looked at Morris and Lucille and Meredith and Jake, and she said that they had all been well loved by their brother and son and uncle. "Aren't we lucky?"

Morris wondered if Libby's strength came from her naiveté, the fact that she might be too young to truly understand the severity of the moment. But no, this was not true. Over the next week, Libby broke down and was inconsolable. Too much had been asked of her.

In the weeks that followed, Morris became clinically obsessed with bullets and rounds and M16s and C7s. When he could not sleep nights, he carried out research. He read that the

C7 gas-powered rifle has a 51-cm (20-inch) cold hammer-forged barrel with a flash suppressor, a bayonet lug, a TRI-AD 1TM MIL-STD-1913 accessory mount, and "coloured furniture to break up the weapon outline." *Coloured furniture?* As if the rifle were something one bought at Urban Barn and then plunked down in front of the fireplace? As well, he researched the bullet that had killed Martin. He thought it might be a 5.56 x 45 mm, manufactured in the States, though he couldn't be sure. He read: "When the bullet impacts at high velocity and yaws in tissue, fragmentation creates a rapid transfer of energy which can result in massive wounding and hydrostatic shock effects."

At this point, he went upstairs and climbed into bed and prayed that Lucille and his daughters would never know these facts. He wondered what "hydrostatic shock" was. And that word "yaw." In the morning, when he was alone again, almost against his will, he looked up "hydrostatic shock" and discovered that it referred to remote neural damage. The bullet was "light and fast" and so effective that it immediately shut down the organs of the animal.

Morris went outside and stood on the front porch in his bathrobe and slippers and watched the sparrows flit from bush to bush, clinging to the bare branches, singing crazily, the happy little brainless fuckers.

The next day he phoned the recruiting centre in Winnipeg and asked to speak to someone who could help him with some research on a book he was writing on Afghanistan. He said that he was Arnold Thompson, and he was an American from the Midwest. He was passed off to various people and had finally gotten some answers from an officer who appeared to be impressed that an American writer would be calling. He said that he was researching elements of the Canadian Forces, specifically types of weapons, and comparing this to the United States military.

"That's fine, Mr. Thompson. How can I help?"

"What kind of guns do your men use?" he asked.

"A C7 rifle. It's a variation of the M16 that the Americans use."

"I assume it's fairly basic, not hard to learn to fire."

"Not at all."

"Can the gun discharge accidentally?"

"What do you mean, sir?"

"Is it possible that the C7 rifle could just happen to fire, without being aimed or the trigger pulled?"

"The rifle has a safety. When the safety is on, the rifle will not fire, sir."

"When would the safety be off?"

"Well, there are situations. During a firefight, for example, the soldier obviously releases the safety, otherwise he would not be able to shoot."

"How about on patrol? Is the safety on?"

"On patrol, the men walk with their rifles in the cradled position. In that case the safety would be on." The officer paused, then said, "Is there a specific question, sir, a situation that you might be referring to?"

"Only hypothetical," Morris said. His mouth was dry. In truth, he wanted to hang up, but he pressed on. "Let's say there's a group of men on patrol. How many would there be?"

"Eight to ten men in a section."

"And they all know each other?"

"Very well."

"Would any of these men know the word 'yaw'?" Morris spelled the word.

"I don't understand the question, sir."

"It's all right, forget that. So these men all know each other. Is it possible for a rifle to fire accidentally during a patrol? For example, the safety isn't on and the finger's on the trigger, and there's a scare of some sort, and one soldier makes a mistake and pulls the trigger and shoots the man beside him, the round yaws through the jaw and up into the brain and the injured party suffers hydrostatic shock. And dies. Is that possible?"

Silence. He waited. Then the officer said, "Who are you, sir? Can I pass you over to someone who is more qualified to answer that question?"

"No," he said. "That's fine. Thank you." And he hung up.

He was breathing quickly. He studied the phone, waiting for it to ring. Certainly the army was adept at tracing phone calls, of chasing down pranksters or the mourning parents of sons who were fallen soldiers. But the phone didn't ring. No one called him back.

Two months later, an official letter arrived from the Canadian Forces National Investigation Service announcing that an investigation into the death of Martin Schutt was taking place and that a Private Tyler Goodhand had been charged with manslaughter and negligent performance of duty. The letter stated that this was simply a charge and that guilt had not yet been proven. The investigation would determine this. There was no apology, nor was there any offering of comfort, nor was there any description of the event. Just a simple statement.

Lucille was wildly erratic. She raged and tore up the letter and threw it out and then pulled it from the garbage and carefully taped it back together as if she were repairing a broken vase. "What are we to believe?" she sobbed. "Was this a wilful act?" When she was calmer, she said that she was happy that this Tyler had been arrested. She hoped he would be found guilty and that he would be put in prison for a long time. And then, a few weeks later, as if resignation might heal her heart, she said that she had accepted that Martin's death was an accident. "Of course it was," Morris said, and he held her and whispered, "There, there." But still she did not rest. She wrote letters to the men who were in Martin's company. One soldier, Richard McCallum, a friend of Martin's from Saskatchewan who had been in the same company, wrote a letter to Lucille. He said that he and Martin had often talked of dying, and they had talked of their fear and how to conquer that fear. He wrote: "It is wrong to think that Martin died for nothing, Mrs. Schutt. His death was an unfortunate accident. He talked about going home, about seeing his family again. He talked about love and women and how many children he was going to have. He always questioned our reason for being here, maybe too much, but if I were to choose someone to be by my side in a firefight, it would be Martin. He was very brave." Lucille had shown Morris the letter, and as she handed it to him, she said, "Why does this make me feel even worse?" He read the letter and then looked up and said, "He's trying, Lucille." Lucille put the letter back into the envelope and tucked it away in a safe place, and to this day, if he had wanted to retrieve it, he would not have known where to find it.

And then, close to a year after Martin died, Tyler Goodhand phoned the Schutt residence. Morris answered, and when he first said hello, there was no response. He said hello again, and a male voice said, very softly, "Is this Mr. Schutt?"

Morris thought it was a solicitor and was about to hang up when the voice spoke again, more firmly this time. "Mr. Schutt?"

"Yes, this is he."

"Mr. Schutt? Martin Schutt's father?"

"Yes. What do you want?" He thought it was probably a journalist, or a writer trying to get information on Martin's death. This had happened once before, a cold call in the middle of the day from a man who was producing a documentary on the war in Afghanistan. Morris had turned the man away, said that he had nothing important to say, at least nothing that would be printable, and he'd hung up. But this was different; there was a tentative tone to the voice.

"Mr. Schutt. Sir. My name is Tyler Goodhand. I was in Afghanistan with Martin." There was a pause, and for a brief moment Morris did not know why he should recognize this name, but once he realized who was calling he sat down and held the phone in his lap and stared at it. He had trouble breathing. He could hear Tyler's voice, and it came as if from a great distance. Morris lifted the phone and whispered, "How did you get this number?"

No answer, and then, "Should I hang up, sir?"

"What do you want?"

"Sir. I want to say sorry for what I did. My name is Tyler Goodhand, and I'm the soldier who killed your son, Martin. I'm very sorry, sir."

"I know who you are," Morris said. And he said nothing more, because he could not speak.

"Do you really understand who I am, sir?" Tyler cleared his throat and continued. "It happened very quickly, Mr. Schutt, sir. It was my fault. We were returning on foot from our patrol, and I was walking about fifty feet from Martin. We were parallel, sir. I thought I heard something, that we were under fire, and I turned to see where the shots were coming from, and in doing that my finger pulled the trigger on my rifle and the rifle discharged. One round, that's all, but that one round must have struck Martin. No, let me say that again, sir. I was afraid, you see, and I disengaged the safety. And because I had my finger on the trigger, it fired, and the round hit Martin. It killed him, sir. I killed him, sir." And he stopped talking.

And in that silence Morris heard his tinnitus, the squeal of a thousand baby bats.

Tyler said, "Thank you, sir, for listening."

"Don't call me 'sir.'"

"Excuse me, sir?"

"I'm not your officer. I'm not in the army. I don't like the army."

"I understand. Mr. Schutt. Can I ask you a question, Mr. Schutt?"

Morris wanted to hang up, to get rid of this boy. He sensed that if Tyler held on to him any longer and kept him on the line, then the conversation would spill over into a place where he didn't want to go.

But Tyler kept talking. "Did they tell you who I was? That my name was Tyler Goodhand? That I was the one who shot Martin?"

"Yes."

"Did you want to contact me, sir? Did they give you my phone number and where I was located?"

"Nothing. We got nothing."

"I'm sorry, sir. I don't think that's right."

Morris laughed a short, harsh bark. "This isn't about right and wrong here."

"I grew up in Edmonton, sir. Mr. Schutt. I'm twenty years old. I grew up in a suburb of Edmonton called Sherwood Park. My parents still live there. I have two sisters who are younger than me."

This was a child he was talking to. And what benefit were these biographical bits and pieces?

"I'm being investigated, sir. I'm not on active duty anymore."

"We knew that you had been charged."

"Oh." Silence, and then, "You're probably glad about that."

"Nothing makes me glad these days, Tyler. But did I think you should be charged? Absolutely. I'm sorry, Tyler, but that's what I think. In fact, this is very difficult, talking to you."

"No, no, you don't have to be sorry. I *should* be charged. What I did was wrong."

Every day Morris had wanted to stand before the man who killed Martin and interrogate him. And now, here he was, listening to his voice, and contrary to what he'd just said, he felt pity for him.

"Are you angry, sir?"

"Well, simple fact is, Tyler, Martin's not coming home."

"I didn't know what you'd say." Tyler paused, Morris waited, and then Tyler said, "We were friends, Mr. Schutt."

Morris tried to recall if Martin had ever mentioned Tyler's name. He couldn't remember.

Tyler continued. "I wanted to call you sooner, but people said I shouldn't. They said you wouldn't want to talk, that it would be upsetting, that I would be invading your grieving space. I'm glad now that I didn't listen, because I can tell that you don't mind. I had to call, Mr. Schutt. I can't sleep, and when I finally do sleep, I have nightmares. I had to call to hear your voice and to ask for your forgiveness. And for your wife's forgiveness. Do you understand?"

It was as if he were reading off a piece of paper, as if he'd prepared a speech beforehand, and yet it was so raw and honest and poorly laid out that Morris believed him. He said, "You didn't mean to shoot Martin. I understand that. You made a mistake and now you are suffering. But I can't help you not suffer. You want me to forgive you, but I can't do that either. Not yet, anyway. Maybe at some point, but not yet."

Tyler said, "I understand, Mr. Schutt. Thank you. I can wait. I *will* wait." And if there was any goodness to be found in this conversation, it was to be found in Tyler's sudden relief, as if he had been staggering about with a great load and Morris had somehow eased him of that load, though it was not clear how or why. When Morris hung up, after giving Tyler permission to call again, and then wondering why he had given that permission, he felt the immensity of Tyler's guilt upon his own shoulders and for two days the weight would not go away. He told Lucille about the conversation and she was astounded. "Who is the victim here, Morris?" she said. "He's still alive, walking and talking and eating. He buys new shoes, he'll marry and have children. So you felt sorry for him. Where does the responsibility lie?"

"With all of us, Lucille."

"What, are you best friends suddenly? You're going to adopt this Tyler Goodhand? Even his name mocks us. This is betrayal."

Was it? He thought that she might be right. He wondered what Martin would want, and he believed that if they could speak, Martin would say, "It's okay, Dad. Talk to him." But even the imagined equanimity of his son was an outrage.

Three months after the first phone conversation, Tyler called Morris again, and perversely, after a moment of guilt, Morris felt pleased. Then anger, and then a confused pleasure once again as Tyler talked. He explained that he was at the base in Shilo, Manitoba. He worked in the kitchen during the day, surrounded by men who seemed to despise him. "Nobody really talks to me," he said. "Except for my girlfriend, Kelly, who phones me every Friday night. And my parents. They visit me. The padre here, he's all right. He talks to me and we play checkers sometimes in the evenings." He said that he and Kelly planned to marry at some point. He had a Dodge Charger at home, sitting in the garage. He liked cars. He said that it was a good thing to be talking to Morris, it was amazing really how generous Morris was. But there was still Mrs. Schutt, and until he spoke with her and explained to her what had happened, he would not be able to rest. "Have you talked about me?" Tyler asked. "Did you tell Mrs. Schutt about our conversation?"

Morris said that he had.

"Do you think she would talk to me? Would I be able to call her? Shilo is not far from where you live. I imagine sometimes that you and Mrs. Schutt would come to see me, so that I could look you both in the face and ask for forgiveness. I'd like you to see who I am."

The boy was smarter than Morris had imagined. This made sense: meet your enemy, let him observe your humanity. "I don't know, Tyler. I should tell you that she's still angry."

"I understand. I would be angry at me. Mr. Schutt, I'm sorry, but I don't know what to do. I know I'm being selfish, this is what my own mother said. You know what she said? She said, 'I wouldn't want to meet the man who shot my son, even if it was an accident.' But I'm asking anyway."

"Tyler, you have to understand that Lucille won't talk to you about Martin."

Silence. Then, "I won't make excuses. I have none to make. I just want to say sorry."

"Listen, she might not talk to you, but you could talk to her. You could try writing a letter."

"I don't know. I'm not good at writing."

"It doesn't have to be perfect, Tyler. In fact, if it's rough but honest, it will be more authentic." What was he doing? What function was he playing here? He was immediately sorry. He said, "Maybe you'll just have to accept silence, Tyler. People can't be manipulated."

"You think so?"

Morris was suddenly tired. He cut Tyler off and said that he had to go. He could hear the disappointment in the boy's voice, but he ignored it and hung up, aware that he was breathing heavily and that his chest was weighted down.

Two months later, just after he moved into his condominium, he received a letter from Tyler that had arrived at his former house and been delivered to him by Libby. In it, Tyler explained that he'd tried and tried to write a letter to Mrs. Schutt, but the words just came out wrong. He wrote that he sounded like a two-year-old. Then he asked if Morris could help him. "You're a journalist," he said. "A writer. Maybe you could help me write the letter to Mrs. Schutt. Think about this, okay?"

Morris tucked Tyler's note into his briefcase and for several months he ignored it, until one day, while sitting at his desk in his condo and rummaging about looking for something, he came across the letter once again. He reread it. Put it away. Picked it up again.

The following day, in the morning, he sat down and wrote the letter to his wife. It was not easy. His own ego kept getting in the way. And his own pain. Finally, frustrated after several attempts, he gave in to Tyler's thoughts and told Mrs. Schutt how her son had been killed. Then he wrote:

> I can't imagine your sadness, Mrs. Schutt. I can only imagine that you must hate me. That you must hate the fact that I am walking around on this earth and your son is not. And you must hate me for killing your son. I am sorry. That's all I can say. I am sorry. I know that you might not accept my apology, and I understand. But I can't do anything about that. All I can do is ask. I am asking for your forgiveness, Mrs. Schutt. I can't bring your son back, I can't fix my mistakes, I can only say I am sorry, and please forgive me.
>
> Sincerely,
> Tyler Goodhand

When Morris sat down to write the letter, he had not known what effect it would have on him. As he was writing, he began to cry. Surprised, he paused and thought, Why these tears? And then, Be wary of the man who cries. After he had completed a draft, he was sorely broken. What is the point? he thought. What am I trying to do?

He imagined a conversation with Dr. G.

"What is the function of this project?" Dr. G would ask, his tone lifting upwards on "project."

"To save the boy. To save Lucille."

"And who are you, Jesus Christ, that you think you can save everybody?" Poking his finger into Morris's heart. "And Lucille wouldn't be furious if she knew?"

"She doesn't have to know. I'm not going to tell her."

"Your motives are questionable, Morris. I suspect that deep down you know this."

The frowsy grey halo, the farting dog at his feet, the *DSM* IV tome behind him, the painting of the horse on the wall—was this the wizened man who knew him better than he knew himself?

When he sent the draft to Tyler, telling him that he could remove whatever words did not feel right, he maintained a perfunctory and cold tone, perhaps hoping that Tyler would conclude that this was done out of duress, and that Tyler should not think that they were suddenly equals. And then he added that he had left Lucille and was living on his own now. And he told him to send the letter to the same address he had used for the other letter. That's where Lucille lives, he wrote, and in doing so he understood that this virtuous act might not be quite as virtuous from Lucille's perspective. So be it, he thought. So be it.

On a Tuesday in late October, a day after he had sent letters to the prime minister, Colt Canada, and Ursula (he imagined the envelopes hurtling through the air), Morris polished his shoes and dressed in his Hugo Boss suit and he put on a tie

and drove over to the Fort Garry Hotel where he parked his
Jaguar in a wide corner spot, far from fender benders and
dangerous others. As he walked inside he thought of Ursula,
whom he had rejected, and he suffered a moment of regret.
He took a seat in the lounge, close to the piano player, and
ordered a Macallan on ice. Only the best for Mr. Schutt. It
was eleven o'clock and the lounge was half full: several cou-
ples, a group of six boisterous men, a single woman at the bar
talking with the bartender. No sign of Leah. He felt foolish,
as if he were scouring her life, though he wasn't; he imagined himself as her protector. He did not expect her to show
up in this lounge; he believed that she would go straight to
the man's room, and so he was delighted, surprised, and dismayed when she came in. There she was, on the arm of a tall
black man, very well built, whom Morris recognized as a
football player that he'd seen on TV, back when Morris had a
TV and watched the occasional game. They were a stunning
couple full of sexual energy. Morris ducked his head as Leah
glanced his way, but she did not see him, in fact, even if she'd
looked right at him, he sensed that she would not have seen
him. Her vision was clouded by lust. She was wearing a short
black dress and high heels and she had a small black-beaded
purse that she put down on the table. She sat in profile, so
that Morris could see her mouth moving and the bluntness
of her nose and the fineness of her jaw. She drank red wine
while the football player pulled on a beer. Of course. When
a plate of appetizers arrived, egg rolls with a dipping sauce,
Leah leaned forward and raised an egg roll and bit delicately,
talking all the while, laughing, ducking her head, and offering

her hand to the big meaty palm of the young man. A running back with the first name Willy. Morris remembered now. Willy had poor hands, tended to fumble, played intermittently, and was often injured. Be careful, thought Morris, of the man who cannot do his job properly. She had lied to him; she ate with whomever, before fucking and after. He willed her to notice him, to be startled and alarmed. Perhaps he should go over and get Willy's autograph. But before he could act, the lovers stood and Leah took Willy's hand, and as they turned, Leah looked right at Morris and then turned away, and she was gone, swept out the door like a football in the arms of wee Willy. Morris ordered another double Scotch and he sat and waited, then he ordered a chicken burger and salad, and while he ate that he saw himself as one of Dante's characters, at the edge of the cornice that makes a belt around the hill, his head wobbling, his *eyelids sewn shut with thread spun from iron*.

Several years earlier, at the height of whatever recognition he had acquired as a columnist, flush with the victories of coddled fame, he had received a letter from an angry woman, one of his readers, who had called him a vicious misogynist. The woman's reasoning was thus: usually, in his columns, he described women by the clothes they wore, by the size of their breasts, preferably small, and by their tall black boots or their high heels, preferably designer stilettos. "Where are the brains of these women?" this writer asked. "Where is the large woman in Birkenstocks who knows how to talk and think and love? For you, Morris Schutt, she doesn't exist."

"Where indeed," Lucille said when Morris read her the

letter. "So you agree?" Morris cried, aghast. "I'm a vicious misogynist?" Lucille had called him ridiculous, he wasn't a misogynist, she would know that from living with him. Still, he did have his fetishes, didn't he? "Don't we all?" he asked, and she said that no, we didn't all, that was pure rationalization on his part.

Morris shook aside these thoughts, stood and paid the bill in cash. Laid a hundred-dollar bill down on the table and walked out. Why did he do this? Whom was he impressing? Did he think that the waiter would write a letter to the editor of the local paper and say, "Morris Schutt left me a sixty-dollar tip the other night. He is a generous man, absolutely aware of the plight of waiters and waitresses. He should be congratulated." What did he want? He realized that if this mad behaviour continued, he would be out of money within the year and he'd have to find work. Perhaps he could work as a speech writer for the prime minister. He should have suggested that in his letter, said: "I notice that you could use a new speech writer as your current one makes you sound staid and formal. Loosen up, sir. Words are delightful, they are meant to please. Use them wisely, see them as currency. Imagine that each word is worth one hundred dollars, sir, and if you spend them wisely, rather than throwing them about like chicken feed for the clucking masses, then you will be amazed at the results."

Or, thought Morris, I could drive a limousine, move rich people like cattle from here to there, listen to them as I drive, eavesdrop on their silliness, their gossip and flirting. I could introduce myself as Morris the Driver, let them either recognize me as the fallen writer, the vicious misogynist, or not. Probably not. You are not as great as you imagine; and not nearly as intelligent. He had hoped, in the last month, that he was gaining knowledge. But his reading was making him more ignorant, or at least making him more aware of his ignorance. Reading *The Republic* several nights earlier, he had tried to understand what the *noble lie* was, and not quite getting it, because certainly it was more layered and nuanced than American politicians talking about the "unknown unknowns," or Canadian politicians nobly lying to the electorate in order to make the public's life better, he had padded off to the cyber café and Googled "noble lie" and had come up with all kinds of ignorant claptrap, lowly plebes offering analysis that made no sense. Everyone was suddenly an authority on Plato. The Internet was democracy and democracy was failing. And so, reflecting on his own ignorance and the ignorance of others, his wallet slightly emptier, visions of ministerial speech writing in his head and Leah coupling with her football player on the king-size mattress of the hotel room, his Jaguar in the parking lot of the hotel, Morris walked drunkenly and legally home.

The following evening, around supper time, he took note of a car parked on the street outside his condominium, with a small man wearing sunglasses sitting inside. It was nearly dark and the sunglasses were unnecessary, but Morris knew that there were men who liked to hide their eyes in that manner, and this must be one of those men. He noticed the Mazda because it had been there, along with the man, two hours earlier when Morris had gone out to retrieve his car from the hotel. The man was still there, late in the evening, when Morris stood on his balcony in the cool evening, drinking a glass of Primitivo and smoking a cigar. In the morning, the car was gone. Morris spent the day writing a column meant for no one but himself, a circumspect inquiry into where he came from, his roots, inspired by the photograph he'd found in the attic months earlier, of his grandfather regal in the medic's uniform of the Russian army. It was as if by reversing time and stepping back towards the apocryphal stories of his grandfather, he could understand better the plight of twenty-first-century Morris Schutt. Grandfather Schutt, from the family Schütt, possibly of Swiss descendants, some of whom ended up in Alsace-Lorraine, was a farmer from the steppes. A scanty existence. Every spring, before planting, the grain to be used for seed was soaked in formaldehyde, to make it hardier. This particular spring, Grandfather Schutt soaked it too long. He planted it anyway, not expecting anything to grow. It so happened that a drought fell upon the land, and where every other farmer's crop was ruined, Grandfather Schutt's grew because it was tardy growing in the first place, and when a slight rain finally fell, Grandfather Schutt's farm was one of the few to produce wheat. A famine ensued, people were poor and hungry, and one day in autumn a soldier showed up at the farm, asking for a little wheat. He'd heard that the Schutt farm had grain. Grandfather Schutt gave him a sack of wheat and told him there was no need to pay. A year later, when Grandfather Schutt was conscripted into the army, he went to sign up with a heavy heart. He stood in line for a day, and when it was finally his turn, he approached the soldier behind the small wooden desk. The soldier studied him and said that he recognized him. Wasn't he the man who a year earlier had given him a sack of wheat? Indeed, he was. And the soldier told Grandfather Schutt to turn on his heel and return home. "Your generosity has been rewarded," he said.

And what, thought Morris, did one make of this? If he, Morris Schutt, had lived the clean and generous life of his grandfather, would his son Martin still be alive? Not so. Life was not theatre. Good deeds were not rewarded so easily. There was no grand arc of a story. Only novelists were inclined that way. A bus could hit Morris tomorrow when he stepped off the curb into the street. So be it. He deleted everything he had written and stood and stretched. He fried himself a hot Italian sausage and red bell peppers for dinner, crumbled some feta on top, sat alone at his small kitchen table, and ate slowly, ruminating, picturing himself as one of Ursula's dairy cows. He felt the memory of her in his heart and loins. His world was not Grandfather Schutt's. He was not a farmer of the steppes; he would never be recruited by the Communists. His existence here in 2007, almost one hundred years after his grandfather's fateful decision to soak the seeds of grain too long, was founded on commerce and vanity. "Moral virtue" was dead. *Grandeur* and *misère* were old ideas. I will live to be a febrile and wild eighty-year-old, thought Morris. He finished eating, wiped his mouth, and felt heavy and slothful. Grandfather Schutt had been a fine dresser, wearing dark suits and ties when everyone else went around in coveralls. He dressed for dinner. Expected the food to be on the table when he entered the dining room and sat down. Expected the rest of his family, his wife and children, to dress well for dinner as well. The clothes made the man. Morris recalled the cut of Grandpa Schutt's suit jacket, shoulder blades pressing against the smooth cloth. His polished shoes. The knotted tie. This habit had been handed down to him. In order to make himself feel better, he went into the bedroom and changed into a suit and tie. As he did this, he thought of the man who had been parked outside his condo and he was struck by an irrational fear. Perhaps a hit man had been hired to take him out. Some irate reader, a slighted ex-politician, a mafia lord, one of these types had paid to have him killed.

Morris picked up the phone and called Lucille, who was in the middle of cleaning up after dinner. Morris would not be deterred. He told her about his fears, listing the possible hit men, spies, or other dangerous types sitting outside his condo. Lucille laughed. "Are you that important, Morris? You still find yourself indispensable? Who has time to navigate your life?"

"What do you mean, 'navigate'?"

"You sprinkled your column with gossip, self-righteousness, and personal attacks, and now you imagine that you are so important that someone is out there tracking you down. That's delusional." Lucille sounded tired, worn out. Her voice was etched with impatience. Morris said that he was sorry to have bothered her.

"Don't, Morris. I'm sorry. Listen, today a woman came to my office, it was her first visit, and she told me about her husband who was a soldier in Afghanistan. Since his return he keeps a knife under his pillow, he is irrational, and she worries that he'll kill her while she's sleeping. I listened to her tell this story and my face went numb. I couldn't help her. I had nothing to say."

"Oh, Lucille. How about now, is your face still numb?"

"It's better. Slightly. She surprised me, you see? The whole episode surprised me. It was like when Martin died. Do you remember?"

He did. In the aftermath, Lucille's face and limbs had gone numb and so she had gone for tests, had an MRI, believing that she was suffering from late onset of MS. But the neurosurgeon had dismissed that diagnosis. The symptoms, affecting both sides of her body, had been too symmetrical, they did not match those of multiple sclerosis. It was stress related, the doctor had said. Morris asked now if she'd talked to Harvey about her symptoms. He wanted to say "Your doctor lover," but he restrained himself.

"Oh, Morris, haven't I told you? Harvey and I are stepping back. I'm not seeing him these days."

"Really? This is news." Deep inside, somewhere close to his heart and lungs, he felt an expansive sense of joy and relief. *Schadenfreude* perhaps. How lovely it was. He postured pity. "I'm sorry to hear that."

"Yes, I suppose it *is* news for you. But no, I don't think that you're sorry." Lucille's voice was resigned and fatigued.

Morris ignored her comment. "Since when?" he asked.

"A week, maybe longer. Yes, longer. Ten days."

"Hmm. Well. When we talked on Sunday this was already known."

"To me, yes. And to Harvey."

"It was mutual then?"

"No. This was my wish."

How cunning she was, making it sound as if she were soft and full of craving: "my wish." For Lucille, wishes always evolved into cold facts.

"Does Libby know?" Morris asked.

"Of course. I'm not hiding anything, Morris."

Which meant that *he* was. And he wondered how much she knew about his life. If she was aware of his sexual exploits, or lack of them. If she understood that he had been quite impotent since she had left. That he required little blue pills ordered off the Internet and that he was desperately attempting to foolishly save a young girl called Leah, and that even he, Morris Schutt, could not be certain of his motives. Did Lucille know that he had, for a time, searched the Internet for sexual solace, skimming the flicker of images and stumbling across a site where women stripped for the camera? This was lawlessness; it was desire, his desire, and he surrendered to passion. What fun. A forty-three-year-old mother did a strip-tease, filmed by her husband, or perhaps by a camera on a tripod, while her seven-year-old daughter slept peacefully in the next room. And Morris, the voyeur, partook. Did Lucille know all of this? She had always been able to read him. In fact, she seemed to know what he was going to do, how he was going to act, what he had been thinking, even before he was aware of his own thoughts. And he had learned that she could be seduced by speech and beautiful words. Eros for her was imagination, poetry. Holding the phone tenderly, Morris said, "I love you, Lucille."

"We know that, Morris. Tell me something new."

"I'm considering getting hair implants."

"Oh, don't, that's ridiculous. Besides, it doesn't work, and if it does, you'll look like you've planted a cornfield on your head. All those perfect rows."

"It's done randomly. The thing is, I have no grey hair."

"There is nothing to verify that."

"Is that why you left me?"

She laughed, somewhat affectionately, and then thanked him for the lovely velvet pants. "They were delivered," she said. "I was surprised."

"Why surprised?" Morris asked. "You know that I shop for you."

"Yes, but not lately."

"Do they fit?"

"I need a belt, and they're slightly loose around the bum. But, I'll wear them."

Morris was pleased, and he said, as if his tongue had been loosed, that Eleanor had invited him to dinner on Friday. She and Jack were having friends in. "I've decided to become more social."

Lucille was quiet, briefly, and then said, "I should warn you, Morris, I've been invited as well."

"Really? Do you think there's some mistake?"

"No. Eleanor knows that Harvey and I are no longer

together, and she has this notion that you and I should be back together."

"Does she?" Morris was pleased.

"You go, you need to see people. You're too locked in. You spend your days reading and walking. Free time is a curse. It can make a person crazy."

"I'm not mad. Not yet. We'll both go. We'll ask Eleanor to seat us beside each other, so that people don't have to feel discomfort, and we'll pretend we're still friends and we're happy. You can wear those pants I bought you."

"I won't pretend, Morris."

"Of course. You don't lie."

"What I meant is that I won't need to pretend."

To avoid the direction the conversation was taking, Morris said that Lucille should phone the next day, early morning, to see if he answered. If he didn't, that meant he'd probably been killed in his sleep by a home invader, specifically the man in the Mazda.

"It's not like you to be this fearful, Morris."

"I have his plate number. Can I give it to you?"

She laughed. "Why all this distress?" And she paused, and began to say something, but then stopped herself, and he knew it was a question about Ursula. It was the quick breath she took, the rising tone, and then the exhalation. How brave she was to stop herself. This was something she was working on: trying not to scour his life. After they said goodbye, he thought about what he'd learned lately, not much, and about what Lucille seemed to have learned. A lot. In the past, she would have ranted like a harridan.

But now, she closed her mouth and let him stew in his own juices. And then that question, "Why all this distress?" The roots of distress were many and they were bitter. He had learned this reading Cicero. Envy is a form of distress, and so are rivalry, jealousy, pity, anxiety, grief, sorrow, weariness, mourning, worry, anguish, sadness, affliction, and despair. These must all be found and pulled out. Had he pulled out any? It was truly bewildering how tedious his growth was, how slow he was to understand. Perhaps envy was gone, and with it rivalry and jealousy. A neat little package of deadly sins discarded. Or had he merely become indifferent? I don't believe so, thought Morris. Of course, he had felt jealousy the other night, watching Leah, but that had been abnormally misplaced—his thinking had run wild. There is opinion about the nature of envy, rivalry, and jealousy, and there is knowledge about the nature of these things. And I have moved beyond opinion and acquired some knowledge, haven't I? I have understood that work, success, money—both the getting and spending of it—and accolades and fame are insubstantial. I have begun, thought Morris, to understand my empty self. And briefly, like a window opening onto the sun, he saw himself, and then the window closed. He would never reach the stage of decision. He was both *bastard and ordinary,* Socrates' *little bald-headed worker in bronze who has gotten some silver,* or in Morris's case, cash. In a fit of fear one night, Morris woke and dug through his safe and pulled out ten thousand dollars, pushed it into an envelope, and taped it to the back of his fridge. Irrational comfort.

Dr. G, when Morris was still seeing him, had posed a question one day. "Wouldn't it be interesting," he said, "if there could be many Morris Schutts, and you would all live different lives. And at the end, just before you died, you gathered together, flew in from different parts of the world, met in a gentlemen's club perhaps, and there put forth an argument as to which of you had had the best life. The aesthete, though poor, would argue that beauty had augmented his life; the fornicator would extol bodily pleasure; the millionaire would maintain that money had not only extended his life, it had made him happy; the bum would say that he had never worried about the getting and keeping of currency, and so he was the freest; the Morris who had committed murder and spent years in prison would say that because he had fallen so far, he was most aware of grace; the religious Morris would claim that his treasures were laid up in heaven; the faithful Morris, the good husband and father, would claim that he had lived authentically and passed on the passion for the best life to his children. And so on. In the end, though, what you would all be claiming is that the beneficial is fair and the harmful is ugly. But, Morris, what is beneficial and what is harmful? You have only one life. You must choose."

At the men's group on Thursday, Mervine said that he had had dinner with his wife on the weekend and then they had had sex in the car after, and when he had dropped his wife off at her apartment, he had asked her if she would move back in with him, and she had said no, she was very happy on her own. "I felt betrayed," Mervine said. "Used."

Ezra harrumphed and said that he should be happy. "You got lucky."

"I don't think so," Mervine said. "For a moment, I was happy because Christa put something good into my pocket. But then she stole it back. That's not lucky."

"You want everything." This was Doug, the wise leader. "Maybe you should be content with going out for dinner with Christa, having car sex, and dropping her off at her apartment. Maybe that's all she can give you right now."

"That's not enough."

"Of course it isn't. But what are you going to do about it?" Doug turned to the rest of the group and asked what they thought.

The group was split. Half thought Mervine should never see Christa again, the others believed that he should be happy with what he was getting. And hope for more the next time.

Morris offered his opinion—hope for more—and then settled into a reverie. He was bored with these men. They were so incredibly average. Always the same questions about wives and fathers and potency and money and wayward children. Pain, erotic necessities, the domestic. Never an elevated idea offered. Never, "I just finished reading Plotinus and I'm wondering about this, et cetera." No quest, no curiosity about thinking or how to think or how to think about thinking. No poetry, no analysis. Just basic gossip and shit and vacuous blather. And the saddest thing? The saddest thing was that he, Morris Schutt, was just like them. Average.

And he didn't want to be average. Doug, early in September at one of the first meetings, had talked about the individual, and how, for all the complaints about the plight one might find oneself in, most people wouldn't change places with another even if begged or paid. "Most of us are, healthily, in love with ourselves. This is necessary." True, very true, Morris thought, though he couldn't imagine why some of these poor men wouldn't want to be him. He was fit, somewhat popular, not bad looking, had money, drove a Jaguar, slept with escorts, had free time, was intelligent, read and sort of understood Tillich, possessed an okay jump shot, and with the aid of several ancient guides such as Plato, he was slowly crawling up out of the cave. On the other hand, when he looked at the men around him in the group, he wanted nothing to do with their lives. Doug, the egalitarian leader? No, too old and boring. Mervine? Too pitiful, too painful to consider. Peter, the Filipino who lived with seventeen other family members? No, too servile, too simple. Ezra, the fallen Jew? No, though there was something attractive about the tribal camaraderie. Morris had been raised a Mennonite stoic in a tribe that wasn't a tribe at all, but more a failed cult whose main sources of entertainment were music, wordplay, and suffering. He had shucked that off quite quickly. And so on. If he would be forced to choose under the pressure of torture, he would surrender to the possibility of something beyond this room, into the realm of film. He would be Jason Bourne, and he would marry Mia from *Pulp Fiction*, and they would live in humid bliss on a small island off the coast of Cambodia.

Later that night, sitting by the fire in Mervine's back-yard, roasting Smokies and drinking beer, Morris told Mervine his thoughts and Mervine laughed and said, "So, Uma Thurman?"

"No, no. Understand that I grew up poor. When I was young, we lived in a parsonage in a small Saskatchewan town. We had no running water, we shat in an outhouse, and we bathed, all of us, in the same water in a tin tub. I had dreams of owning a horse. We killed chickens outside and they squawked and ran headless through the snow, leaving bloody trails, and then we dipped them in hot water and plucked them. Mice ran across the hardwood floor at night. I slept with my brother and borrowed his heat. To escape this Siberia-like landscape we went to the Congo. I still remember sitting in the airport as a young boy, with no plane tickets, waiting for a good Samaritan to come along and offer us passage to Africa. For three days we sat and ate raw wieners and carrots while my father engaged other passengers and told them our story. On the third day, miracle of miracles, a woman travelling to Ecuador listened to my father's speech, then bowed her head in prayer with him, walked over to the ticket counter, and bought us all round-trip tickets to the Congo. She was the daughter of an oil tycoon from Texas. She was a Baptist. She wanted to play a role in saving the poor people who lived in the heart of darkness. Even at that age, I suffered tremendous embarrass-ment for our poverty, our need for other people's goodwill. I don't want to sleep with Uma Thurman. I want to be the man who doesn't need others, who is independently wealthy, the man who has everything. Jason Bourne is indestructible, and Uma happens to be the goddess he has acquired. Do you think for a moment that Uma has ever taken a shit in an outhouse?"

It was a cold night. There would be frost on the grass in the morning and Mervine, stepping out of his tent, would leave footprints on the grass. What madness to live this way. Morris squirted ketchup onto a bun and laid a Smokie onto the bed. He chewed slowly, huddling closer to the fire.

Mervine said that he had never known someone like Morris's father, who must have had some crazy faith.

"He was mad, certainly. A tyrant. If Sam or I did not like the food at dinner, it would still be waiting on our plates in the morning. Nothing would be wasted. Sam sometimes woke up in the middle of the night and finished my food for me, to save me from myself, from my father's wrath."

Morris reflected on how wrath itself was passed from generation to generation. Grandfather Schutt, visiting one Christmas, had offered Morris a raspberry-shaped candy from his coat pocket. Pulled it from a cellophane bag and handed it to Morris. And later, Morris had stolen three more candies from the pocket of the coat that had been placed in the closet, and in the process of stealing a fourth, Grandfather Schutt had caught him and taken Morris into the bathroom and pulled down his pants and strapped him with his beautiful leather belt. Grandfather Schutt, dressed in his dark suit and dark blue tie, his pants loose because of the weapon in his hand, spanking Morris's six-year-old bare bum. What surprise and shame. For what? A little candy? And the wrath was passed on, generation to generation, and so it landed on

Morris's head, and Morris, in a moment of unthinking passion, had spanked his own son off to war.

Mervine was talking, saying that Christa had loved the letter he'd sent her. Had especially loved the care he'd taken with the presentation. A little sprinkle of perfume. And where had he learned to write like that? She never knew.

"So it worked," Morris said.

"The moon thing. She loved that. She said it made her all soft. She said she wanted to play with my little button nipples."

"Didn't I tell you?"

"I was wondering, Morris, if you could write another one, telling her that I'm lonely and that I'm sleeping outside in a tent."

"Now, you want pity?"

"I want her to know my sadness."

"The point, Mervine, is not to talk about your own anguish, but to reflect everything back onto her. You love her because she is this and this. You want her back because she is the only key that fits into your lock. Be poetic. Borrow a Shakespearean sonnet and use it as your own. Talk about her as if she were still twenty, hark back to a memory that you know will stir her. Try to recall the first time you held her, describe that, and then tell her you still feel that way. I can't be your Cyrano."

Mervine had no idea who Cyrano was and so Morris explained. "And, in the end, the girl receiving the letters has fallen unwittingly in love with the writer of the letters," he concluded.

Mervine laughed, barely, with some consternation, imagining perhaps that Christa would be Morris's lover. They parted at midnight, beneath a cold half-moon, Mervine back towards his tent, and Morris into his car, driving over the bridge, across the muddy polluted river, past abandoned buildings and the cold storage where carcasses of sheep and pigs and cows hung from giant hooks.

He knew, of course, that he'd been talking about himself, that he should be the one writing to Lucille. He knew how to win her heart. And if he were to dredge up any moment that would soften her, it would be Morris at the age of twenty-three, having just recently met Lucille, tearing across the city by cab to buy a second-hand bicycle for fifty dollars, a wish that she had uttered nonchalantly one day, about an object that she would absolutely love. Wrapping her arms around his neck and kissing his nose and whispering that what she'd always wanted was a baby-blue woman's bike with a black saddle and a wicker basket, just a dream, "Morris, oh, wouldn't I look beautiful?" Her father, a rich man, could have bought her twenty-five of those bikes. But he hadn't. And there Morris was, having laid the fifty in an old woman's lap, wheeling the undersized bike out onto the street, pedalling madly and absurdly back across the city, his tall frame swamping the little bike, like Professor Karle, he thought, exactly, and he'd arrived at her place breathless, before Lucille returned from her shift at the hospital, and he'd washed and cleaned the bicycle, strung ribbons across it, and when Lucille came home and saw it, she wept. Why, he was still not sure. Joy perhaps. Or gratitude. She called him "a beautiful dear man." Her lover. Though he hadn't been yet, and he wondered now, passing down Main Street past the late nightclubs where long lines of young people huddled hopefully in the cold, how it was that he had chosen not to sleep with Ursula Frank. He was a coward. Or too chivalrous. Or too cautious. The bicycle story was, in any case, the anecdote that would turn Lucille's head. She would smile as she remembered, and then she would tell him that he had been such a gentle, attentive man. And what had happened? Well, she had left him for a manipulator, a fixer, a materialist who stuck his small hands into people's chest cavities. But the good doctor saved people's lives, didn't he? And of what use was Morris Schutt, educated amateur, to the world? Of no use, pitiful prick.

The following evening, a Friday, Morris dressed in jeans and a white T-shirt and a dark blue cardigan and polished his wingtip shoes, and he drove over to Eleanor and Jack's house, which was on the Crescent, a smaller low-slung house flanked by mansions. He parked his car on the street, reached over to the passenger's seat for the box of butter tarts that he'd picked up at the German bakery, and the bottle of *frizzante,* and as he did so he looked out the passenger window towards the house where the dinner party was to take place. Through the picture window Morris saw Eleanor moving about, shifting empty chairs around the dining room table. She was talking to someone outside of his vision. He paused. Put the bottle and tarts back onto the seat and felt a sharp pain in his chest. His breathing was shallow and he imagined for a moment that he was having a heart attack. He would die here in his Jaguar, and later that night, after dinner, Lucille would step outside, see his car, and find him, head thrown back against the leather seat in the ignominy of death. "Breathe," he whispered to himself, and he closed his eyes. He may have slept, because when he opened his eyes again he saw through the picture window that everyone was now seated; five people and an empty chair beside Lucille. The pain in Morris's chest had abated slightly. Perhaps he had eaten too hastily at lunch, though he realized that he hadn't really eaten at all, only a little leftover sushi from a takeout dinner earlier that week. Perhaps the fish had been off. He should have thrown out the sushi instead of saving it. He placed a palm against his chest. Lucille kept turning to look at the front door, as if expecting him to appear at any moment. She would be telling everyone that he'd thrown out his cellphone, adopted the life of a Luddite, and so there was no way of making contact. He felt sorry for her. He climbed out of the car and shut the door softly. A cold wind blew up the street, scattering leaves across his feet. He walked up the driveway and then stepped out onto the middle of the lawn. It was dark. He stood on the grass and looked in on the scene of the dining room. The hosts, Eleanor and Jack, had invited Lucille and Morris, as well as another couple Morris was familiar with, Patrice and Suzanne. Patrice worked for the UN in Paris. He had married Suzanne, a local woman who was Jewish, and he himself had converted to Judaism almost right away. He had done what Morris had sometimes wished to be brave enough to do—find a tribe that could envelop him.

Eight months ago, before Lucille had left Morris, the two of them had come to this house and sat at that exact table, with these same people, except back then another couple had also been present, a film director named Darko and his lover Maria. That evening had turned into a disaster that centred on an argument that had begun just after dessert. Patrice, heart so soft and useless, had brought up torture and then used the word "Gitmo" and Morris had said, "Don't say 'Gitmo.' It trivializes, like '9/11.' It diminishes everything that our soldiers are fighting for." Lucille, sitting beside him, said his name, but he had not paid heed. Patrice had earlier been talking about Afghanistan and the breaking of international laws and the futility of the conflict, and most of the group had agreed. Except for Lucille. And Eleanor, who was gauging the conversation and Morris's reaction; she kept glancing at him. And then Morris had gotten started and he was not to be stopped. He said that Patrice had no idea what sacrifice meant. How many French soldiers had died in Afghanistan? And how many Canadians? And where did he get off saying that the protection of land and schools and hospitals for the local Afghani people was pointless? And whose children were dying? All along, Morris had been aware of the film director's lover. He'd been aware upon arriving that Maria was too beautiful to pay attention to, and he imagined that in arguing drunkenly like this with Patrice that he was trying to impress her. Or perhaps to repulse her. If he made himself unattractive, then she would dislike him and there would be no reason to even fantasize about her. He should not have come here. But he had, and now he needed to finish what had been started. He tilted forward to pour more wine into his glass. He felt giddily out of control, yet he knew that he was standing on very solid ground and that the moral indignation of Patrice could not withstand his own virtuous stance. After all, Morris's son had died as a soldier. Morris lifted his glass and drank, and as he did so he raised his free hand, and then lowering his glass he looked at Darko rather than Patrice and he said, "Let me tell you about a boy named Tyler." And as he said this, he saw Darko's dark eyes, and he wondered how it was that this man had acquired such a beautiful woman and such a laughable name. He was short and had a pockmarked face and his upper lip was chubbier than the lower, and he didn't seem very intelligent, at least from what Morris had perceived throughout the evening, but then what was intelligence truly, an ability to hold one's own at a dinner party? But of these things, Morris was certain: the man had power and he had money. He knew that what he was about to do was quite wrong, and Lucille, beside him, had placed her hand on his thigh and was whispering, "Don't, Morris," but he charged on, perhaps because he wanted to imagine Maria, later that evening, raising her sharp small face in astonishment and sucking in a deep breath of pity for Morris Schutt. He said, "Tyler Goodhand joined the Canadian Forces and was sent to Afghanistan in February 2006, and while on one of his first patrols his gun went off accidentally and he killed one of his fellow soldiers. Every day, Tyler relives this incident, and every day, he wishes to go back to Afghanistan and fight the Taliban. Tyler is twenty years old now. He will never forgive himself. But Tyler, rightly or wrongly, wants to act. Because, as he told me, if we don't act, then what are we doing?"

Morris paused and looked up at the ceiling. He wondered if he was going to cry. He said, "I love Tyler. He might be completely deluded, but he is sincere and honest and he isn't afraid to ask for forgiveness and I love him." Morris pushed away from the table, excused himself, and went to the bathroom. He sat on the toilet and fell asleep, until Lucille's hesitant knock woke him.

That evening, eight months earlier, had not ended so badly. He had returned to the dinner table and Patrice had apologized. And Morris had apologized in turn for his self-abandonment. "I do not want to seem a victim," he had said, "though that is exactly what I'm doing." He drank an espresso that Eleanor had handed him, and by the end of the evening there had been a semblance of forgiveness and perhaps even forced joviality.

And tonight, here was almost the same situation, as if Eleanor had conveniently forgotten the fiasco of the last dinner. Only this time Morris was out on the lawn, looking in, and Darko and Maria were absent, perhaps making a film in Rio, perhaps no longer together. But Patrice was present once again, his mouth moving, pontificating. And Suzanne lifting her head, white teeth shining, and no doubt talking about the cruise they were taking up the British Columbia coast to Alaska. Lucille speaking then, looking at the hostess, exclaiming about *the delicious halibut*. A light came on at the neighbouring house and a man stepped out on the verandah. Morris slipped behind a tree. The bark of a dog, a voice calling, "Angel," and suddenly Morris was cornered by the tiniest ball of fury, yapping shrilly, snapping at his ankles, and then the dog lunged and bit deep into the Achilles tendon of his right ankle. Morris swung his leg out violently and the little ball of fury flew sideways, hit the tree, and yelped. The neighbour, in a panicky voice called out, "Angel, Angel," and stepped through the hedge, onto the driveway, and found Morris with his back up against the bark of a rotten elm, holding his foot. An old man, dressed in pyjama bottoms and a dark blue overcoat. A sparse halo of white hair. Slippers. A plastic bag clutched in his left hand. "Who are you?" the old man asked. Angel continued to bark and yelp and whimper. A light came on above Eleanor and Jack's porch and Eleanor pushed her face out into the cold.

"Harry?" she called.

"There's a man out here," the old man said. "A peeping Tom. Call the police, Eleanor. Angel's got him cornered. She's wounded him."

Eleanor stepped down onto the grass and approached the tree, moving carefully on high heels. When she saw Morris she said, "Is that you, Morris? What are you doing? We've been waiting for you. Did you knock?"

"Hi, Eleanor. Yes, I did. No, actually, I was about to, and then realized I'd forgotten my wine and was heading back to the car when this man's mad dog attacked me."

"She didn't," Harry said. "That man was skulking." He stooped to pick up Angel and, holding her to his chest, he said, "Atta girl, good girl, there's a girl. Good job."

"I wasn't skulking," Morris said. He pointed at the window, beyond which Lucille stood, peering out into the darkness. "That's my wife in there. Eleanor is my friend. We're about to have a convivial dinner and your sweet little Angel bit me."

"He bit you?" Eleanor asked.

"Punctured my Achilles," Morris said. He would sue this man, and he'd have the nasty bitch put down.

"Nonsense," Harry said. "Angel doesn't bite. Look at her." He held her up for inspection and then drew her back under his chin and turned to Eleanor. "He was hiding behind the tree."

Morris began to limp back towards the car. "The wine. I was retrieving the wine. It's *frizzante*, from Italy. It's on my front seat. I wasn't hiding."

Lucille had stepped outside now and was walking down the driveway, calling to him. He reached his car, opened the door, and slipped behind the wheel. His heart attack symptoms had disappeared, but now his foot was shredded. Lucille tapped on the window and he lowered it.

"What happened, Morris? Are you okay? Where have you been? We've finished the main course already."

"Why would Eleanor invite Patrice? Who are these people we're spending time with? What do we have to say to each other? Christ, Patrice is a boring man. All he talks about is global warming."

"He's very intelligent, Morris. He speaks five languages."

"Polyglots can be just as boring as mutes, Lucille. Does he speak Arabic, the language of our enemy, Lucille? We must know our enemy."

"Don't talk like that. Come inside. The food is wonderful. Jack made a beautiful tajine dish with prunes. Come." She began to open the door. "Let me see your ankle."

He shook his head. "I'll get it checked. I'll run over to the hospital, get tested for rabies, and if they don't chain me to a tree, I'll return."

"No, you won't." She was wistful. A tendril of hair fluttered like a moth across her brow. He wanted to reach out and stroke her cheek. He resisted.

"I'll call," he said. "Tell Jack and Eleanor sorry. Tell them I'm not well. Tell Patrice I'm at home reading Cicero in the original. Tell him that this is just how foolish people behave: *they observe the faults of others and forget their own.* That's a quote, by the way." He started the car. A low rumble, not a tappet to be adjusted. What a gorgeous machine.

"That boy, Tyler. I got a letter from him last week," Lucille said. It was as if she had just received the letter, as if she had just opened the envelope and read the letter in which he was asking for forgiveness. Her face in this light seemed confused, perplexed. She hadn't liked the letter.

"Yes?" Morris said. "And what did he want?"

"What do you think he wanted?" Then she said, "You call me, okay? Promise?"

Morris nodded. Reached out the window, touched Lucille's hip, and felt the soft velvet. "You're wearing these. Nice." And then he left.

He did not go to the hospital. He went up Wellington Crescent and then drove quietly through the park. Near the Pavilion, a couple was crossing the street, arm in arm. Morris imagined that they must have just had dinner in the pavilion restaurant and were now heading home, intent on each other, having satisfied the necessary desires of eating and drinking, with the woman looking up into the man's face and saying, "Take me doggy style, please." Morris feared he had lost sight completely of what was necessary and unnecessary. At some point, his behaviour had gone beyond bounds. Reading Plato recently he had been troubled by the regimes of the soul, the idea that too much freedom seems to change into nothing but too much slavery. But now he saw that his own soul had descended into tyranny and gluttony of feeling, of revolt and chaos. His soul was sick, and therefore his body was sick. You are what you do, Morris, he thought, and you have been doing poorly. He had tossed aside all of his modern encumbrances, seeking liberation from technology and the free market. Storing his treasures on earth in the safe in his condo was a symptom of excess. He had become a slave to freedom. On Monday he would return his money to the bank and let the captains of commerce invest and worry about it. And then he would call up his editor and say that he was ready to return to his column, only he had no intention of revealing his private life anymore. He no longer believed that shamelessness was courage. He drove up around and past the botanical gardens and along the edges of the zoo, where beyond the chain-link fence he saw the dark shapes of buffalo and reindeer. Poor trapped animals. His foot throbbed. He felt feverish and his mouth was dry. Earlier, cornered by that dog, he had seen the folly of his ways. And then Lucille, leaning into his car window to study him, had shaken her head, yet she had said nothing. But he knew her thoughts. Morris, she'd been thinking, what are you doing standing on the lawn looking in at a dinner party, when all you had to do was knock on the door and enter? Do you think that you are so special that you will not rub shoulders with or be tainted by humanity? That your thoughts are so elevated that no one else will understand you? You don't even understand yourself. You have so successfully shut yourself off from human contact that you have begun to believe your own lies. These had been Lucille's thoughts. He had seen the doubt in her eyes, only she'd been too kind to utter the words that he was now thinking. He retraced his route, passing once again by Jack and Eleanor's, where the lights still blazed and where, still at the table, the company was talking about *poor Morris*. He continued down the Crescent and turned right on Hugo and then up towards his condo. He parked and climbed cautiously from the car, clutching his butter tarts and his bottle of wine. Glancing upwards, he noticed that the lights were on in his condo. He wondered if he'd forgotten to turn them off. Or perhaps Libby was visiting. She had a key to his place.

He hobbled up the stairs, reached the landing of the third floor, and saw that his door was slightly open. He approached tentatively, perplexed. The jamb was broken, the door splintered near the lock. He pushed the door open cautiously and called out Libby's name. He stepped down his hallway into the living room and found not Libby but Ursula sitting on the couch, a suitcase at her feet. She held a gun in her lap.

"Morris," she said, and she stood, the gun in one hand, and walked towards him.

He stepped backwards. "Ursula, what are you doing? Put that away."

She paused and looked down at her hands and she smiled as if surprised by the gun she held. She said, her voice shaking, "I thought he'd come back."

"Who'd come back? What are you talking about? Why are you here?"

"Oh, I know, I was asking myself that same question just now. I'm sorry to surprise you, Morris." She dipped her head and lifted her shoulders. "I shouldn't have come."

Morris looked at the broken door and back at Ursula. "Who did this?"

"I don't know. I was outside, by your entrance, when a small man ran out wildly, carrying a bag. He pushed by me. I came in and found your place and the door was broken." She paused and looked at him tenderly, her eyes wide. "I hope it's okay that I came in. I didn't know what else to do. Where to go. I'm leaving Cal."

Behind her, against the wall, the safe was closed. "Look at that," Morris said, and he limped past Ursula and stooped towards his safe, pulled out his wallet, took the key and slid it into the slot, turned the combination, and opened the safe. Nothing had been touched. "Look at that," he said again. Then he stood and went into the bedroom. His closet had been torn apart. Clothes everywhere. He bent and lifted his futon and saw his cash neatly laid out beneath it. He dropped the futon and turned. Ursula stood in the doorway, still holding her gun. "You sleep on it?" she said.

"Christ," he said. "You realize how lucky I am?" He grinned merrily. "So lucky." Then he said, "Do you still need that?" and he gestured at the gun.

"Oh," she said, and she shrugged, almost helplessly, as if she had suddenly realized that she was in the wrong place. Her face was smoother, Morris thought, as if she'd perhaps gained weight. Thin eyebrows, the slight glitter of blue dust on her eyelids, red lipstick. Her hair was lighter; she'd dyed it dirty blonde. He saw that she was wearing a red dress that pressed against her hips. She had fixed herself up for this meeting and now she lifted her shoulders helplessly again and said, "It's me, Morris. I'm sorry."

"Of course it's you. Why sorry?" He went to her and walked her back to the kitchen, took the gun from her hand, felt its inadequate weight in his own palm, placed it on the windowsill, and then said, "I didn't know you were coming."

She began to weep, and as she wept, Morris thought, Be careful of tears, they might mean something completely different than you think. And then she stopped. "You told me to go away," she said. "You wrote and you said goodbye and I was devastated. What have I done?"

"Nothing. You've done nothing, Ursula." Morris paused and reflected and then asked, "Did I tell you to go away? Truly? Or did I talk about myself. You know that I think only of myself, don't you, Ursula?" He felt he should go to her, do something, but he simply stood, aware that he must choose his words more carefully. "Here," he said, and he sat her on one of the yellow vinyl chairs at the kitchen table, and while he made tea Ursula described how she had arrived to find the door broken down and then she'd had to decide should she stay or leave, not knowing, of course, if this was even his place, though she thought it was, and then how she'd stepped inside and seen a photo of Morris and a young man on the bookshelf and she'd known then that this was his condo. "And I sat down and waited, though I was afraid that man would come back. Shouldn't you call the police?"

Morris shook his head. "I know who it is. The police don't need to be involved. Nothing was taken."

"You have money, Morris," she said. Her voice was meek.

"That's all of it. My life fits into a safe the size of a filing cabinet. Ha."

"Your foot," she said, pointing at his ankle. "Are you hurt?"

He shook his head. "A dog bit me."

"Oh, Morris. Let me see."

He waved her away. This was too intimate, and it might lead to other things.

She studied him carefully. "Were you serious, Morris? In your letter?"

Again, Morris tried to recall his exact words. Had he been cruel? Perhaps he should have been crueller. He said, "Why are you leaving Cal, Ursula? Where's your son?"

"Wilhelm's safe. He's with his aunt." She reached into her purse and pulled out her cellphone and laid it on the table. "He'll call soon. Before he goes to bed."

"And Cal?"

"He's become wild and unpredictable. I'm afraid of him." She paused and looked up at Morris. "And now that I'm here, I'm afraid of you, of what you will say."

She was lying, testing his strength, his moral resolve. She had escaped Cal and run to Morris, and now she would try to charm him. He would not allow that. He couldn't afford any more commotion in his life. He would name himself as the culprit; he was dishonest and wrong-headed and more errant than she would believe. He slept with whores, he had alienated his family, he was a liar, he jigged and ambled, and he was full of sophistry and games. He was untrue, both to those who loved him and to himself. He no longer loved himself. Not true, not true, he loved himself too deeply, and this was why he was shunning her. Get away from me. Do not ask a dissembler to join you. He will bring you down. That is all. I am done with you. Do not contact me again. Go. Goodbye.

"Ursula, I'm not going to throw you out on the street. You're tired. It's hard to think clearly."

"Can I take a shower?" she asked.

He stood and showed her where the towels were. While she showered, he boiled water and poured it into a large stainless-steel bowl, and then added two tablespoons of salt. He removed his right sock and rolled up his pant leg and inspected his ankle. It was bruised, four neat little marks where Angel's teeth had clamped down on his tendon. There appeared to be no puncture marks. Still, to be safe, Morris eased his foot into the bowl of hot water. He winced, counted to four, and removed his foot. Tried again, and then again, and finally managed to keep his foot soaking. He did not think while he did this. His mind refused to operate. He was aware of the heat of the water and the pain in his foot, and of the sounds Ursula made as she showered and puttered in the bathroom. When she returned, dressed in jeans and a sweater, she kneeled and held his foot and said, "When you're afraid of a dog, the dog smells this and it makes him aggressive and so he bites you. All animals are like this. Even cows can smell fear."

Dove soap on her skin. She had brushed her teeth; he could smell this as well. She must have packed a whole kit of toiletries.

"Cal knows where you are?"

"Oh, no."

"And your son?"

"I told him I would be away for the night. Morris, oh, Morris, I know you said goodbye to me, but I felt that you weren't telling the truth. There was something between us, something much bigger than ourselves. You are a kind man. You could have taken advantage of me in Minneapolis, but you didn't. You slept in the bed beside me, you didn't touch me. I don't know many men like that. You're reliable. That's what I love about you. I can rely on you." She took a tea towel and wrapped up his foot. Sat down on a chair beside him. Asked if she could hold his hand.

What a cunning speech, Morris thought. He let her take his hand. How was it that he always found that women were better with words than he was? She was so willing. He looked into her eyes. Ah, he thought, is she still thinking that I am reliable? And it was this singular thought, the fact that he might not be trustworthy, that halted him. "Okay," he whispered. And he stood and said that she must be hungry. He could fry her eggs, make some toast. Or pasta, he could whip that up. She said that she wasn't hungry, that food didn't interest her these days. He asked if she wanted a drink then, any kind of drink, and she hesitated, her lips wet, and then she said, "Some wine?"

He poured her a glass of wine and then sat across from her and confessed that in trying to find order for his soul, he had been thinking and reading and thinking again, and he felt at times that he might be on the brink of an epiphany, but then it always slipped away. He was not wise enough. He said that his life was driven by desire. He admitted to sleeping with escorts and she said that she found this fascinating, though her face seemed disturbed. "What do they do for you?" she asked, and he did not know the answer. "You see?" he said. "I'm false. You think I'm good and true, but I'm artificial, a man who does not know how to care for himself, and so how can I care for others? Martin, for instance."

"He was beautiful." She said she had looked at his photo in the other room, before, when she was alone. "That's him beside you, laughing, right?"

Morris nodded.

"You're too hard on yourself, Morris."

"Am I?" He smiled. Then he said that Martin had been a very good poker player. One of the best, and he'd been well on his way to becoming a pro, but Morris had been against this. What a life, making money off others' losses. Where was the contribution to society? "And after he died, what did I do? I sat up late at night watching poker on TV. These are strange people with strange tics, and they appear to have little education and a whole different speech pattern. Their language mystifies me, and the fact that they make millions. Martin might have been one of them. I would take that now. I would give up everything to have him sitting at a poker table in Las Vegas or Monte Carlo, stealing from others."

"It's not stealing, Morris. See? You judge. You're judging me right now."

"I'm not."

"You think I'm dumb. Just a dairy farmer's simple wife. Why are you talking to me then? What do you see? What do you want?"

And before he could conjure up an answer that would have been wholly inadequate, Ursula's phone rang and she picked it up and looked at it and answered. "Sweetie," she said. She listened, her mouth open slightly, and then she said, "Mommy's fine. Listen, I was helped by this man. My car broke down and this nice man picked me up and now I'm safe and warm and I'll be home soon. All right?"

She was quiet and then she said, "Morris." She made a noise in her throat and then said, "Honey, listen. Okay. Here." She held out the phone to Morris. "It's my son. He wants to talk to you."

Morris shook his head.

"Please," she said. "It's Wilhelm. He's eight. Please." She pushed the phone at him, and she stood and walked over to the window and picked up the gun off the sill.

Morris held the phone. He heard breathing and static, and after a long wait he said, "Hello?"

"Are you the man?" the boy said. His voice was high and asthmatic.

"My name is Morris."

"How old are you?" the boy asked.

Morris gave his age.

"What's your house number?"

Morris looked around. "I live in a condominium, Wilhelm. Number thirty-six."

"Eighty-seven," the boy said, without hesitating. Then he said, "My brother died. His name was Harley. He was a soldier."

"Yes, I know, Wilhelm. Ursula told me."

"My mother?"

"Yes, your mother." Ursula was opening her purse. She put the gun inside and set the purse down.

Wilhelm said, "My mother's sad. But my father will take care of her. He's strong and brave."

"Listen, Wilhelm, here's your mother," Morris said, and he handed the phone back to Ursula, who took it and said, after a brief silence, "I know, it's a wonderful thing. Absolutely. Okay, yes, soon. I love you." She tilted her head and went, "Hmm-hmm. I know," and then said, "Bye." She snapped the phone shut, looked at Morris, and said, "Thank you."

Morris was standing when she hung up, staring at Ursula. "What was he talking about?" he asked.

"He likes numbers, he adds them in his head very quickly."

"No, not that. About his brother being dead, and his father keeping him safe. That's not normal, Ursula. For his age." Morris had been seeing darkly, peering into a room in which there was little light, and in the room people were shuffling back and forth, and now suddenly the light had been turned on and he was seeing too clearly and he did not like what he saw because he too was in that room. What despotic notions we have. How can I know the other when I do not even know myself?

Ursula lifted her chin, more serious now. "He's really mature, Morris. I can tell him things I wouldn't tell Cal."

"He's a child. He should be riding a bike. Playing video games. His mind is worried."

And now Ursula was hostile, though her face remained calm. It was her voice that rasped and grated. "I know how to raise my child, so don't tell me what Wilhelm needs. You've never met him."

Placating now, softer, Morris admitted that she was right. He'd never met the boy. But he sounded so serious, he said, so full of shrill anxiety. "You should go home to him," Morris said.

Ursula's face flattened. "You're chasing me away? You want me to go now, to drive eight hours in the dark? Is that right?"

"Tomorrow. You'll go back to him tomorrow. There's nothing I can do for you, Ursula. I have nothing more to give you. I used to have this long speech about America as the bull in the pasture, the last to be slaughtered, the killer of my son, but you didn't come here to be lectured, and I've been trying to stop talking." Morris stopped. He was tired now. The light in the room was once again dim, the shadows were moving sluggishly. He'd lost his vision.

Ursula shook her head. Her eyes were bright and angry. She said, "You're so full of shit, Morris. You write me letters and you use your beautiful words to seduce me and then you're surprised when I show up here. The stupid bull in the pasture, what does that mean? I want your heart, your feelings, but you won't let me." She cried, her face in her hands, and then she stopped and looked up at Morris and said, "Can I sleep in there?" She pointed at his room. He guided her to his bedroom, cleaned up some of the scattered clothes, put clean sheets on the futon, and then closed the bedroom door, leaving her inside. She had tried to say more, to explain herself, but he had shushed and told her to sleep. He sat in his brown leather chair and closed his eyes, thinking about how he had come to be the man he was. And he thought that contrary to what one would like to believe, there are no exceptions in morality.

An hour later, he went back into the bedroom. The light from the living room fell across the bed. Ursula slept on her side, still dressed, her left hand pressed beneath her cheek. He stood and waited. He called her name softly but she did not answer. He crouched, felt for her purse, opened it, and put a hand inside. He found the gun immediately, felt its hardness, and pulled it out and held it in his hand. So light. Then he stood, moved from the room, closed the door, and waited there, breathing heavily as if he'd just returned from a long journey. He took a key from his wallet, kneeled before his safe, opened the door, set the gun down on top of his money, and closed the door. Then he sat again in his chair and looked at his safe, tightly sealed. This creeping like a thief into a lover's house. Oh, Leah, what betrayal. For it had been her, sending that burglar, possibly her pimp, who had rummaged through Morris's clothes, who certainly knew the combination, but could not find the key. Morris picked up the phone and dialled Leah's number. The answering service cut in immediately and he left a message, saying that there had been one key in the sock drawer and another in the fridge, frozen into a cup of ice. If she wanted the money, why hadn't she just asked? In fact, he had offered it to her. "Goodbye, Leah," he said, and hung up.

What was left? He was a man who had run out of friends, lovers, and opinions. How was it that, at the age of fifty-one, he could not know himself? Opening *The Republic* the other day, almost in desperation, he had been alarmed at the number of dog-eared pages, the scribbles in the margins, the notes to himself. When had he done all of this? When had he found the time? Some of the notes were inexplicable, illegible. Some of the sentences he'd underlined no longer seemed important. But there was brilliance and knowledge. For instance, in Book II, Morris had circled a sentence heavily in pencil: *Isn't it of the greatest importance that what has to do with war be well done?* Exactly. And Martin, like so many other young soldiers, had been an amateur. And Harley as well. They were chosen poorly. One should have stuck to dice and draughts, the other to being a cowherd. And then there was Tyler, who had not understood the tools of war, and had killed Martin. Who had failed here? The guardians, the leaders, had failed. What fools we are. And this, from Book V: *Then is that city best governed which is most like a single human being? For example, when one of us wounds a finger, presumably the entire community—that community tying the body together with the soul in a single arrangement under the ruler within it— is aware of the fact, and all of it is in pain as a whole along with the afflicted part.* Did any other person in this city, in this country, feel the pain of Martin's death? Morris thought not. What should be public had become private. And now, here tonight, he was alone, on his leather chair, suffering privately. And Ursula, alone in the next room, suffering as well. How then should he escape from the darkness into the light? And more to the point, did the right hand know what the left was doing?

His head dropped. He slept. And when he woke a grey light filtered through the thin curtains. He recalled that Ursula was sleeping in the next room. He stood and walked to the bedroom door and pushed it open softly. The bed was empty. Her suitcase was gone. She must have left as he slept, passed by his slouched figure and stepped out the door. She had left no note, no accusations, no thank you. She was simply gone.

A week passed. Silence and thought, and deficiency of thought, and then more thought. The phone rang but he did not answer it. He walked in the evenings, taking in the city and the people within the city. In the eyes of strangers he found resignation and duty, and discovering this, he himself felt freer. No one is responsible for my nature, he thought. I alone must take possession of myself. I am a man who writes to airlines who have mistreated me and lost my luggage, to men who manufacture guns, to ex-lovers, to my bank manager, to the prime minister, and in my writing I cajole, rationalize, protest, and I apportion blame. I will stop harassing these people. Only Morris can care for Morris. Enough of this complaining, sighing, lamenting, and suffering. I have been, in the words of Socrates, *envious*, *faithless*, *unjust*, *friendless*, *impious*, a vessel of every vice, and on and on. And in conclusion, a tyrant. By scribbling my thoughts down and then sending them through the mail, I am most self-absorbed and self-centred. I want an audience, and I will have one; I have a place waiting for me on YouTube and Wikipedia. We are beasts *crawling between heaven and earth*. Happiness does not depend upon the exploitation of other human beings, or the exploitation of oneself. I will stop exploiting, I will remove myself from the rack of cruelty, I will no longer chase after pleasure simply for pleasure itself. Soul over body, reason over desire. This is not oppressive, it is imaginative. The poor you will always have with you. I have donned the garb of an aesthete and I have ridden into Jerusalem on the back of a donkey.

What's all this? Morris thought. Are you suddenly a Christ figure? His son, three days before he died, had been talking to him on Skype, and at one point, perhaps because they were talking about a combination of things—chance, family, Thanksgiving—and perhaps because what was unsaid lay like a sleeping beast between them, it slipped out that Martin had killed a man. In the swirling sand, one thousand miles from Jerusalem, his boy had taken someone's life. What a strange event. Other children might call home to say that they had received a scholarship, or that they had found a new job, or that they were engaged to be married, but his son reveals that he killed someone. The flat jerky movements of Martin on the screen of Morris's laptop. No ducking of the head as he admitted this, no blinking, just a cool meekness. But there was an edge to his voice. And in the next few minutes he became capricious, panicky. He opened a can of Coke and drank for a long time from it and finally put it down. "I'm sorry. I shouldn't have said anything. You can't understand."

"Martin, listen. I worry about you. Have you talked to anyone? Do you want to tell me what happened?"

"We were on foot patrol and we came under fire. And so we returned fire." He paused and drank from his Coke and then said, "It's crazy, Dad. After, I felt so alive. So happy." He looked away from the camera and back again.

"Happy's good. I'm very happy to be looking at you. Talking to you."

"I feel lucky, but the weirdest thing is that my luck is someone else's bad luck. You know?"

"You *stay* lucky," Morris said.

"Don't tell Mom, all right?"

"If that's what you want." And then Morris told him to be good, to come home safely.

Martin said that he would come home. Thumbs up. No problem.

Several months after Martin died, Morris told Lucille about the conversation. He chose his words carefully, but this did not help. "This is wrong, wrong," Lucille cried. "I didn't birth him and raise him and feed him so that he could one day go out and kill other men." And then she said, "Did he see me as feeble? That I could not handle the truth?"

"He loved you," Morris said. "You were his mother."

Morris had arranged to see Jake, to take him to the botanical gardens, and so on Thursday he picked him up. A harsh wind blew as they walked hand in hand across the parking lot. Jake talked and talked, and every sentence, every query, began with "Grandpa?" and always Morris answered, "Yes, Jake?" The solidity of the boy, his fresh smell, the innocence, impressed upon Morris the imperfection and brevity of his own existence. Make way for the young. Later, after looking at the birds and reading the signs beneath the trees, in English and Latin—Morris announcing ineptly words that he had never studied in school, never learned, and why not, why just the heavy German language?—he took Jake's hand and bought him hot chocolate and they sat in a café and looked out at the park, where leaves blew across the open field. And in that field, walking his dog, was Dr. G. Morris leaned forward to verify this and saw that, indeed, it was the man he had loved so deeply. How strange to see him after all these months. He whispered his name and Jake looked up and asked, "What, Grandpa?" Dr. G had paused and was stooping now to remove his dog's shit from the ground. How mortal he looked, in his dark corduroys and his too-small hat, gathering up dog poop. Morris thought that if he and Jake made it out to the parking lot in time, they might cross paths with the good doctor. He could introduce his grandson, tell Dr. G that he was no longer tripping and stumbling, thank you very much. No, no, the simple fact that he was with Jake would communicate this. He told Jake that they would drink the chocolate in the car. Jake, perplexed, gulped a mouthful before leaving and burned his tongue. He gasped, and then cried and cried. Morris made him suck ice cubes, and he held and rocked him, looking out towards the field, now empty. He drove him home later and confessed to Meredith that he had been careless with a hot drink; Jake had burned himself. Meredith surprised him with her calm response. She invited him in and offered him tea and announced that she and Glen were getting married. At Christmas. Morris said, "Oh." And then he said, "That's wonderful, congratulations. We'll be having a wedding." How odd to suddenly understand that life carries on with its normalcy and regulation, that he was in fact not the centre of the world. And he held Meredith and he registered her heft and build and he thought, This is my daughter.

That same week he gathered his money together and returned it to the bank. Put half into his corporate account and kept the rest in American dollars. The bull in the pasture. Perhaps he would buy some gold as well, talk to Jonathan and get his opinion. Sitting across from Jake, he'd been acutely aware that he was a custodian, a protector of his own grandson. Who else would look out for the boy financially? Certainly not his mother, who worked as a waitress in a lounge and was now marrying a mechanic who repaired domestic cars and had probably never looked under the hood of a Jaguar.

On Friday, when he finally picked up the phone, Leah's voice whispered in his ear.

"Morris?"

Morris's first thought was to hang up, but he didn't. He waited.

She said again, "Morris?"

"Yes?"

"Morris, I'm so sorry. It was my cousin. He broke into your place. I guess I told him about your safe. I told him as a joke, like I was telling an interesting story. I didn't expect him to break in."

Her voice was so familiar, so easy and yielding. Morris held his breath.

"I'm sorry," she said. "What do I owe you?"

"Nothing. He took nothing. You owe me nothing."

"But the damage. The embarrassment."

"What do you mean?"

"I'm ashamed," she said.

"Really? But you did nothing."

A long pause, as if she were contemplating this, and then she surprised him by saying, "I saw you. At the hotel."

"I was worried. And then I find you with a football player, of all things. Not a lot of intelligence there, Leah."

She might have laughed, he could not be sure. She said, "I'm not looking for intelligence, Morris."

"You should be. Conversation, thought, reflection, these things will save you."

"The message you left sounded so angry. Was that it? Because of the football player?"

He ignored her question and asked, "Do you need money, Leah?"

"No. No."

Too emphatic, this denial. Perhaps she was an addict and needed to support her habit. He tried to recall if she had shown any signs; track marks, runny nose, jittery movements. But no, it was he, Morris Schutt, who was the addict. Funny, how that felt so outside of himself. He hadn't even masturbated this week. Where had his vigour gone?

"What about school?" he asked. "Australia."

She laughed weakly. "I'm not going." Then her voice brightened. "I got a job. A real one. At the Gap."

"Clothes?" Morris said.

"Yeah. Pay's lousy, but it will lead to something." She paused and he imagined her biting her lower lip. "Aren't you pleased?"

"Of course I'm pleased. Good for you."

"I'm sorry, Morris, for all the trouble."

"It wasn't trouble. It was only a door."

"Did you call the police?"

So, this was the reason for the call. He sighed and said no, he never had. There'd been no reason to. "We all have feet of clay, Leah. You. Your cousin. Ozymandias. Wee Willy. Me. Mistakes are made."

"Oh, well." A tiny stutter. Her throat clearing. She was unaware. "Maybe I'll see you around, Morris."

"I don't think so, Leah."

And then she'd said goodbye, tenderly and hesitantly, yet happily, as if she were escaping. And she had, hadn't she? Escaped the longing loins of Morris Schutt. Fortunate girl.

The following day two men in dark suits knocked on his door, and as he answered, he wondered, with a reeling sense of imbalance, if someone else dear to him had died. And when they said his name, Morris Schutt, and introduced themselves as RCMP officers, the panic deepened. They asked if he was Morris Schutt the journalist, and when he said yes, he had been, once, but now he was unemployed, they asked if he had written a letter to the prime minister in which he had threatened the prime minster and his son.

"You're kidding," Morris said. He felt such relief, and with that relief came astonishment at the stupidity of this visit.

"No, Mr. Schutt, we're very serious." This was the shorter officer, whose shoes, Morris noticed, needed polishing. Never trust a man who may be perfectly dressed in every way except for the shoes. The shoes are the groundwork, the root of everything good and evil. One of his laces was loose as well. Feet of clay. They stepped into his condo and pulled the door shut. Morris had not asked them to come in, and he found their aggression disconcerting. He stood his ground, taller than either of them.

"That letter was a lament," he said. "It was not to be taken literally." He moved his head to the side, as if dismissing the plainness of everyone else's imagination. Then he said, "So he read it? The prime minister read my letter?"

The one with the thicker neck spoke. He was slightly taller and he had a soul patch and his lips were wet. He said, "That's irrelevant, Mr. Schutt. In fact, he did not. However, someone did, and the contents were considered incendiary, and we are here now to ask you a few questions."

"Do I need a lawyer?" This was said lightly, meant lightly, but these men did not walk through the world lightly.

"You may. However, at this point, we are simply following up on a request from Ottawa."

Ahh, thought Morris. A request. No need for a lawyer.

The shorter one said, "Are you planning something?"

"What do you mean?"

"You said you were full of rage and that you were provoked. This can lead to other things."

"Did I say 'full of rage'? I don't think so. This is ridiculous."

"The point is, Mr. Schutt, there was a sense of threat, however veiled," the taller officer said.

Veiled, thought Morris. This man had a grasp of language. Perhaps he was also a reasonable man. He said, "Those were words. They were the wrathful words of a disheartened person. I'm not dangerous. I am a peaceful man. My son was killed in Afghanistan. Did you read that part of the letter? And it wasn't even a letter. It was a column that I wrote, did not publish, and happened on a whim to send to the prime minister."

"Do you own a gun, Mr. Schutt?"

"Of course not. I never have. I detest guns." And when he'd finished speaking, he thought of Ursula's gun in his safe. He held the eyes of the bully, the man with the thick neck. "The prime minister could have sent me a note. He could have said, 'Thank you, Mr. Schutt, for sacrificing your son for our country.' But I received nothing. Do you have a son?" The man turned away briefly and shook his head. "And you, sir?" He looked at the smaller officer who was standing, feet wide apart, as if prepared for a fight. "Do you have a son?"

"Yes, I do. But that's not the point."

"Oh, but it is the most important and only point. I lost a son. I'm not asking for your pity, but I want your respect. Now, unless you mean to arrest me, I'd like you to leave."

The man with wet lips smiled weakly. He leaned forward and held Morris's elbow. "We understand, Mr. Schutt. Please be aware that this was a call of inquiry only. We'll go now." And he turned to the other officer, who was surprised, nonplussed, and he led him from the apartment. The man, so bullish and predictable, had done the unpredictable, and set Morris free. Would that man be admonished by his superiors? Perhaps. How strange it was to be surprised by authority, as if authority did not have the capacity to surprise. But here it had. And what a surprise. And the gun. He had been foolish to steal it from Ursula. And to what end? Did he think she was going to kill herself or someone else? It was for protection, she had said, yet a gun was made to fire, was meant to maim and kill. It wasn't meant to sit like a dumb animal in a dark safe.

His brother too had a gun nestled in amongst the cornucopia of lingerie and sexual toys. And so Samuel was unpredictable as well. Well, he would call him now and ask what kind of gun he had exactly and how it compared to Morris's, the one he'd stolen from his ex-lover, who wasn't truly his lover. He phoned Samuel in the evening, when he knew he'd be home, and as Samuel answered, he felt a flood of love for him. Here is my blood, he thought, and he wondered why it was they spoke so rarely. "It's good to hear your voice, Samuel," he said. "I should hear it more often."

A hint of suspicion in Samuel's voice as he asked, "Where's your energy coming from, Morris? You sound overexcited."

"Do I? Well, I need you to check something for me. I need you to use your powers to find out if I'm in trouble here in Canada. I need to know if CSIS is watching me, if I'm going to be captured and tortured."

"What are you talking about?"

And so he explained about the RCMP visit, the letter he had written, and when he was finished, Samuel said, "That was a foolish thing to do, Morris."

"Well, maybe it was. And I'm sorry for it. We live in a fearful time, Samuel. A time and place where politicians ask for sacrifice yet refuse to step up and make sacrifices themselves. Do you remember the day Grandpa Schutt spanked me for stealing raspberry candies from his pocket? Well, I recall that you also stole a candy, yet I was the only one caught, and I was punished."

"Why are you telling me this?"

"It was something I thought of recently. Maybe I'm tired of being punished."

"Nobody's punishing you. You're punishing yourself."

"You think so? That's interesting. And sobering. You sound like Lucille."

And then they talked: of Grandpa Schutt, and of their father, and of their mother who used to listen to funeral announcements every Wednesday morning on the local radio station. And then she called up friends to discuss the recent demise of someone barely known. Until she herself died. And her death was announced on that same radio station, and she was buried, and beside her sat a vacant plot that would be her husband's.

"I took a longevity test on the Internet the other day," Morris said. "You type in a bunch of answers, your calorie intake, whether you smoke or not, your weight, your height, age, how much you exercise, and when all is said and done, you find out how long you'll live. I'll be ninety-seven when I die. I don't want to live that long."

"You might."

"That's forty-six more years. Already my pectorals are failing me. Can you imagine what they'll look like at ninety-seven? What kind of gun do you have, Samuel?"

"What are you talking about?"

"You have a gun. I found it when I was visiting in the summer."

A pause and then, "You were snooping through my drawers?"

"Guilty," Morris said. "I was bored, restless. Maybe I wanted to find who my brother was. We don't really know each other, Samuel."

"Then ask me who I am. Don't riffle through my stuff."

"Riffle," so close to "rifle." Unfortunate choice of words. "I'm sorry. And all that other stuff, Samuel. Those toys. I didn't know that about you."

"Enough, Morris. Those were Dorothy's." A short silence and then Samuel said, "I kept them when she left."

Now they were getting somewhere, moving below the surface to a deeper and more painful place. This was good, thought Morris. His brother probably never talked to anyone. Morris said, "I've been seeing this psychiatrist. It's really useful, Samuel. You should try it sometime." And then he asked again what kind of gun Samuel had. "Who's the manufacturer? Not a Colt, is it?"

"No, it's not a Colt. What kind of question is this? Are you okay?"

Yes, he was fine. More than fine. "That's good, Samuel. I'm good. Listen, about those men. Do you mind checking?"

Samuel hesitated, shifted the phone, and then said that Morris was far too worried, but that he would check into things.

He phoned back two hours later. Morris was soaking in the bath when the phone rang. He got out and put on a bathrobe and stood in the kitchen, water dripping onto the cork floor.

"Do you know a Cal Frank?" Samuel said. "Your name comes up with a connection to his wife, Ursula. Who is she, Morris?"

"Christ. My name?"

"Yes. Who is she?"

"A woman from Minnesota. She wrote me after Martin died. She had a son who was killed in Iraq. Why?"

"Are you friends?"

"I don't know what we are. She writes me. I write her back."

"Well, her husband is on a security list. Seems that, like you, he's made threats against the government."

"I never made threats. I wrote a letter. What kind of threats?"

"That's unimportant. The thing is that he's a security risk, you've spent time with his wife, and so your name is attached to his. You just wrote to her?"

Morris tried not to sound indignant. This would not help. His brother's tone was no longer brotherly, it had become officious.

"I drove down to see her," Morris said. "In Minneapolis. What, I'm going to be accused of talking to a woman whose husband has every right to be angry? You people keep lists of names? For what? And how did they get *my* name?"

Samuel ignored this and went into speech mode. "Her husband's what we call an 'idler.' He's like a car that idles in a garage. The threat might be imperceptible until it's too late, so we keep an eye on him, which is like opening the garage door slightly. Usually the engine peters out. A man like Cal Frank is a non-threat. Like you, Morris. We watch. We don't approach. I'm surprised those officers came to see you."

"Ursula's a threat? I don't think so."

"Probably not. She's just one of a million in the system. The world is full of rot, Morris."

"How do you do it, Samuel? It must poison you."

He was quiet. Then he told Morris not to be foolish.

"I'm more sad than foolish," he said. "You can't arrest a man for being sad."

"No one's going to arrest you. You're not that important. Are you okay? Do you want me to come up for a visit?"

What was essential, he thought, was to not let Samuel get too concerned. And so he told him that he was fine, everything was good. In fact, he'd said goodbye to that Ursula woman. "I'm going to try to be alone, without impediments," he said. "I have lots to learn in that department. I have a two-month plan. I expect to be back at my writing by Christmas. December will bring fresh ideas, snow, a biting wind that will clear my mind. Remember the hockey rink we built in the backyard, that year we came back from Africa? Maybe I'll take up skating again. Use Martin's skates."

He heard a soft noise that resembled a curtain being pulled back. He tried to imagine where his brother might be in his big house in Idaho with the three-car garage. Then Samuel said, "You miss him."

"I do," he said. "I do."

And so, Morris thought, I am an idler. Like a million others who chafe and bother the system, I am merely a pebble in the grinding wheel. Would Ursula be amused to know that she too was an idler, along with her husband? But they were idlers with rifles and ammunition. They had paraphernalia. He imagined writing her to let her know that she was being watched. But this was paranoia, wasn't it? His brother loved spying, and of course he would say that everyone was being watched. That night, long after midnight, he stood by his balcony window and looked down onto the street below. A car passed by slowly. A man and woman stood on the sidewalk, talking. And then gone. A taxi idled at the curb for a while. Odd word choice, "idled." Implying inactivity, futility, uselessness, empty thought. "Stop your idling, Morris"; this is what his mother would say to him as a young boy when he lounged on the couch at home, or lay on his back on the rug, staring at the ceiling. No time for daydreaming. Industry was essential. And so Morris had reprimanded his own son for idling. *Enough. Go. Be done with thee, Martin. Get thee to an army.* And what a getting had been got. He slid away from the window and walked into the kitchen. He surveyed the counter, considered making coffee, and then, with great and sudden intent, as if the notion had sprung from some involuntary bidding, he went to his safe, opened it, and removed Ursula's gun. He put on a parka and a toque and pulled on his Timberland boots. And then, with the gun in his pocket, he walked outside and moved up the street towards the river. At three a.m. how quiet the streets were. The world was sleeping. His family was sleeping. A police car drove by and Morris looked straight ahead. Was he walking too fast? Too slow? The cruiser continued down the street and turned the corner. In the distance a train shunted cars onto a siding. He heard the bang of the cars and the squeal of the wheels. The engineer would be going somewhere soon. How easy it must be to know, as an engineer, that there is no choice, that there is only the single track, the two rails, and the hand on the throttle. One of the extremes of moderation was madness, and for over a year now, ever since the death of Martin, he had lived on madness alone, bingeing on grief and anger. The last time he had seen Ursula, the day after she left him without saying goodbye, Morris had written her a letter in which he confessed that he had taken her gun.

I am not a patriot like you, Ursula. I do not understand the notion or the ideal, and I do not believe that we should have the right to carry guns in our pockets and purses so that we might protect our property and ourselves. You come from a civilization, Ursula. Act that way. Your son Wilhelm needs sensibility and love. He doesn't need to be taught the parts of an assault rifle, how to break it down and restore it. I am not so naive as to believe that if I want to kill someone, I couldn't do it with my bare hands, or with a rock that I pick up from the roadside. This has been done, but it is more intimate and real than a handgun or a rifle fired from a distance. If I had my way, I would melt all weapons into ploughshares.

And so on. Words that would fall on deaf ears. Morris the pontificator, Morris the nutcase. Unlike Bellow's Herzog, Morris sent his letters. He wrote them by pen, sometimes he typed them, and then he folded the paper and slipped it into an envelope and applied stamps and walked up to the red mailbox, pulled back the handle, and dropped in the letter. He was a doer. An actor. And idler.

Up Osborne to the foot of the bridge and then right, down a path to the edge of the river. On the far bank, a fire burned and around the fire several figures huddled. Morris heard voices, low and indistinct, and then the laughter of a woman. Under-the-bridge homeless people. He stood and listened and watched. Then he took the gun from his pocket and threw it, like a rock slung from the hand of a young boy out into the middle of the river. He heard a splash and then nothing save the low voices and the traffic above him on the bridge. He stood for a long time looking out at the fire on the other bank. There was joy and drinking and comradeship. The sound of a bottle breaking. A voice lifting in song. Morris turned finally and walked back home.

4

Lucille came to find Morris at noon, two days later. She knocked on his door, and when he opened it, she said, "Get dressed, I'm taking you for lunch."

He was barefoot and wearing old corduroys and a muscle shirt. He hadn't shaved for a number of days and his beard was growing in delicately. He was not man enough to grow a proper beard. He invited her in, asked to take her trench coat. She stood in the foyer and said that she'd made reservations at 529 Wellington. She motioned at the chair in the living room. "I'll wait, Morris. You go shower and shave and find clean clothes. Make yourself handsome."

Morris did as she commanded. He shaved, eyeing himself carefully in the mirror. Over the last while, when he did shave, he'd been cutting himself in his haste, or perhaps his hands were getting shaky. The onset of Parkinson's or perhaps it was his agitated state. He couldn't concentrate for long. He trimmed his eyebrows as well. Lucille didn't like bushy eyebrows. Then he showered and towelled himself dry, imagining what he might wear. Standing naked before his closet, he felt reduced. He'd noticed in the mirror that his biceps were thinner. He would look into purchasing a Bowflex. He chose a light blue shirt and black dress pants that he'd found at Harry Rosen. Alistair, his personal salesman, had said, "Morris, the fit is marvellous." All flattery and flotsam. He put on his socks and shoes and presented himself to Lucille, who was peering through her reading glasses at a book in her lap. It was Cicero. "This is where you steal your words from," she said. "And I thought it was you talking, Morris." She laid the book on its face and stood.

"I have nothing original to say, you know that, Lucille."

She approached him, looked him up and down again, and touched his shoulder. "Nice," she said.

He ordered a six-ounce prime rib and Lucille ate rice and vegetables and a crème brûlée for dessert. She was full of energy, as if she'd gone to a shop somewhere and bought her youth back. Morris studied her. "You're different," he said. And she said thank you as if "different" was important, as if change were crucial. As Hamlet had spuriously spurned Ophelia, so had he spurned Ursula. Thrown her out on her ear. All this movement; to act or not to act. Lucille was wearing sunglasses on the top of her head. In this dimly lit room, amidst the hush of waiters, businessmen with mistresses, she leaned towards him and said that she had something to tell him, though she wasn't sure how he would respond. Startled, he tried to appear calm. Perhaps she had a new lover. They had driven to the restaurant in her Passat, shiny black. She had many bracelets on her right wrist that clattered as she shifted. He loved women, envied their accoutrements, their clacking heels, swaying hips, their inwardness, their need to talk themselves towards intimacy. He had wanted to touch Lucille's wrist where the bracelets lay, but he restrained himself. Flanking the restaurant was the Shaarey Zedek Synagogue, at which a funeral was taking place. Parking-lot attendants waving their orange sticks, a policeman at the entrance. Morris, climbing from the car, had said, "When I die, I want a Jewish funeral." He said that he had made an appointment to see the rabbi of this synagogue, and then cancelled. He planned to read the Torah. He said that what so many Jews had forgotten was that the Torah was more important than the state of Israel. "They've got their priorities mixed up." Lucille listened to him and smiled affectionately. She did not believe anything he said; he was extremely impetuous, his head full of fantasies. And now, tapping at her crème brûlée, she was remarkably confident. She said, "Remember I told you about the letter I received from Tyler Goodhand? Well, I phoned him, and then on Monday I drove to Shilo to meet him. Oh, Morris, what a sweet boy. And all along how I hated him. But he's a boy, just like Martin. And he's suffered so. Are you upset?"

"Why would I be upset?" He was astounded, in fact, at the power of the written word. His written words. "It was the letter then."

"That. And then the phone call. You were right, he's innocent and vulnerable. And I was so harsh." She said that she'd spent an hour alone with Tyler, just the two of them. A beautiful boy. "I felt so close to Martin. It was a mistake, Morris. A terrible accident. Tyler's been incredibly brave. And I should have known that, but my sadness was too great."

"And now?"

"Oh, Morris, it's still big, but there's a corner of my heart that has been set loose. I should have done this months ago, when he called you." She dipped her long head downwards, towards her dessert, and said, "I'm stubborn sometimes."

"What does he look like?" Morris asked. He felt jealous.

"Short. Stocky. He's got that smooth head all army boys seem to have. Cropped, like Martin when he left for Afghanistan. And I saw his tattoo. It's on the inside of his left wrist. Martin's name in small script. He showed it to me and I cried." She removed her sunglasses from the top of her head and blinked. The relief on her face made her look younger. Then she leaned forward and touched his arm. "There's one other thing. Tyler said that the charges against him are going to be dropped. Something about the charges being contrary to the Criminal Code and the National Defence Act." She removed her hand from his arm.

"So he's free," Morris said.

"He is. He said that he wants to go back to Afghanistan."

Inexplicably, he felt disappointment and rage. "So he can shoot some more of our young men."

"Morris. Morris." Lucille watched him carefully.

He waved a hand in the air and looked across the room to where two men in suits were sawing at their meat. "It's a surprise," he said. "Your sudden change of heart. The dropping of charges."

"Yes, I know. As long as I was angry, you could be forgiving. You know what Tyler told me? He said that Martin wanted to be there. Martin told Tyler that if he had to choose again, a hundred out of a hundred times he'd choose Afghanistan. The army. You'd prefer to think it was your fault, Morris. That you forced Martin. You didn't. He was a big boy."

"This is not helping, Lucille. So Tyler, with his bullet-shaped head, tells you what Martin wanted, and you believe him? These are young boys caught up in the adventure of war. The army needs naive boys who move easily from video games to real warfare. They count on it. And now you're good friends with Tyler? *I* wrote that letter, Lucille. I wrote it for Tyler. It was to help *you*."

"Oh, Morris, I know. Tyler told me. You did a good thing. You're a wonderful writer."

And what to say? Such smugness: "you're a wonderful writer." But she was not mocking him. She was not skeptical or cynical or full of doubt like he was. She knew his intent before he himself knew it. Whereas he would have resented her writing that kind of letter, she saw it as a good thing. A good thing, Morris. He had done a good thing. He imagined this might be a form of love, that Lucille still loved him, that she was *making an effort to form a friendship, due to an impression of beauty.* What did Cicero say? *If such a love exists in the world—one without worry, without need, without care, without sighing—then so be it!*

For the rest of that day, and into the next, his thoughts ranged far and wide. In his determination to be rational he failed and he found himself slipping downwards. He willed himself to be happier. This proved impossible. He washed his car, inside and out. He scrubbed the tires and rims.

Everything gleamed. He walked down by the river and watched the last of the ducks preparing to fly south. There was one family of six, and the ducklings were so small that he feared for the young ones' lives. How could something that tiny fly five thousand miles south? The parents had been irresponsible; they had bred too late in the season. A week later, at dawn, he again walked down to the river and found ice forming near the shore. The ducks had fled, poor things. His heart was constricted, as if it sensed the possibility of rejection, of falling into the hands of someone irresponsible. A man on a bicycle passed. Morris nodded hello.

That afternoon he met Libby and Meredith at Viva on Sargent. They shared a large soup and ordered sizzling shrimp. Both girls talked and talked. Libby said that Shane had tried to contact her. She'd hung up on him. She laughed lightly as she said this, wrinkling her nose as if she'd tasted something slightly off. Meredith wondered what was more repulsive, a young man with an older woman, or vice versa. "It's more acceptable for an older man to have a younger lover. But I don't understand the girl. Where's the attraction? That old flesh? Yuck." Libby said it was the mind. She'd loved Shane's mind, the way it worked. "He was way more mature than any boy in high school." It was as if their father wasn't present, Morris thought. These girls, talking, not asking for his valuable opinion. And then, as if the scene had been preordained, Leah entered the restaurant. She was with a man who might have been her cousin. They stood at the counter, ordered, sat and waited for fifteen minutes, and then walked out with two bags of food. Morris saw her, she didn't see him. She was dressed plainly, she wore no makeup, and she looked very young. This was the way of the world. He was shaken by the sight of her. His heart ached briefly and he imagined, absurdly, that he might still be attractive to her. Meredith noticed his agitation and wondered if it was the conversation. "Too much for you, Dad?" she asked. She was different from Libby. She saw only herself and would never have been able to imagine her own father having sex. "Talk on," Morris said. "You both sound so wise."

"Daddy." This was Libby, who knew she wasn't wise, and this made her wiser. Meredith was talking about Harvey, their mother's ex-lover. She said that he had had money, lots of it, but she'd never understood what their mother saw in the man other than his fat wallet. She lifted her eyes and fluttered them at her father. Crass girl, thought Morris. She had a loose mind, like her grandfather when he descended into senility. She rarely visited her grandfather; she said he smelled old, and besides, she had a child to care for. She was handsome, bigger boned than Libby, and though she wouldn't admit it, she'd been devastated by Martin's death. Morris had always wondered if that was why, for a period of time, she hadn't allowed Morris to see Jake. She was punishing her father.

It was Libby who brought up Tyler's name, hesitantly. "Did Mom tell you?" she asked. She was looking at Morris.

Morris nodded. Shrugged.

"She's nuts," Meredith said. "She's letting him off the hook."

"It's not about him," Libby said. "Can't you see how relieved Mom is? It's like she's been born again."

"More like she's in love. And now she wants us all to meet him," Meredith said. "I'm not. I'll tell you that. I'd tear his eyes out."

"You might surprise yourself." Morris the peacemaker. He didn't believe himself, but he knew that Meredith needed some words of guidance, some regulation.

At the curb, before he said goodbye, he said that he planned to take their grandpa to the memorial service at Vimy Ridge Park on Remembrance Day. Did either of them want to come along? Meredith said she had no interest, and she skipped towards the car with a quick wave, avoiding having to hug him. Libby said yes, she would like to be there. She leaned forward and kissed him on the cheek. "Are you okay, Daddy?" she asked. He said he was good. He was satisfied. That was enough, he said.

The first column he would write upon his return (and he would return) would be an apology. He would apologize to his wife, his children, to the good readers who had trusted him, to his son Martin, to the writers he had stolen from. Bellow, for instance. What did he say? *We must get it out of our heads that this is a doomed time, that we are waiting for the end . . . People frightening one another—a poor sort of moral exercise.* What he would not do is apologize to the prime minister, or to the CEO of Colt. These were managers of death. Rewarded for their sins. If Morris still *sounded* slightly mad, so be it. He was in fact sane.

On November 11, he drove to the Remembrance Day Service at the memorial to the forty-fourth Battalion of the Royal Winnipeg Rifles in Vimy Ridge Memorial Park.

His father and Libby were with him. He'd asked Lucille to join them, but she'd said softly that she was fine with not going. "Okay, Morris?" And so three members of the Schutt family hovered at the edge of the gathering and watched a man in a white robe read a Bible passage from the Sermon on the Mount. The words floated upwards and were carried away by the wind. In the bare branches of a nearby tree, a young boy perched and watched the goings-on. A group of soldiers performed the three-gun salute. Morris heard the sharp cracks as the guns fired and he observed the people present and he realized that he both belonged and did not belong. His father was cold. He had a blanket over his lap and Morris had found a toque and mitts, but still his father was shaking. He gave him coffee from a Thermos and his father looked up at him and said, "Thank you." Then he asked, "Is it Martin? Is he gone?"

Morris said that yes, he was, and his father, with brilliant clarity, saw that he had missed something. And then the lucidity in the eyes disappeared. A soldier with a trumpet played a song. The wail and wonder. The wind blew. Reaching for the last note, the trumpet faltered, slightly off key, and then faded away. A lone soldier, dressed as if he had just stepped out of World War I, stood at attention near the cenotaph. A middle-aged couple who had perhaps lost a son laid out a wreath. The crowd, as if responding to some silent call, surged forward suddenly and laid poppies on the wreath. Touchingly, surprisingly, Libby joined them. Grandpa Schutt called out, agitated, and when Libby returned she took her iPod and gently positioned the earbuds for her grandfather. He sat quietly, and then began to sing, humming at first and then breaking into words, haltingly and finally with more force, drawing the attention of those nearby. He sang "Everybody Knows," his voice strong and clear. People stared. Some fidgeted. Morris wondered if he should quiet his father, and then decided no. Libby crouched and held her grandpa's hand. Across from the park was a church. He thought that if at this moment he could gather in his arms all those who loved him, he would have maybe fourteen or fifteen people in his circle. Wasn't that enough? He would turn fifty-two in a month. Time was slipping away. He could die soon, and his life would be incomplete. He was only halfway through Book IX of *The Republic*. He had intimate things to say to Lucille. A place must be found for Martin's ashes. Libby must grow up. Meredith required love; Jake as well. He stood in the cold and the wind, and he knew that when he got home he would pick up his ballpoint pen and write all of this down in his journal. There was still much to solve and much to consider. Take note, thought Morris. Here I am.

ACKNOWLEDGEMENTS

The author is thankful to Levon Bond for his guidance regarding military details.

I have begged and borrowed from many writers: Plato, Cicero, Petrarch, Dante, Shakespeare, Søren Kierkegaard, Jacob Boehme, Theodor Adorno, Paul Tillich, Leo Strauss, Reinhold Niebuhr, Allan Bloom, Terry Eagleton, and finally and most avidly, Saul Bellow.

All quotes from *The Republic of Plato* are from the translation by Allan Bloom, Basic Books, 1968.

The quote on page 3 attributed to Jacob Boehme is taken from *Personal Christianity*, by Jacob Boehme, Frederick Ungar Publishing Co.

The excerpt from Petrarch on page 8 is taken from *My Secret Book* by Francis Petrarch. Translation copyright 2002 by J.G. Nichols.

The line on page 102, attributed to Theodor Adorno, is taken from *Minima Moralia: Reflections on a Damaged Life*, by Theodor Adorno, Verso. Translation copyright 2005 by E.F.N. Jephcott.

The quote on Socratic Restoration on page 128 is taken from *The City and Man* by Leo Strauss, University of Chicago Press.

The lines on pages 140, 154, 213, and 249, attributed to Cicero, are taken from *Cicero on the Emotions: Tusculan Disputations 3 and 4* (Books 3 and 4), University of Chicago Press. Translation copyright 2002 by Margaret R. Graver.

About the author

About the book

Read on

Ideas,
interviews
& features

Author Biography

DAVID BERGEN was born in Port Edward, British Columbia, and, due to the peripatetic lifestyle of his pastor-father, spent his early years moving about Western Canada. The family eventually settled in Niverville, Manitoba, a small farming town south of Winnipeg that would become the template for his first novel, *A Year of Lesser*.

His early reading was unguided, he says, and consisted of books that were plot driven: Zane Grey, thrillers, crime novels, and the occasional Margaret Laurence novel. This reading would partially shape him as a novelist. He felt the need to tell a story that had impetus and force and a strong narrative. And shaped by the religion of his youth, questions of faith, too, would come to influence Bergen's writing, especially his earlier books, which include his collection of stories, *Sitting Opposite My Brother*.

Bergen sees himself as a late bloomer. His first published story appeared in *Prairie Fire* when he was thirty-one. He published his first book at the age of thirty-six, and three years later his first novel. He says it took him a long time to find a voice, and the search involved poor but necessary imitations of some of his favourite writers: John Updike, Anton Chekhov, Flannery O'Connor, and Cormac McCarthy.

In the late eighties, Bergen moved with his wife and children to Southeast Asia, where he taught English to Vietnamese refugees soon to depart for Canada. The solitude and the removal from Western life allowed

David Bergen

THIES BOGNER

him time to write, and it was here, in a small town in southern Thailand, that he typed out his first stories and mailed them to various publications. The rejections came back slowly, along with the occasional acceptance. In 1997 he returned to Southeast Asia and lived in Vietnam. While there he sought Bao Ninh, the author of *The Sorrow of War*, a novel written from the perspective of a North Vietnamese soldier. Though he never found Bao Ninh, through his search he met numerous Vietnamese poets, artists, novelists, and short story writers.

Upon his return from Vietnam, he published two more novels, *See the Child* and *The Case of Lena S.*, which was a finalist for the Governor General's Award for Fiction. His years in Southeast Asia would eventually provide the background for the novel *The Time in Between*, awarded the Scotiabank Giller Prize in 2005. *The Retreat*, published in 2008, was hailed as "further proof that the late-blooming Bergen is now one of Canada's very best writers." Published in 2010, *The Matter with Morris* was shortlisted for the Scotiabank Giller Prize. Bergen has won the McNally Robinson Book of the Year three times, the Margaret Laurence Award for Fiction three times, and the Carol Shields Winnipeg Book Award twice.

For Bergen, structure is one of the most important aspects of novel writing. He worked as a carpenter for several years and says that this taught him something about building a novel. "The foundation has to be there, then the frame, and after that you can lay all the pretty stuff down. If you don't ▶

"It was here, in a small town in southern Thailand, that he typed out his first stories."

Author Biography (*continued*)

have the frame, then the pretty stuff just collapses and the novel ceases to be a novel. It's just beautiful language and that doesn't make a novel."

Vestiges of his Mennonite upbringing are evident in his writing. Raised on the Bible and the stories of the Old Testament and the religious writers such as John Bunyan and Augustine, Bergen is compelled to explore moral complexity through character, which provides a realism that evokes both beauty and cruelty. Live in the world, write about it, he says, and what arrives is a possibility for doubt and belief, for uncertainty and disappointment, and for moments of clarity and joy.

David Bergen, who lives with his family in Winnipeg, received the Writers' Trust Notable Author Award in 2009.

❝If you don't have the frame, then the pretty stuff just collapses and the novel ceases to be a novel.❞

Meet David Bergen

When did you first know that you wanted to be a writer?

At the age of twenty-one, as I was trying to figure out what I "wanted to be" in life, I came across a description of a journalism program that included creative writing. (This was before Creative Writing programs began to flower.) I didn't want to be a journalist, but I was drawn to the writing course. Interestingly, it was the only course I ever took, and though it pushed me in certain ways, I discovered that I produced better work and had more fun if I followed my own vision—reading writers I loved, imitating them, trying to find a tone and a style that made sense. I liked the "feeling" of writing, of attempting to tell a story. I learned quite quickly of course that "feeling," though necessary in small ways, has little to do with good writing.

> **I liked the 'feeling' of writing, of attempting to tell a story.**

What were your earliest stories about? Did they plant seeds for any of your novels?

My earliest stories were clunky, poor imitations of writers I admired. One of my first good stories was called "Fat." I was teaching in a high school at the time, and at lunch I closed my door and wrote with this feverish ache. So in this story "Fat," there's a high school teacher who has an affair with a student. He goes to the student's house for dinner where he meets the mother, who flirts with him. That's the story. But I remember I was aiming for the dialogue to be edgy, and at some point I realized that there was a layer of grief that hovers over ▶

Meet David Bergen (*continued*)

the house, much like a layer of fat. I never published the story. I recall an editor saying that it was strong, but wrong. I thought he had issues. Did this story plant a seed for something that I would write later? Probably. My themes are my themes: grief, loss, longing. I can't avoid them. That said, I don't believe that I went back to any of those first stories and made them brilliant. There was too much that wasn't working there.

You've called *The Matter with Morris* "a real departure" for you. Can you explain?

Writing *The Matter with Morris* felt almost like a free fall; the story came quickly, and the characters arrived fully formed. Morris himself is wry and self-deprecating and lost. His humour, when it shows itself, is understated. This is perhaps what I meant when I called it a departure. Although the book has serious themes, the writing of it felt easy and almost effortless.

Do you typically begin your writing with a character? A scene? A theme? What pulls you to the page?

Character. Everything else will follow if I can find a character that is compelling and believable and large.

How did Morris pull you to the page?

I wanted to understand this man who is flawed and angry and sad and yet who is implacable in his optimism. Morris, though damaged, is honest. I've had readers say that

> **❝ I wanted to understand this man who is flawed and angry and sad and yet who is implacable in his optimism. ❞**

they didn't understand Morris, or that they didn't like him. I've never understood how "liking a character" is the most important aspect of a novel. Fiction is one of the safest places to explore characters we don't understand, or characters who frighten us, or characters who do things we couldn't imagine doing.

Morris is, initially, a character who shares much with you, the author. In what ways is he similar? Different?

This is tricky, because as soon as an author notes similarities, the novel becomes "autobiographical." It isn't. That said, Morris, like me, comes from a Mennonite background, he is in his early fifties, he reads a lot, he has children, he comes from Winnipeg, his wife is a psychotherapist, and he is a writer (though, in his case, he is a journalist). Those are basic facts, but at some point the facts leave off and the character becomes more complex and made up. Fortunately, the author gets lost, as he should, and the fictional character is free to develop.

Critic Philip Marchard called Morris "in one crucial sense, very much a Bergen character." Do you feel there's such a thing as a "Bergen character"?

I don't know what "a Bergen character" is, though my characters are usually attempting to understand their own morality as they bang up against something that is much bigger than themselves. ▶

> " Fiction is one of the safest places to explore characters we don't understand. "

Meet David Bergen (*continued*)

Do you feel you know your characters well before you begin writing, or do you get to know them as their stories unfold?

I knew Morris more intimately than I had known previous characters, but I didn't know everything—a good thing, as the pleasure of writing is discovering the characters and seeing how they behave.

In what ways did your Mennonite upbringing influence your writing about Morris?

I am always influenced by my upbringing, and this spills over into my writing. I had fun putting my words and doubts and skepticism into Morris's mouth. He is working out his beliefs and questioning his greed, and he wonders if, like his parents, he could have lived a simpler life, realizing of course that nothing is simple.

I understand you and your father agreed to disagree on the content of your books. Was it a struggle for you creatively to come to terms with this?

I would have been surprised and disappointed if my father had not disagreed with what I was doing. If he had agreed, then I would have known that I had failed at my attempt to push against the strictures of my background. I was very aware that I could not allow my father to look over my shoulder as I wrote. There is something hurtful in that, and in his wisdom he perhaps is more generous than I am.

> ❝ I knew Morris more intimately than I had known previous characters, but I didn't know everything. ❞

Steven Hayward of the *Globe and Mail* said of the Herzogian sensibility of the novel that you mastered this material, giving it a specifically Canadian context and infusing it with new life. Others were critical of the similarities to *Herzog*. How do you feel about these reactions?

I give a direct nod to Bellow; Herzog shows up in my epigraph. I was basically saying, "This is what I'm doing, Herzog is my model." Was this a sort of "anxiety of influence"? Sure. Those who believe we must create "new" stories and be original are deceiving themselves. We stand on the shoulders of the writers who came before us, and that's what I was doing, in a very large way. *Herzog,* to be sure, is a much more complex novel. Stylistically I could not emulate Bellow. Impossible. However, I saw no problem having Morris struggle as Herzog does: with fidelity, friendship, mortality, love, and children, all the while genuflecting to the great historical thinkers.

In Morris's grief over his son's death, he rereads the classics of philosophy; some that you read are listed under Further Reading. Which ones resonated most with you?

Cicero, when he is grieving the loss of his daughter. And Plato's *Republic,* along with Allan Bloom's commentary. I reread *The Republic* several times, finally coming to understand that it would take a long time to work through the layers. The whole idea of the city-as-soul made for great fun; and of course Morris walks through his own city, trying to understand himself. ▶

"I saw no problem having Morris struggle as Herzog does: with fidelity, friendship, mortality, love, and children, all the while genuflecting to the great historical thinkers. "

Meet David Bergen (*continued*)

You infused this story with more humour than your other novels. Does this signal a change in you as a writer?

I doubt that I will change. Morris, the character, has a certain wry, self-effacing humour. I suppose if I find another character like that, I will lean once again towards humour, aware of course that being "funny" is all about taste.

For all that *The Matter with Morris* is about loss, as well as grief and mortality, do you feel it's an optimistic novel?

I do. I didn't intend this, but Morris made it that way—which is a testament to how characters will determine the movement and tone of a story.

What compels you to return to certain themes, such as loss, as you've done in your short story collection and six novels?

If a novelist isn't writing about death, he isn't doing his job. I read this somewhere once, and it's true. We shouldn't take this in an obvious way, where the story has to be about "death" or "loss of a loved one," but in a broader sense where the story grapples with an awareness of mortality, even if the character is seventeen years old. And so I return to these themes. It's a working out of my own minor story, one attempt after another to come to grips with my own transience.

> " If a novelist isn't writing about death, he isn't doing his job. "

About Writing *The Matter with Morris,* an essay by David Bergen

A number of years ago, my then nineteen-year-old son began to study philosophy at the University of Winnipeg. He brought home books that he was reading, and he left them lying about. I would pick them up and read certain sections, and then I would ask him about a specific idea or an author, and so we would converse. As we spoke and argued and debated, I remembered that I had once been enamoured of certain old books and authors, and discovered that I had missed out on others. Now, at a much later age, I was returning to these writers.

My reading began with Petrarch, *My Secret Book,* a book not written for broad consumption and yet full of heart and wisdom. From there I moved on to a very close encounter with *The Republic.* With some consternation, I admit that I had never read all of *The Republic,* and so I entered it now with a particular ignorance and a specific hunger. I was surprised by the humour, the irony in the writing, the complexity of the thought. I was also taken by its clarity and its relevance so many years and civilizations hence—and for example, the idea of the balance that we must find between reason and passion. I was raised in a religious home, where the Bible was the guide, and I found in Plato many similar ideas: justice, truth, moderation. I also read Cicero, specifically *Cicero on the Emotions,* which was written after Cicero's daughter died quite suddenly. ▶

> ❝ I was raised in a religious home, where the Bible was the guide, and I found in Plato many similar ideas. ❞

11

About Writing *The Matter with Morris*
(***continued***)

While doing this reading, I was considering a character for my next novel. I knew the character would be male, middle-aged, that his son would be killed while fighting in Afghanistan, and that the death would implicate other people, in this case the young soldier who accidentally shoots him. The novel would take place after the son's death, and it would cover approximately a year in the life of Morris Schutt. Cicero's description of grief and distress (gauntness, pain, depression, disfigurement) suited Morris, though the disfigurement would be more moral and spiritual, and not physical.

In the novel, Morris Schutt is stumbling towards a discovery of himself, attempting to understand how one should live the best life. Because I was fifty-one when I started the novel, and my main character Morris Schutt is fifty-one, it was not hard to imagine Morris harking back to the books he had read as a young man, before he got caught in the vicious cycle of what he refers to as "the pursuit of money and status." And in some ways I was simulating his intellectual voyage: I read and didn't understand Plato; and then I was overwhelmed and piqued; and I became confused. Like Morris, I had no wisdom. I was lost. Morris's reading, his heavy underlining of various passages, his dipping into a book and then becoming overwhelmed, all of this represented my own reading experience.

Early on in the writing, Morris became the character, I disappeared, and so the story took over. Morris, bereft and angry and tired

❝ Cicero's description of grief and distress (gauntness, pain, depression, disfigurement) suited Morris, though the disfigurement would be more moral and spiritual, and not physical. **❞**

of the failures he sees around him, never-
theless remains hopeful. He is looking for
a teacher and a guide. He is not looking for
someone to bring light into the cave, but for
someone to direct him up out of the cave.
He finds this in reading Jacob Boehme, and
Adorno, and specifically Plato. Boehme has
a very religious, mystical element to him,
which reminds Morris of his youth and his
pastor-father; Adorno offers him a more sec-
ular, almost mischievous, sacrilegious view.
And Plato, of course, is a guide, someone he
can trust more than he can the writers of, for
example, the Bible, which for Morris comes
with too much baggage. He is not an intellectual, but he is sincere and industrious in
his search, and this is all that is required. He
is also full of contradictions—he tries to be
rational and moral, and then is overcome by
passion and desire.

I knew, before I began this novel, that the
death of Morris's son in Afghanistan would
be the engine driving Morris. This singular
event forces him to reassess the first half of
his life. Throughout the novel, Morris is
struggling with the sacrifice of his son. He
had no part in the sacrifice and yet the sacrifice was made. If he has laid up treasures—
his family being the greatest treasure—then
what does it mean to lose that treasure? The
irony of course is that it is only when the
treasure is lost that he understands that he
didn't fully appreciate its value.

I was also aware of Saul Bellow's character Herzog, who writes letters that he never
sends (to dead thinkers, to priests, to great
writers, to philosophers). Morris writes letters as well, though Morris, unlike Herzog, ▶

66 Morris is
struggling with
the sacrifice of
his son. He had
no part in the
sacrifice and yet
the sacrifice was
made. 99

About Writing *The Matter with Morris* (*continued*)

actually sends the letters that he writes. The homage to Bellow is intentional; in fact, Morris Schutt says at one point, "I am not Bellow's Herzog. . . . I am not a free thinker, and I am not going mad, but like Herzog, I will persist. I will keep thinking." Because to think, to reason, to find a balance between wisdom and passion, this is Morris's main objective. And he fails. And then he tries again. Finally, Morris discovers, it is the seeking of balance, rather than the achievement of it, that matters.

"The soul is *the* philosophic question, and it is his concern for this question that distinguishes Socrates from his predecessors." That quote comes from an interpretative essay by Allan Bloom at the end of *The Republic*, and this idea hangs around the edges of my story. In a loose way this is a "conduct" novel. It asks, through Morris as its mouthpiece, how to live the best life, how to live the good life, and how to seek one's soul. It also asks what freedom is, which is why Morris walks the streets, absurdly asking people, "Do you have freedom?"

Yet I was aware while writing that the characters had to win out over the ideas. In fact, the characters had to contradict the ideas; they had to reveal the messiness of life as opposed to the moral ideal that Morris wishes to impose on his own existence.

This is a contemporary story, set in 2007, and its main action takes place over three months, with a number of flashbacks. Morris is the main character and it is his tone that

> Yet I was aware while writing that the characters had to win out over the ideas.

controls the narrative. I wanted the reader to feel that the story was being told in the first person, even though it isn't. I wanted the reader to descend into the mind and soul of Morris Schutt, to feel his anguish, his lust, his lostness, his craving for connection. I wanted Morris to be raw, to love his daughters and his grandson ferociously, to miss his wife Lucille very much but not understand how to reclaim her, to fear what he sees in his ailing father, to fear in fact his own mortality and to rail against it. I wanted a man who, like most of us, is slightly bewildered by where he has ended up. A man who hungers for knowledge but instead chooses desire. I also knew, almost immediately, that though I was dealing with weighty themes, the voice of Morris Schutt was distinct, playful, and surprising. I did not fight the voice, but simply let it fall into place.

And what a pleasure it was to let Morris loose, to allow him to stumble and grasp and to make mistakes and then bull his way back into the fullness of his life. He is a man who teeters, falls, and then rises again. This is Morris Schutt, forever hopeful.

> ❝ I wanted a man who, like most of us, is slightly bewildered by where he has ended up. ❞

Further Reading

What follows is a list of books that I read while working on *The Matter with Morris* (though I certainly did not complete all of them):

After Theory by Terry Eagleton

Cicero on the Emotions: Tusculan Disputations 3 and 4 by Cicero (trans. Margaret R. Graver)

Herzog by Saul Bellow

Minima Moralia: Reflections on a Damaged Life by Theodor Adorno (trans. E.F.N. Jephcott)

My Secret Book by Francis Petrarch (trans. J.G. Nichols)

On the Aesthetic Education of Man by Friedrich Schiller (trans. Reginald Snell)

Personal Christianity by Jacob Boehme

The City and Man by Leo Strauss

The Courage to Be by Paul Tillich

The Divine Comedy by Dante Alighieri (trans. Allen Mandelbaum)

The Republic of Plato (trans. Allan Bloom; preface and interpretative essay by Allan Bloom)

The Symposium by Plato (trans. Seth Benardete)

"What Is Political Philosophy?" by Leo Strauss

Also:
Bits and pieces of Reinhold Niebuhr
Bits and pieces of Søren Kierkegaard

To receive updates on author events and new books by David Bergen, sign up at www.authortracker.ca